I0622948

MEET me at JiMMY'S arCADe

Nostalgia and Musings From an 80's Kid Who Accidentally Solved a Murder

Grant Fieldgrove

Meet Me at Jimmy's Arcade: Nostalgia and Musings From an
80's Kid Who Accidentally Solved a Murder
By Grant Fieldgrove
Copyright 2023
Watch the Sky Media & Publishing
All rights reserved.

ISB 979-8-218-16977-0

Published by Watch the Sky Media – Publishing Division

This is a work of fiction. Names, characters, places and incidents are either the product of the author's imagination or are used fictionally and any resemblance to actual persons, living or dead, business establishments, events or locales is entirely coincidental. The publisher does not have any control over or does not assume any responsibility for author or third-party websites or their content.

Copyright 2023 by Watch the Sky Publishing & Grant Fieldgrove

No part of this book may be reproduced, scanned, or distributed in any printed of electronic form without permission. Please do not participate or encourage piracy of copyrighted materials in violation of the author's rights. Purchase only authorized editions.

For
Bebe
& Skye

My name is Grant Fieldgrove, and on the Fourth of July 1990, I accidentally solved a murder.

Introduction

This is my first foray into non-fiction.

When writing fiction, you can start the story off in a slam-bang fashion. You can literally make up any scenario to start your novel. It doesn't even really have to tie into the main plot. You can have your detectives solve a brief but complicated murder in the first chapter, then go off on the actual story. Or you can have a giant explosion or big action scene to establish the good guys and the bad guys.

But with non-fiction, I feel the options are limited.

If this were a typical true crime story, you could start with a grisly murder or a tense stalking scene. But this isn't that kind of a book. This is a book about childhood. It's a book about solving a murder where there were no real suspects, no exciting red herrings.

So, what can I do?

Introduce myself?

That sounds horribly boring, but I can't think of anything better. Seeing as this book is mostly about me, however, it seems appropriate.

The good news is that I can hide all this under the boring and often-skipped *introduction* section. That way, if you read it and say, "Wow, this sucks," I can counter with, "It's an introduction. What did you expect?"

So here we go. The big intro!

I was born on August 10, 1979, in Bakersfield, California, Memorial Hospital room 209, at 8:10 am. I only remember the exact time because it's the same as the date. My older brother was with our grandparents to stay off my parents' nerves (which he was often on). After I was born, my dad walked down the street to a little restaurant called Happy Steak. The waitress noticed his 'It's a Boy' button and gave him his steak for free. If you ever talked to my dad, chances are you've already heard about the Free Steak Incident.

August in Bakersfield is no joke, so I'm sure my mom was glad to have me finally stop mooching off her womb. We didn't have a pool then, but she spent many hot summer days, about ready to pop, floating in the community pool (as I would do later in life even though we got our own backyard pool a few years later).

My childhood consisted of playing baseball and soccer, family trips to national parks, Hawaii, and various other locales, and TV. Lots of TV. If there was a show on TV, I loved it. Anything from *Strawberry Shortcake* and the *Care Bears* to *Columbo, Murder, She Wrote, Miami Vice* and *Magnum P.I.* Hell, I even watched *Cop Rock!* I couldn't get enough. I had a bedroom packed with action figures, baseball cards, Garbage Pail Kids, and even a Cabbage Patch Doll named David. The entire wall above my bed was covered in a mural of Earth taken from the moon's surface. X-Wings and Star Destroyers hung from my ceiling, collecting dust. A nineteen-inch television with an antenna that picked up four channels and a VCR was sitting on my desk.

I was the typical, All-American boy of the 80s, complete with shaggy brown hair and shorts with wild designs that my mom made with her sewing machine. They were called Jams!

As I said on the previous page, this is my first attempt at non-fiction. My usual gig is fiction, romantic-comedy-detective fiction, to be exact, and I've been doing it so long that I feel like I'm a pro at it. I've written an entire mystery novel in two weeks before. No joke. And it was decent.

So yeah, that's how I started out – writing novels. At first, I just self-published them, and they really went nowhere for a long time. But somehow, by the fate of the Book Gods, years later, they started catching fire, which led to me being able to write for a living instead of wasting my life and draining my soul of all joy at a grocery store that insisted on working me the worst hours possible.

Yeah, the grocery store life was not for me, which isn't a knock to anyone working there. I don't knock anyone with a job, no matter what it is (hell, I don't knock anyone without a job, either), but damn, it just wasn't workin' for me. If you've ever worked retail, you know exactly how it is.

Customer after customer with the most inane comments, the same jokes over and over (Must be free! Must be free! mUsT bE FrEe!), and ridiculous complaints. Like they really thought I was the head of this massive grocery chain, and I spent my nights secretly raising all the prices just so I could sit in my mansion and watch the money come flooding in. I mean, I was literally there scanning their stupid, disgusting ground beef with the leaky package and puh-tay-ta chips, listening to their asinine bitching. How much authority could I possibly have?

The answer is none. Zero. El zilcho.

I was told I needed to show more enthusiasm about the store. I was told I could try to help the customers instead of being such a smartass. I was also told that starting soon, we would have to start trying to up-sale an item at the register.

It's like they were thinking of ways to make Grant even more uncomfortable.

When that stupid rule went into effect a few weeks later, all the checkers were supposed to pick one item from the store, preferably something 'store brand' or on sale, put a couple on the register, and try to sell them to the customers as they checked out. The only problem was that these customers were barely alive. Sometimes they would come through and just stare at you slack-jawed and silent. If you asked them how their day was, you'd get ignored, but yeah, let's try to sell them more.

My buddy (and coworker) Derek and I decided to take this new rule very seriously, though. So seriously, in fact, that we had a bet as to who could sell the most of our selected product. There was no rule that said we couldn't have a little fun with it, so what the hell?

And what was the product we chose?

We went down the magazine aisle and picked out the latest paperback from some lady name Lynsay Sands titled *Lady Pirate*. This was back when grocery stores proudly sold smut books right next to the magazines. Most of them had shirtless Fabio-type studs (or Fabio himself!) on the covers, nipples rock hard and long hair flowing in the wind, embracing the seemingly helpless young heroine who always looked a little dead behind the eyes and rather plain (but not too plain - the goal was for the reader to see themselves as the female lead).

Honestly, they looked cheesy as hell, and we were here for it!

We each grabbed a copy and set them on our registers, and whenever someone with no kids came through our line, we would try to pressure them into buying it. So hard was our sales pitch that we started finding erotic passages in the book and reading them aloud to the customers to entice them enough to purchase our up-sale item. (We knew exactly what we were doing.)

This went on for three days before the up-sale policy was immediately stopped. Not a word was said to either of us (after all, we were doing exactly what we were told to do), but we both knew. So did everyone else.

We were the heroes of the day, and Derek somehow managed to sell a copy.

Unfortunately, things didn't exactly get better after that. In fact, they were right back to the terrible norm the very next day, and that slight spark of life our stunt had given us was snuffed out.

I hadn't had a raise in so long that the state's minimum wage was six months away from catching up to me, so when some walking corpse of a woman approached my line a few weeks later, threw down a loaf of Iron Kids Crustless white bread in disgust, and yelled at me, "How do the kids get the nutrients without the crust?!?!" I had pretty much had enough.

I clapped back in my best 'you're a moron' tone, and said, "Do you think the bread on the outside of the loaf is somehow different than the bread on the inside of the loaf? C'mon, lady, it's shitty white bread, nothing close to a nutrient has ever been near it!"

I was booked for the night shift, far, far away from anyone that could possibly be offended by me calling out their bullshit or refusing to 'smile more', which was also a popular demand.

It didn't work entirely because every now and then, in the early morning hours of the store opening, I would get called to work the checkout if I was needed. I'd stroll up there in my shorts and slip-on shoes that both go against the ridiculous dress code, and I would remind them why, exactly, I was on the night shift. At that point, I had nothing to lose.

Being fired was a dream!

Literally.

On some of those late nights, while changing price tags, I would play out all the different ways I could get fired. I would fantasize about being called into the office and seeing all the managers there. They would tell me to have a seat, then they would read off some ridiculous offense I had done, and then, "We have to let you go."

Other times I would daydream about storming in there, ripping my stupid apron off and throwing it on the floor like I was in the midst of a temper tantrum and yelling, "Take this apron and shove it where the sun don't shine! And I don't mean London, suckas!"

I never did.

And I never got fired, no matter how hard I tried.

I remember one time around Valentine's Day, we got tons of boxes of those conversational hearts that taste like chalk – you know the ones. Anyway, mixed in with all the boxes was one package of Spanish ones. I saw them, grabbed them, and put them on my register for no real reason, just because they were different. I thought it was funny to have them despite having zero customers who spoke Spanish.

Ten minutes after putting them on my register, two crusty old fogies complained about them. Seriously. They complained about disgusting, chalky conversational hearts made for people sixty years younger than them that just happened to be in a language they didn't speak.

I stood there and took it, silently scanning their groceries while they continued to bitch and moan about candy they weren't buying, and when they finally shut up, I handed them their receipt. As they walked away, I waved and said, "Adios!"

It didn't go over too well, but wow, was it satisfying.

My second complaint in as many days came the next morning when the store closed out all of the off-brand cigarettes we had stocked for some unknown reason. The shitty ones, like Kent or Old Smokey, or those ones that are toothpick thin but a mile long.

They were all dumped in a handbasket, and someone had written a sign that announced these were 'close-out cigarettes' (even though I'm sure something on that three-word sign was misspelled because every sign in the store had something misspelled).

Anyway, here comes another couple, the guy wearing overalls with no undershirt, unloading their groceries onto my belt. They see the cigarettes, and the lady asks me if anything is wrong with them. I said, "Yeah... They cause cancer."

No more morning checking for me. Strictly night shift!

That went on for six years.

Six years!

I didn't sign up for that, and I certainly wasn't rewarded handsomely for it. I mean, I guess I should be grateful. Daydreaming during those night shifts (the ones that didn't involve me being fired) is what actually got me out of that place.

When I started writing my first book, the self-published one with all the typos, I would walk around the store with a little notebook and pen, writing down anything that popped into my head about my fictional little murder mystery. I filled up an entire notebook before realizing I didn't need it.

My brain is a funny thing. If I think of something, I remember it. Forever. Even after thirteen years of writing fiction mystery novels, I still remember every scrapped plot detail, every bit of cut dialogue, just...everything. I've written a book a year and never used so much as a piece of paper to remember anything. My brain just stores it in little filing cabinets.

I'm hoping that works in my favor for this story – my memory, I mean. I remember exact conversations from my childhood, I remember which theater I saw movies in (the actual theater number, not just which theater chain), and even typing this right now, ten or so pages in, memories are unlocking, like some dusty old chest being reopened, my filing cabinet of a brain going through everything that has been locked away for decades.

My parents thought I may have a photographic memory, so it was something I discussed with doctors. It turns out that actual photographic memory may not even be a thing.

Eidetic memory was the most likely thing I had, but the more I read up about it, the more I was convinced that that wasn't it. Eidetic memory was more about recalling precise details about an object or image after only seeing it briefly and without using a mnemonic device for help.

I didn't care about a label for it. I always remember things, no matter how trivial, and that's fine.

It's a strange thing, however, to have memories with people that don't remember them. Something that is still so vivid in my mind is entirely absent from the mind of the person I shared the moment with. The other day, I asked my buddy Eric if he remembered driving around Hart Park with our friends Joy and Maggie, listening to Everclear and Blur CDs, just because we had nothing else to do on that random Thursday night in December.

He had no recollection of it, but I remember every single detail like it was last night.

But still, that should help with this book because every memory I recall here, I will recall accurately; even entire conversations I wasn't a part of, I can remember flawlessly. And suppose, for some reason, I can't remember important details, like a few press conferences that are a bit fuzzy. In that case, I will research them and make sure everything is just right.

I am writing this because true crime is all the rage right now. Mix that in with some good old fashion nostalgia, and I think I have a winning combo.

And honestly, with all these podcasts, TV shows, and social media people mining these old true murders and exploiting them for money or views, I decided I wanted to beat them to the punch. I want to be the one to tell my story, not someone else.

My name is Grant Fieldgrove, and on the Fourth of July 1990, I accidentally solved a murder.

And it was a big one.

Maybe you remember me from a long time ago, but probably not.

I was hot stuff for a while - or at least a bunch of people thought I was. I tried to put on a happy face and take it all in, but the truth was that I was heartbroken and wanted to escape it all.

That murder devastated the entire town, and suddenly I was thrust front and center, entirely against my will. I was just a dumb kid. I didn't ask for any of this, but I was the one who figured it out, so I suppose that's my burden to bear.

The murdered girl's family thanked me profusely. They hugged me and cried tears that fell onto the top of my head. I didn't know what to do, so I stood there and let them do whatever they needed.

I contacted the murdered girl's sister just before writing this book. I wanted to ask her if it was okay. Her parents have since passed away, and she is all that's left of her family now.

She gave me her blessing and told me she was glad it was me to be the one to do it. Then she told me, "It better have some laughs! It's what she would have wanted."

I hope she enjoys this book.

I hope you enjoy this book.

That murdered girl's story deserves to be told, and I

will be the one to tell it because I know what happened; I remember conversations I had the week she went missing almost verbatim. I remember everything we did before learning the news. I remember the weather, how the sun felt on our faces, and how the air smelled of coconuts, chlorine, and freshly cut grass. And I remember the exact moment I realized my life had been changed forever - because I was there.

I lived it.

And this is my story.

And it is her story.

Together.

I will put you in my shoes, dear reader, and tell you the events leading up to that hot summer night when everything changed.

And I don't want it to be sensationalized for binge-watching.

That girl deserves better.

That's also why I'm not writing this as some lame network TV-style torn-from-the-headlines mystery or a non-fiction novel. I am writing this book about myself and my friends and the summer we uncovered a horrible secret.

My own little story wrapped up in a murder mystery.

So, let's end this introduction and get on with it.

Above: Grant reporting for duty.
Below: a barely conscious Grant (left)
and Roxy (right) on a camping trip.

Meet Me at Jimmy's Arcade

Let's start in the middle of winter 2021 before heading back to the 80s. We're in Maine shooting a slasher movie called *Time's Up*, and the temperature is a balmy negative number. I, being from California, packed one pair of pants, two pairs of shorts, a couple of hoodies, and precisely zero socks.

The scenes we are shooting take place at a public library, doubling as a high school library, where several outdoor and indoor scenes will be shot. We have one day to complete them all.

The cast and crew are all piled into one study room on the far east wing of the library. It's the middle of a pandemic, and we're all masked up and taking as many safety precautions as possible. One Covid case would derail the whole production.

Cast and crew are getting their make-up done, getting the lighting just right, and I'm running around with my walkie-talkie, ensuring everything is running smoothly.

The library is open for business while this is all going on.

It's a long day.

Death scenes are being filmed in the basement, which is so small, only the director and the necessary cast and crew can fit. Library-goers kept asking me what was happening and if someone was hurt down there.

No. Everything is fine. Everything is fine. Everything is fine. It's a movie, and everything is fine.

Before the sun drops, Tyler must film his big scene out on the library steps. Snowflakes are falling on my head. I have no socks on. Tyler kills his scene, then it's back inside until nightfall.

It's now 9pm, and we've been filming all day. It's time to move production back outdoors, but nobody really wants to help with that. It's stupid how cold it is. But the necessary cast and crew fight through it, and we get the scenes shot. I'm miserable and wet by the time we get back inside. I take a seat next to some twenty-somethings that are playing teenagers in the movie. They're talking about the show *Stranger Things* and making fun of all the 80s references in it. I sat there listening and wanted to smack them both.

You kids weren't even around in the 80s! You don't know anything about it, and you're both stupid! Stupid, I tell you! Someone take me back!

That night, after working a fourteen-hour day, it finally dawned on me that I was...old. I've always considered myself quite youthful. When I compare myself to forty-year-olds with office jobs or actual careers, nothing I do jives with what they do. I don't own a suit - hell, I've only ever worn an actual business-like suit once, and that monstrosity was so ill-fitted to my body that I looked like a three-year-old putting on his dad's clothes. To make it worse, my look was captured forever in my buddy's wedding photos when I stood next to him as he got married. I looked like the Grimace from those old McDonald's ads. The Hamburglar could have been lurking at me from the tree line, ready to steal my lunch, or Mac Tonight could have been serenading me from his piano.

Before the wedding, while all the groomsmen were gathered in a huge garage at the venue getting dressed, I was sitting on the pool table, desperately trying to safety pin my suit into fitting correctly.

It didn't work.

Everyone else looked fine, but there was Grant, with zero sewing skills, trying to tailor down a blue suit we could all have camped under.

I was using shitty safety pins I had picked up at CVS on the way to try and taper the legs of the pants because they were straight-cut, and it was 2019 out there, not 1982 or whatever! But I had no say and had to deal with what I was given.

To make things worse, I literally went into the suit shop the week before to be fitted. The lady measured my legs, my crotch (tee-hee), my shoulders, my gut; there was no excuse for the pool tarp I was handed the day before the ceremony.

Remember that cartoon wolf who wore the zoot suit with shoulders so broad you could serve lunch on them?

Yeah, that's what my top looked like. At least the wolf's suit was adequately tapered around the midsection. I just looked like a suffocating Kool-Aid Man.

Needless to say, my CVS safety pins, and my complete lack of tailoring skills didn't pay off. While everyone went into the main house for whatever reason, I tried to switch my pants with another groomsman, pawn those pieces of shit off on some other poor bastard, but everyone was already wearing theirs. So, I tried to switch jackets, but the one I could try on before everyone returned belonged to a dude about half my size.

Strike three.

I was doomed to wear these gigantic clown pants, and there was nothing I could do about it.

Sigh.

I made jokes about my suit, and we all had a good laugh, but damn it, I didn't want to look like Hobo Joe at my friend's wedding, so most of my laughs were forced and probably quite sad to everyone who heard them.

Some of the guys called my pants Hammer Pants, but they lacked the knowledge of what Hammer Pants truly were. I would have killed for Hammer Pants!

Hammer Pants were tapered at the bottom and actually fit around M.C.'s waist! While he slid across that dancefloor doing his signature shuffle, he didn't have to constantly tug on them to keep them from falling off and slowly, and ever so gently, drifting to the floor (like a parachute!) like I had to do while walking my fellow bridesmaid down the aisle.

I guess the point of that ridiculously long-winded story was to inform you that I don't wear suits. I wear t-shirts of fictional killers and punk rock bands, and shoes with white laces, and up until that night a few years ago, I still considered myself quite youthful.

In December of 2022, when I attended the premiere

of *Good Side of Bad*, another movie I help produce, I wore slip-on camo shoes and a Michael Myers hoodie. While everyone else looked glamorous, Grant looked like he somehow slipped passed security.

I've never tried to be something I wasn't, so when I came to that realization that I was old, sitting there in a Maine hotel room, alone, in the middle of winter, it was like a punch in the gut. Since then, I've been desperately trying to reconnect with my youth, which I suppose is another driving force behind this book.

So, let's go back to the eighties!

I'm not sure at which age permanent memory is supposed to kick in for a child, but I know it's at least after three, maybe even up to five, which means everything you do for a child in those years prior will not be remembered.

My earliest memory was in 1983, a couple of months before turning four. May 25, 1983, to be exact. The day *Return of the Jedi* opened in theaters worldwide, and I was there.

The theater was at the Valley Plaza, our local mall, but in a separate building, almost out in the parking lot. Still, that day's line was so long it reached the mall and almost circled it completely. My dad and big brother were at the front of it, waiting patiently while my mom sat with me at the mall McDonald's so I could enjoy some Chicken McNuggets dipped in honey.

When we returned to the line, my dad and brother were still there, closer to the front now... And that's all I remember about it. The weather was gorgeous, the crowd was excited, and although I don't remember seeing the movie that day, it was one of the all-time greats. The perfect capper to the most perfect trilogy of films ever. It's no joke that I must have watched them all at least five hundred times each. There was just something so unique about them.

So yeah, that's my first memory, I think. There are bits and pieces scattered throughout that may have come sooner, but I have no definitive timeline like I do for the theater one, so we'll stick with it. It's an excellent first memory to have, especially considering how much *Star Wars* took over my life afterward.

As I mentioned earlier, my parents had a pool installed at the house by the time I was six. I remember watching the tractors dig up almost half of our backyard. I remember them fitting the rebar and pouring the cement. I remember my idiot brother, shirtless (as he often was), trying to drop his BMX into it like he was in *Rad* and falling face-first into the deep end. He needed seven stitches and a permanent cap on his front tooth. I remember the excitement my best friend Xavier and I felt as we watched the final product fill with water.

We were no strangers to pools, we liked to hang out at the community pool and continued to do so periodically until high school, but the private pool was better when you just wanted to swim and relax.

My birthday is in summer so every year I got a pool party. My dad would fill the pool with balloons, which he usually blew up himself, while my mom made elaborate decorations and a cake that fit the theme of the party, which was anything from *Star Wars* to Baseball, and everything in between, and my brother, well, he would be useless as always.

Eighties birthday parties felt so different than birthday parties today. Everyone back then was so...present. There were no distractions, no phones, no pressure to keep up appearances, and the only photos being taken were usually by the grandparents, to be shared with everyone involved a week later via free double prints or sometimes even triple prints. Back when cameras resembled bricks, and if you wanted to take a picture in low light, you had to screw on a magical cube that would light up exactly once and then be discarded and replaced. Then the film (film!) would have to be carefully wound manually to avoid being exposed and ruined. You would take that carefully rolled film to Long's Drug Store, which was our drug store of choice in the 80s, yours may vary, and wait a week to get them back.

Later, one-hour photo arrived in a big way, popping up in malls all over the world. Then after dropping off your film, you would have to wait but one teeny-tiny, minuscule hour to get your photos. That hour was usually spent cruising the mall, picking up a few sausage samples from Hickory Farms, a giant cookie from Mrs. Fields, window shopping at K.B. Toys, or perusing the aisles of B. Dalton or Sam Goody. And by the time you were done, presto, so were your photos. Like magic.

Sure, everything today is easier and far more convenient, but there was something special about the wait, like it was part of the experience. It allowed you to forget about taking specific pictures and be surprised at how they turned out. And now that entire experience is gone forever, replaced with instant gratification and phoniness. (I was at Disneyland last week, and I watched a guy stand in the middle of Main Street, hold his phone out, point to the castle, and laugh, like, seriously laugh, to try to get some authenticity to his photo, then take the picture. He did this exact same thing five times. Five! Point, laugh, click, review, no good, redo, point, laugh, click, review, no good. Five times. Ridiculous)

I know why people refer to this general time and age range in their lives as the good ol' days. I get it, but I'm smart enough to realize that they were only the good ol' days because, as a child, you were carefree, and even tragedies were easier to shrug off. The truth is, there haven't been any actual good ol' days when everyone was happy and lived in peace. What is good for some is bad for others. Entire races of people struggled to exist, fighting not just for equality but to simply catch up.

The 80s were no different.

We were constantly under the threat of nuclear war with the Russians, Reagan's Trickle-Down Theory was choking out the middle class, and in 1985, a disease initially called Gay-Related Immune Deficiency (GRID) began spreading rapidly, especially among gay men. It was now being called the 'white gay disease,' and it caused massive and toxic homophobia across the entire country. Even though it was primarily detected in bi or gay white men, other races were seriously affected, but nobody bothered to include ethnic minorities in outreach programs, blocking them from vital information and early treatment options. So, the disease spread, and spread, with little to no help. It wasn't until July 25th of that year, when actor Rock Hudson announced he had the disease (now called Human Immunodeficiency Virus Infection–HIV/AIDS), that the world stopped to really take notice, and AIDS stories in print and media triple over the next few months.

When an Indiana teenager named Ryan White contracts AIDS through a blood transfusion to treat his hemophilia, he is refused entry into his junior high. Parents and staff are terrified he will give them all this deadly new disease.

Panic ensues. Rock Hudson dies on October 2nd of the same year at 52, leaving in his will $250,000 to help set up the American Foundation for AIDS Research. Elizabeth Taylor serves as the founding National Chairman.

Ryan White died on April 8th, 1990, at age 18.

Over 39 million people have since died from the disease.

Pile all of that onto massive pay discrepancies and commonplace sexual harassment towards women in the workplace, casual racism, people of color often being treated as second-class citizens, whackos trying to convince the world that people who listened to a particular style of music or played certain fantasy games were involved in devil-worshipping and deadly occult sacrifices and who knows what else (Satanic Panic!), and let's not forget the shittiest looking cars of all time, and yeah, the 80s weren't the good ol' days for everyone. But as a kid, it's easy to forget all that stuff, to shrug it off and move on, or even better, be utterly oblivious to it, like I was.

I was a kid, and I was enjoying it. I look back on it

fondly, and that fondness is what I will focus on the most. Bad news and disaster are everywhere, and I'm afraid if I talk only about bad things, it will lessen that poor girl's death somehow, and I can't, and won't, allow that to happen.

I will say one last thing about disaster before moving on since it is relevant to the story. The earliest disaster memory I have was from January 28, 1986. I was in school, and the janitors had brought in those heavy televisions strapped to rolling carts, and we got to watch the launch of the Challenger Space Shuttle.

The reason this launch was so important was because a teacher was on board. For the very first time, a non-astronaut was allowed to fly to space, and we all wanted to be a part of it until we all desperately did not want to be a part of it. It was called the Teacher in Space Project and was the only time it happened.

Right there, on live television, we all witnessed the deaths of not only our beloved Teacher in Space, but six other crew members, in an explosion that is permanently seared into my brain, and probably millions of others. (Even worse, later on, we discovered that some of them survived the initial explosion and then had to plummet to their deaths while trapped inside the spacecraft.)

So, WTF happened?

The record-low temperatures in Cape Canaveral leading up to the launch had caused the rubber O-rings of the space shuttle to stiffen, thus lessening their ability to properly seal the joints. The primary and secondary O-rings both failed shortly after takeoff. Hot, pressurized gas seeped through the joints and into the propellant tank causing it to explode and collapse upon itself, which in turn caused the shuttle to rotate into an angle its speed simply could not handle. The shuttle was torn apart by the massive force pushing against it, huge clouds of smoke and chemicals filled the air, and then...nothing. It went down.

Zero survivors.

The school was in a panic. We were all pulled from

our classrooms and forced to gather on the large grass area behind the playground while teachers and other staff struggled to figure out what the hell to do. Counseling was offered, kids were picked up and taken home by their parents, and then... That's all I remember. Nothing else seemed to matter at that moment. We had all witnessed death firsthand, and none of us knew how to handle it.

Now, you would think something like that would have turned the school against ever broadcasting a live event to its students again, but you would be wrong because the very next year, in the middle of October 1987, the heavy TVs were rolled in again so we could witness another live event.

A ballsy move, I thought, because a year and a half after the Challenger, a bunch of grade school kids, especially the boys, had turned the tragedy into jokes. Where we were so petrified by that day in January, now we were completely desensitized. Freddy Krueger and Jason Voorhees had been introduced to the majority of us and made death easier to cope with, although we didn't understand it at all, hence the jokes.

So popular was Freddy in the 80s that this child killer, burned alive by the parents of the kids he brutally murdered, was marketed towards...you guessed it, KIDS!

Are you ready for Freddy?!

I'm guessing the majority of parents weren't, but me? Hell yes, I was. Freddy was everywhere – lunchboxes, posters, an album called *Freddy's Greatest Hits* (which I still have and honestly love), even his very own 900 number, which I called several times without prior permission from my parent or guardian (more on that later.)

I'm a rebel, I know.

Freddy was everywhere, though. He had taken over the world in perhaps one of the oddest marketing decisions of all time, which later gave way to a mass of R-rated movies being marketed towards kids, including *Robocop* (the most f-wordiest and violent movie I had ever seen at the time – I still love it to this day) and *Rambo*.

For a kid obsessed with on-screen violence, it was heaven.

One hot summer night at the great Kern County Fair, the smell of hay and horse shit mixed with sugar, grilled onions, and popcorn filling the air, the bugs buzzing in our ears, my dad and I were strolling the midway and came across a framed Freddy poster as a prize in a shooting gallery game. I was such a Freddy connoisseur that I knew that this specific photo was taken during the promotional shoots of *Nightmare on Elm Street Part IV, The Dream Master*. I could tell by the make-up job on Freddy's face and the way his sweater was tattered. I needed it desperately. My dad knew it without me even having to say a word. He seemed just as excited about it as I was, even though I knew our chances of winning it were slim to none. These games weren't exactly designed to allow winners, but we had to try.

My dad pulled out his wallet and paid cash; there were no pre-purchased game tickets, just cold hard cash, and the carny handed me the gun.

Now, guns are not my specialty. I've never liked real ones, but I was a crack with fake ones, like the Nintendo Zapper – those ducks in *Duck Hunt* didn't stand a chance. I was basically a pro at *Wild Gunman* at Jimmy's Arcade, but those guns were all fake. They didn't shoot anything from the barrel, just invisible lasers, I suppose. The closest thing I ever shot to a real gun was a stupid Super Soaker, so my confidence in shooting out the entirety of the little red star about fifteen feet away with actual projectiles was as close to the ground as a caterpillar's butthole.

But I lifted that stupid BB gun to my eye, I set my sights on the red star and – *bang bang bang* – the notecard size paper exploded in front of me as I sent those tiny metal balls through that red star until my barrel was emptied.

It looked good.

It looked really good.

As far as I could tell, I absolutely destroyed all traces of that damned red star. That wood-framed Freddy poster was as good as mine. I knew it. My dad knew it. Unfortunately, the carnie didn't. "Sorry, kid," he said, "there is still some red left. Better luck next time."

I, being a child, accepted the loss at face value, as disappointing as it was. My father, being an adult, did not accept the loss. He didn't accept the loss so strongly that he hopped over the counter and began yelling at the carny and pointing to the paper I shot. Like an absolute madman, he told that carny what he thought of his call. Still, to this day, I have never heard more uses of the phrase Son of a Bitch in a single chunk of dialogue than I heard my dad use that night. He used it as a verb, a noun, an adjective, pronouns, you name it. It was truly a rant for the ages.

He pulled the shot-up card from its little clothespin clip and shoved it in that carny's face, demanding to know where there was any red left.

It was the greatest thing I had ever seen.

"Winner winner!" the carnie said enthusiastically, perhaps just to get my dad off him, or perhaps he truly saw his error. I didn't care either way. That Freddy poster, still in its original frame, hangs in my house as we speak. I see it every day and smile.

My dad died in 2013 at the way-too-young age of sixty-three, but that Freddy poster will hang in my house forever.

The point of all that was horror movies had dulled the painful reality of actual death to myself and a large group of my idiot friends, so by the time that giant TV was rolled into the classroom again, we were almost hoping for the worst, as awful as that seems.

In Midland, Texas, a little girl had fallen down a well and had taken over the lives of every American with a television. They were close to rescuing her that day, and we were all forced to watch.

I remember the classroom vividly. The boys laughed like it was all a joke, some even going as far as to mimic the corpse they hoped would be pulled out, while the girls looked at them scornfully, demanding that we "grow up!"

The teachers learned a harsh lesson that day as well. I don't recall ever watching the news in a classroom ever again.

Baby Jessica was rescued on live TV, and we witnessed it. The world cheered. A bunch of idiot kids at Quailwood Elementary School shrugged it off and went on with their lives. Some were downright disappointed with the results.

Everything was a big joke to us.

The good ol' days.

Sure.

Nothing had really affected me on a television screen before or after the Challenger, except for when ABC canceled *ALF* after a major cliffhanger, forcing nine-year-old me to assume that ALF had been captured by the government and killed in horrible fashion (I'm still scarred!) or the *Alvin and the Chipmunks* episode where the Berlin Wall came down, freeing their friend who was trapped, which turned out to just be a dream of Alvin's while on a flight, and the wall had not, in fact, come down yet. (Not gonna lie; those two shows messed me up. Bad. There is even an *Alvin* episode where their dog dies that didn't affect me as much as the wall episode, even at the end when the creator dedicated it to his dog that just died in real life. Ugh!)

Note: The finale of the TGIF show *Dinosaurs* was also soul-crushing. So much so that I couldn't believe a show with talking dinosaur puppets would ever go so dark.

(*Roseanne*'s finale was also a downer, but by the time that show ended, it had become so unbelievably lame I barely cared. By the last season, Roseanne was fighting off terrorists on a train with Steven Seagal! Just...bad. So, so bad. And I love Steven Seagal!)

I bring this up because seeing death behind a television screen, even when it's real life, is far different than when it practically comes knocking on your front door, which is precisely what happened in 1990.

When you're a child, everything seems so much

bigger than it really is. That may explain why I thought the entirety of my town existed in, and was solely limited to, my neighborhood. The town wasn't anywhere near as grandiose as it is now. In fact, back then, it was downright tiny, but still, life existed outside of my little slice of paradise, Quailwood. Maybe that's why it felt like a mini adventure every time I left.

Looking back, I can see how easy it was for me to assume my neighborhood was a town – I mean, it had its own school, right smack dab in the middle, literally called Quailwood School (go Cobras!). Next to the school was a great park, filled with the newest and best playground equipment, and behind that was a community center that housed the pool we all loved so much, and right in the middle of all three... is a sump.

Seriously, a huge sump with a rickety-ass fence around it, and who knows what living inside. Before we had to go in there during that summer of 1990, we assumed it was filled with dead bodies, mutated creatures, and discarded drugs. That sump was the subject of countless scary stories told in the wee hours of the night during slumber parties until the magic and mystery left on that hot July day when I was almost eleven.

On the outskirts of the neighborhood, however, there wasn't much. A dirt field remained there up until about five years ago when the landowner finally died. It could be sold to someone with a little grander ambition than dirt – now there is a Sully's gas station, a pizza place, an urgent care, and a seemingly random hotel.

Behind the neighborhood was also a lot of nothing, but this nothing was at least a little more exciting. Trees, bushes, shrubs, even a couple of lakes, you name it, occupied acres upon acres of unused land which was just begging to be explored by people more ambitious than us.

The street separating that little forest from Quailwood was busy (Truxton Ave.), so some genius installed an underground metal tube for easy passing. However, now, you couldn't pay me to cut through there (it's the sump all over again.) But in the 80s, when kids were allowed to roam free, we used that tube at least a few times a week without a single care or worry in the world. We'd push our bikes through that muddy metal passage and either hang out among the trees or take the newly installed bike path as far as our little legs could take us. All the while, our parents had no idea where we were.

So, you can see how my little island of a neighborhood could fool a child into thinking it was the nexus of the universe, especially when other factors were figured in, such as the town sheriff living two doors down from us, having two churches in the neighborhood (one a Mormon and one whatever a typical church is – Christian? I don't know) and a third, this one Catholic, just around the corner with a white cross so large you could see it from school. I never liked that. It looked, and still looks, ominous and creepy.

Next to that church was the fire station, and I knew that at least three firemen working there lived in our 'hood. Hell, even our mailman lived here.

In 1985, when my dad and I were obsessed with pro wrestling, 7-11 had special WWF Big Gulp cups, and we were on a mission to collect them all.

We had already gotten all of them but one. The Junkyard Dog was proving to be a tough find. There were tons of Roddy Pipers, Andre the Giants, King Kong Bundys, Iron Sheiks, Mr. Wonderfuls, Macho Man and Elizabeths, Ricky Steamboats, and Nikolai Volkoffs. Still, that damn Junkyard Dog was nowhere to be found!

We traveled to all the 7-11s on the far outskirts of town, which took a long time to get to.

We finally got the Junkyard Dog when my dad saw it on a hanging display in a 7-11 that was way out in some farming area. He told me to go distract the worker with some asinine question about an Almond Joy. While I did that, my dad would jump up and bust the display and free the Dog. Everything went according to plan, displayed ruined, and we got the cup!

The point of that story was that all those 7-11s out in the middle of nowhere or in the middle of that farmland...are now considered 'Central Bakersfield.' That's how much this place has grown since then, but my little neighborhood has remained the same. The only change was Quailwood School's mascot – it went from the awesome-sounding Cobras to the cringe-inducing Horny Old Women (Cougars) for some unknown and not-thoroughly thought-out reason. Boo!

So yeah, there was definitely something special about Quailwood, which made what happened even more shocking. We went from a quiet, quaint little neighborhood in the southwest of Bakersfield (a town made famous by my grandma's cousin Buck Owens, among other country artists) to the temporary epicenter of a media frenzy.

Above: Little Freddy & Mom
Below: Freddy says Vote for Grant...or else!

Our heist paid off!
After thirty-plus years
and a few puppy
attacks, The Junkyard
Dog still lives!

Her name was Bebe Lynn Sanders, (B.B.) and she lived on the opposite side of the school as me, over on Pheasant. She was older than me, so I didn't really know her, but I did know who she was. She was beautiful, with long golden blonde hair and a dimple on her right cheek that became more prominent every time she smiled, which, from what I could tell, was often. She seemed to be popular with kids her age, too, and when she walked, she radiated an air of self-confidence. I would later find out that this wasn't entirely true, and Bebe was dealing with a lot of bullshit at the high school level, a level I was not privy to. But still, she really pulled herself together nicely. While I was certainly more preoccupied with girls my age that I couldn't even gather enough courage to talk to, I recognized her beauty from afar. Perhaps that's why so many people remembered seeing her the day she vanished.

I recently asked Bebe's sister, Skye, to describe Bebe for me. Skye told me that Bebe loved her family and friends and always tried to look at the positive side of life. Her favorite movies were *Dirty Dancing* and *Sixteen Candles*, and she loved to read. She was funny and loved to laugh and make others laugh.

Bebe-Lynn Sanders was born on May 31st, 1973, to parents Becky and Phil Sanders. Skye and Bebe were separated by only two years and spent most of their childhood as best friends. Skye moved out and into an apartment with another girl named Trudy in the spring of 1989 when Bebe was finishing up her sophomore year at Bakersfield High School.

Skye told me she felt bad leaving her sister at home but was sure Bebe would be fine. And, for the most part, she was fine. She had friends, went to parties, and dated, so everything worked out.

I don't remember ever seeing Skye, but I saw Bebe around the neighborhood and at the pool occasionally. Where I saw her most, though, was at Jimmy's Arcade, one of the most popular hangouts in town. It seemed like every kid in the entire city could be found there, especially on weekends and summer nights.

Arcades, and in Quailwood's case, the pool, are the places I noticed in the eighties and early '90s where every group of people could come together harmoniously. I spent a lot of time at both, especially Jimmy's. Everything was an equal playing field at the arcade, and kids my age could mingle and interact with kids far older, and everything would be swell.

If I saw those same older kids at, say, a Bakersfield Dodgers game at Sam Lynn Ball Park, they would often throw Coke cans at us, knock our ice cream sundaes served in miniature batting helmets out of our hands, or threaten to kick our asses.

But not at the arcade.

Never at the arcade.

A quick note about the ballpark I just mentioned. As I said, it's named Sam Lynn Ballpark, after the former local owner of a Coca-Cola bottling company in town that donated a ton of his income to youth baseball leagues. When it was built and opened in 1941, it was the home of the Bakersfield Badgers. It cycled through six more farm leagues before becoming the home of the Bakersfield Dodgers from 1984 through 1994. We would attend games constantly and saw several up-and-comers. In 1995, however, the team changed to the Bakersfield Blaze and ceased their relationship with our beloved L.A. Dodgers.

Anyway, this is all a lot of information just to get to the punchline. The field, as historic as it is, being the oldest stadium in the Class-A Advanced league, faces west!

Brilliant work!

It's one of only two baseball diamonds in the entire country that faces west, the other being in Wisconsin. If you're confused about why this is such a big deal, I'll tell you.

The sun set directly over the centerfield wall, which blinds the crowd, and, even funnier, the batters, causing them to go out there and hack at whatever pitch came down the pike, hoping to get lucky. It's an architectural disaster, a failure on every level, and I absolutely love it.

If you're ever in Bakersfield, swing by sometime and check it out. A team called the Bakersfield Train Robbers plays there now, and if you're a fan of heat, beer, ragtag baseball, and occasional heckling, you're bound to have a grand ol' time, and you might run into me.

Anyway, sorry.

Jimmy's Arcade was just barely within walking distance from my home. In fact, it seemed to be barely within walking distance from anyone's home. It was off the second busiest street in town, about a quarter mile from the mall. Despite being within walking distance, almost everyone rode their bike there. So many bikes had been piled up along the bike rack, 'Jimmy' had to add a second row. And then a third. Before long, the entire building was surrounded by bike racks, every one of them filled.

Developers eventually recognized the gold mine the arcade was and began building it up. Soon, a Peter Piper Pizza moved in next door, then the coolest surf shop in town next to that, then a movie theater.

The old mall theater had been torn down years ago when new theaters popped up. A Dave and Busters sits there now. I can hardly stand to look at it.

To say Jimmy's Arcade was the place to be would be a massive understatement. It was the only place to be. At least, that's what it seemed like to me. It was the only place I could interact with high school kids and feel kinda, sorta, semi-cool. In fact, in the arcade, not only could a grade school kid feel kinda sorta semi-cool to high schoolers, they could sometimes even feel downright superior! I mean, if their sweet gaming skills were top-notch, which mine were.

While researching this book, I discovered there is no Jimmy! Seriously. The guy who opened the arcade originally was a Swedish fellow named Runar, or Rune for short. He wanted to open an arcade with a "typical sounding American name," thus Jimmy's was born. In

1992, Rune sold Jimmy's to Bob and Diane Taggart, who owned it until the end. B&D Vending, short for Bob and Diane, still rents out machines all over town. If you've played a video game in a Bakersfield pizza parlor recently, you probably played one of theirs.

More on the arcade later. It becomes an essential part of this story, in case you couldn't tell by the title of this book. For now, I'll focus on Bebe-Lynn.

Like I said, while I didn't know her personally, I did know who she was, but I certainly did not know about her... reputation... if you know what I mean. I didn't find all that stuff out until she failed to come home one Friday night in 1990 after leaving Jimmy's.

The news hit my mom the following day during a phone call with one of our busybody neighbors named Ms. Franks, who had to have been at least four-hundred years old. I had just finished up some Saturday Morning Cartoons when my mom came into the living room and asked me if I happened to see Bebe in the neighborhood or at the arcade last night.

When I turned in my chair to answer her, my dad took the opportunity to snatch the remote control away from me (which was roughly the size of a brick, the exact opposite of the tiny, fart-breeze sensitive touch remotes of today) before quickly returning to his La-Z-Boy.

I told Mom I didn't see Bebe, but the more I thought about it, maybe I did. Summer days at the arcade kinda bled into each other, so it was difficult to distinguish one night from the next, and at that time, Bebe was just some high school girl that didn't come home the night before. I had actually come home early that Friday night, not wanting to miss a show on TGIF. Also, my mom had recently (finally) ditched her Jennifer Hart Hair in favor of a much more manageable short bob, so seeing her without her face in the middle of a giant hair wall still threw me off. She apparently loved the change because I think she's stuck with it ever since. (The only thing that ever changed with my dad's hair was the color. It went from shaggy and brown to shaggy and gray, and that's about it. His barber, Joe Brown, down on Stockdale Hwy about three miles from our house, apparently knew only one cut for shaggy hair, and that's what he got, refusing to go anywhere else, for any reason...ever.)

Mom's face turned sad. "I saw her yesterday morning," she said. "I've seen her and her friends every morning for a week. She was almost always with a big group of girls, but yesterday she was alone. I'm not sure what to make of that."

"I'm sure it's nothing," Dad said, flipping the channels with one hand and reclining his feet up in the air with the other. He was on vacation from work and planning to take it very seriously.

Mom, however, was not on vacation. She was showing a house right across from the community center, and things weren't exactly going well. She was having a ton of trouble selling it which is shocking. Shocking, I tell ya! Who wouldn't want to live across from a noisy ass public pool filled with screaming jackasses?

Apparently, everyone, because she had been trying to get rid of it for almost six weeks. It really dragged her down, and I remember desperately hoping that it would sell soon so she could be done with it and we could all enjoy Dad's vacation, which would include a trip to Sequoia National Park for a few days in a cabin.

"I wish I would have known she might have been in trouble," my mom said somberly, perhaps taking a cue from the massively over-dramatic Ms. Franks, from whom she received the news. (I once saw Ms. Franks literally clutch her pearls and stagger backward, the back of her right hand pressed against her forehead, when she learned that the new guy who moved in down the street was a homosexual. A move {minus the pearl clutching} my mom mimicked when she found my Guns' n Roses cassette tape hidden under my mattress and read the lyrics. LOL, moms.)

Ms. Franks is somehow still alive, but for the life of me, I cannot figure out how!

"That's ridiculous," my dad said regarding my mom's

mind-blowing revelation that she saw a high school student near a high school hangout. "You couldn't have known she'd disappear. And even if you did, what would you have done? Locked her in our garage until it was safe? She'll turn up. Seventeen-year-old girls do really dumb things."

"I heard she's been givin' it out to all the guys!"

This is how I will formally introduce you to my older brother, Neil, Mr. (Thinks He's) Too Cool for Everything. I hadn't really mentioned him before because he is such a colossal pain in the ass. But here he was, Tom Cruise Aviator shades on (indoors!) and a mullet hanging halfway down his T&C tank top (which really pissed me off because I also wore T&C), paired with acid-washed short shorts, informing all of us that a missing girl 'gave it up' to a lot of guys.

It was the most I'd seen of my brother in a month.

I, being an idiotic ten-year-old, asked, "Giving what out?"

"That's enough, Neil," my mom said, trying to kill the conversation.

"It, little bro!" Neil made a thrusting motion, like Travolta in Saturday Night Fever. It was somehow even more disturbing.

"Neil!" my mom gasped - if she had pearls, they would have been clutched! "Geez, your shorts are so short I'm surprised your dealies aren't hanging out."

"It's the style, mom! Jesus Christ! You wouldn't get it."

"I still don't know what she's giving out," I said, adding fuel to this steadily growing fire.

Neil made a circle with his left thumb and forefinger and inserted his right pointer finger through it repeatedly, complete with squish noises for added effect.

"Neil Alan Fieldgrove!" my mom yelled. I caught a quick glimpse of my dad smiling. He quickly killed it and tried to turn it into a serious Dad Look. It didn't work too well, but luckily Mom didn't see, anyway.

Neil went on, "She's the town bicycle. Everyone got a

ride!" (I wish I was making this up, but I'm not. A full-grown man living with his parents just called a high school girl the town bicycle in front of said parents! Major cringe.)

My dad's smile was gone for real now. He'd had it with Neil and told him that was enough.

"I'm just telling you what I heard," Neil said. "It's a well-known fact that ol' Bebe-Lynn was very generous to the opposite...sex." He winked at me.

"I don't give a rat's fat ass one way or the other," Dad said. "What a girl does is none of our business unless she's doing it with you, which I highly doubt."

The look on Neil's face was priceless.

Dad continued, "You want to talk that trash, then go do it with your idiot friends."

Neil, stunned, said, "They're not idiots."

Dad laughed. "Oh yeah? I saw one of them smash his head into a concrete wall because a bunch of you other idiots were egging him on."

"He won five bucks for that, Dad! Does that sound idiotic to you?! Because to me, it sounds like a...job!"

The way he said job made me laugh. Like, for reals laugh. Neil was twenty damn years old at this time and had accomplished absolutely nothing. He lived with our parents still, kept baby oil under his mattress, and had never worked a day in his life, despite my parent's desperate pleas to "just do something!"

"That's enough," Mom said, "both of you. Neil, a girl is missing. What she does or does not do doesn't take away from the fact that she didn't come home last night or this morning. I will have no negative talk about her, regardless of your feelings about her."

"Oh, please, mom," Neil said, "she's dead, and we all know it."

Dad was over it. He yelled, "Go to your goddamn room!" then turned Vin Scully up almost as loud as the TV could handle, signaling that this conversation was over for good, and Neil could either hop in his stupid Trans-Am and leave or return to his weird, creepy, lotion-scented bedroom.

Neil grabbed a bag of Laura Scudder potato chips from the counter and looked straight at my dad as if he was all prepared to fling him the zinger to end all zingers. All he could come up with was to bend his right leg up and make a loud fart noise before finally leaving.

Brilliant.

My brother, everyone.

"She's not dead, honey," my mom says like I'm an over-sensitive five-year-old wimp. I gave her a weird glance to subtly tell her that I was basically a man and that I didn't care either way.

Desperate to change the subject, I told Mom, "They sold that house around the corner. By Xavier's house."

My mom nodded. "I know."

"I saw the SOLD sign when me and Roxy were riding our bikes to Jimmy's after school yesterday."

My mom just nodded again, saying nothing.

I, the master of deduction, asked, "Did you sell that house?"

"No. I did not."

"Oh," I said. "Why not?" (Jesus Grant, just stop talking!)

"I honestly don't know, honey. I don't know why the Parkers didn't ask me to."

"Oh," I said, glancing at my dad, who was still watching Vin. "Sorry, mom."

"It's okay," she said, faking a smile. "There's nothing to be sorry about. I'll sell that house by the C.C. this week. For sure. I just know it. I'm showing it for the second time to a couple from down near Hollywood."

I make a show of crossing my fingers. My mom mirrors the gesture, and we both smile.

"You should try showing it at night," my dad said, "when there aren't so many damn kids there. Might help a little."

My mom perked up a bit, then said, "Good idea." And it was. The pool was the place to be in the daytime, but once evening came, most people moved the party home or to Jimmy's or wherever else.

Let me take this opportunity to tell you about my dog at the time. In every coming-of-age or adventure movie featuring kids, there is always a faithful companion in the form of one of the boys' dogs. The dog is always great, sticks by their side, sometimes even saving the day.

My dog was the exact opposite. He was fat and lazy, and if you left the front door open, he would suddenly gain superpowers and run away, usually directly into oncoming cars. For the life of me, I can't figure out how he lived until the age of seventeen.

He was seriously dumber than a bag of rocks. When we got him, my surfer dude dad wanted to name him Ocean Pacific, after the popular brand, and I wanted to name him Optimus Prime, after the leader of the Autobots on TV's Transformers.

What are the odds that both of us wanted to name the dog such a stupid name that could both be shortened to O.P.?!

So, that was his name, O.P. He was a good dog but utterly useless. So later in the story, when you may wonder why there isn't a ridiculously intelligent dog at our side, it's because this isn't fiction, and my dog was stupid.

By this time, my best friend since birth, Xavier, and I had sort of gone our separate ways. We still lived down the street from one another, but he ended up going to a private school, and I went to Quailwood. I never understood why he didn't just go to the school in the neighborhood, but I later figured out it was a private Catholic school. When he enrolled at the Catholic high school in town, it dawned on me like a big idiot.

I was okay with growing apart. It almost felt natural. And it's not like I never saw the guy again. He still lived down the street, and we hung out occasionally, especially over summer, but the title of Grant's best friend had been passed on.

There was a new hoser in town.

A Canadian family moved in around the corner, and their son and I became instant best friends. If he wasn't at my house, then I was at his house. And if we weren't there, we were at school or Jimmy's (no need for the community pool when we could just play in my backyard.)

Roxy Roxburgh was a little over a month younger than me, born on September 19th, 1979. Although Roxy wasn't his real name, I refused to call him anything else, as did pretty much anybody that knew him.

Although we're fully grown adults and no longer live with our parents, we still live in Quailwood and only one street over. When together, we hold about the same level of maturity as we did as kids.

It didn't take much to entertain us then, and it doesn't take much to entertain us now. We still like most of the same stupid garbage we liked back then, and we still watch the same movies. The only thing that has advanced is the video games we play.

What started as stick figures swinging a bat at a square baseball on my family's old Odyssey Entertainment System (Xavier had a ColecoVision, which wasn't much better – that system's Smurf's game involved a Smurf walking and... jumping, and literally nothing else), morphed into the super-advanced sports gaming of today, which neither of us really understand. However, we still play, set to idiot mode, swinging at every damn pitch that's thrown, just like those Triple-A ballers at Sam Lynn, because why the hell not.

Our families became good friends, too, which worked out very well for us. That meant we would get to travel a lot together and spend holidays with each other.

The very first time our parents met was at Pizza Hut shortly after they arrived in town. This was in late 1988. In fact, it was November 18th, 1988.

It was basically a fun way for the parents to meet each other and see who their child had been spending so much time with. We didn't care about that. Roxy and I, along with his older sister Hilary, who was the closest thing I ever had to a real sister (Neil was MIA, as usual, because he's an idiot), were running amok, enjoying the greasy pizza, the unlimited sodas in those textured red plastic cups, the video games (not nearly as good of a selection as Jimmy's), and those plastic *Land Before Time* dinosaur hand puppets that were being given away as a promotion.

Back then, Pizza Hut was extremely popular with kids due to their program called Book-It, which was basically designed to bribe kids into (lying about) reading books. It was started in 1984 by the president of Pizza Hut, Arthur Gunther, after the actual president, Ronald Reagan, called on American businesses to get involved in education.

Arthur's son was having trouble learning how to read, so Gunther met with educators in his hometown (and home base of Pizza Hut), Wichita, Kansas. His plan: To develop a program that would encourage kids to really try and develop their reading skills. The bribe: Free personal pan pizzas (along with other stuff, like buttons, shirts, stickers, whatever.)

Free. Pizzas.

(Disregard the fact that every pizza was free to a kid, those lousy freeloaders, but for some reason, this promotion was a hit!)

It launched nationwide in 1985, less than six months after it was dreamt up, and such a smash it was, by 1988, Bill Clinton had declared October 3rd Book It! Day in Arkansas, and even the awesomely awful syndicated afterschool sitcom *Small Wonder* (which I'm not ashamed to admit I own on DVD) featured the program in an episode when Vicki's class had to finish all their reading assignments and one of the students does some ridiculous hip-hop book report about Mr. T and Robin Hood and, I dunno, the show was fucking awful.

So, as cool as the Noid was for Domino's, the dumb Noid wasn't handing out free personal pans (which probably ended up costing the parents a lot of money to buy everything else, but what did we care? We were kids.)

Now, do you want to hear more about *Small Wonder?* The year was 1985, and legendary TV writer Howard Leeds was thinking of a way to... Nah, I'm kidding. I won't bore you with useless *Small Wonder* trivia!

Let's get back to Pizza Hut.

With my parents and Roxy's parents both being pretty damn likable, the night went unsurprisingly well, with everyone seeming to get along great. The evening, however, ended early for possibly the lamest reason ever - The Beach Boys were on *Full House* that night, and we had to get back early.

So did Roxy's family, for the exact same reason.

Once 7:30 hit, we dumped the rest of our quarters in the Flintstone's 'Dino's Lucky Egg' vending machine (A prize every time!), collected our future garbage that the game dispensed, and hit the road!

Full. House!

Beach. Boys!

Not even joking!

I *wish* I was joking, but unfortunately, I'm not. The Beach Boys were at the height of their comeback due to the popularity of the (now rather lame) hit song, Kokomo. And well, *Full House* was, and always will be, excellent.

So popular was the one-two punch of *Full House*, preceded at 8pm by *Perfect Strangers*, that a few months later, in 1989, the network would put together a special two-hour block of sitcoms and market it heavily towards families in a bid to get them to stay home on Friday nights and watch TV. It worked. TGIF was a hit that ran for over a decade. It launched with moving *Full House* to 8, followed by a new show, *Family Matters*, a spinoff of *Perfect Strangers,* that would follow directly after.

Family Matters, developed by Thomas Miller and Robert Boyett, of *Full House* and *Perfect Strangers* fame, began as a surprisingly fantastic and meaningful show featuring a middle-class African American family dealing with the everyday troubles of life, like struggling to pay the bills, discrimination, and even outright, tough-to-watch racism. It dealt with all these issues in funny ways that didn't lecture or patronize its audience. By the end of the show, however, the whacky and obnoxious nerd next door that hijacked the entire series literally teleports the family to Paris so he can fight his clone, then they travel back in time to fight pirates.

That fourth show on TGIF was always a toss-up. The three main shows were so popular that finding a new one that measured up proved challenging. *Mr. Belvedere* was there at first, but it was nearing the end of its run and was losing steam rapidly. It was replaced by *Just the Ten of Us*, which was complete and total lame sauce, then the *Look Who's Talking* rip-off *Baby Talk*, which somehow managed to be even lamer.

The point of all that was on a foggy November night, a second family for both us boys was forged. It was fantastic because it would make hanging out with Roxy much easier, which isn't to say it was difficult to begin with. Still, once parents get involved, and there is respect, trust, and friendship, it usually works out quite well for the kids, i.e., holidays, trips, vacations, etc...

Long before that night at Pizza Hut, however, Roxy and I had been plotting how to get our hands on a Nintendo Entertainment System. *Mario Bros* and a handful of other games had made their way to arcades by then, so we were already familiar with the Nintendo brand. It wasn't until heavy marketing for the home system invaded our lives that we were convinced that we would not be able to live if we didn't get one.

There are two Christmases from my childhood that really, really stick out. The first one is the Nintendo Christmas, and I believe that fateful night at Pizza Hut is what set the wheels in motion to make my dream come true.

Although, it certainly wasn't easy.

It had been a long, hard road to obtaining my NES, but I steadied the course and played it cool, dropping only the most subtle of hints (I remember pretending to faint during a Nintendo commercial) and a few days leading up to Christmas, right there under the tree, a wrapped box, approximately the size of a Nintendo game, had appeared! I looked under the tree for an NES-sized box but came up empty. I focused on the small box, holding it in my hand, trying to see if I could see through the wrapping paper. No luck. I tried shaking it, but I had no idea how the box was supposed to shake.

At that time, all I had ever done was look at unopened games at Toys R Us. You could never touch them because they were always kept in a separate room. Only the covers were displayed on the aisle. If you wanted to purchase a game, you would pull the corresponding ticket, take it to the register, pay for it, then walk to the side where they stored them. An employee would unlock that door and disappear into the back of the long, thin warehouse, emerging a few moments later with... the game!

As a child, this was one of the most enchanted moments in my life. But I wasn't there yet.

Not knowing what the box should feel like, I tried smelling the present, seeing if I could catch any whiff of Toys R Us on it. I failed.

I took the package and placed it by the phone at the bar dividing our kitchen from our living room. It could wait there, in plain sight, where I could gaze at it from any position in the kitchen, living room, or family room. Back then, we had two different rooms off the kitchen. We had the wall knocked out in 1993, making one giant room that was so much better (and it forced my parents to remove that wood paneling that, I believe, every house in the 80s was required to have on the walls). The wall was removed because my mom bought my dad a giant screen TV. It was so damn big that our house required major construction just to watch it.

But at that point, the game was placed at the pinnacle of all three rooms, dead center, where I could always watch it closely.

Any story you may have heard about the late eighties' Nintendo craze is true. We kids craved it like a drug. Nothing would get in our way of getting one. No matter what the cost, no matter the sacrifice, like an addict, we needed even the occasional taste just to survive.

When word got out that a kid at our school had one, we were on the case. The kid, I'm ashamed to even say this, was 'the booger eater' who didn't have a lot of friends. What he did have, however, was an NES, and Roxy and I needed it. And wouldn't ya know it, the same day we found out snot-snacking Danny had one was the same day we realized we wanted to be his friend?

Like, what a lucky coincidence for us!

Danny lived on the same street Bebe lived on, down at the far end of a cul-de-sac on the other side of the school. Roxy and I walked down there one weekend morning and, without a single drop of shame, knocked on his door. When his mom answered, we told her we were there to play with her son. We were so cute, and she was probably thrilled her dorky kid had visitors that she welcomed us with open arms.

Subtlety was not our forte, so before she even told us where Danny was, Roxy shouted, literally shouted, "Which room is the Nintendo in?!"

The volume of his voice was startling, even to me, probably even to him, but we had no choice but to play it cool. We stopped in our tracks, turned, faced Danny's mom, and smiled the biggest, goofiest smiles our dumb faces could manage.

Yep, we were totally innocent. Just a couple of friends coming to visit. Nothing out of the ordinary here. Now, if you'll kindly point us in the direction of the NES, uh, I mean, um, Danny, we'll get out of your hair, ma'am.

Little bullshittin' Eddie Haskell punks.

Our dumb (and ridiculously selfish) plan worked because we got what we wanted. In fact, we completely steamrolled poor Danny, basically hogging both controllers for ourselves, forcing him to be an observer in his own home until it was time for us to go.

Our parents figured it out somehow (I'm still unsure how. Did Danny rat on us? Had his mom called our moms?) and were not pleased. We could only hang out with Danny if we didn't use him for his Nintendo.

We never stepped foot in his house again.

Not an ounce of shame.

Not even a drop.

Back to that mysterious wrapped present. A funny thing happened that Christmas morning. I was consumed in the excitement that was only possible at that age, at that time - so consumed I had somehow forgotten all about the present. I opened everything under the tree and didn't get my Nintendo. It was weird. I wasn't mad or anything, I was still having a great time, and I liked everything I got. I remember my brother got a huge stereo that kids his age would often rest on their shoulders as they strutted through town. At the time, they were called Ghetto Blasters, but thankfully they eventually switched to the much less problematic name of Boom Box. I could hear his stupid music playing from his bedroom while I was still basking in the Christmas Morning Afterglow.

It was such a fun morning that somehow, someway...I had totally forgotten about that damn mystery present. Exactly how it happened, I don't have a clue. But in my forgetfulness, it allowed my parents to flawlessly pull off a *Christmas Story* miracle. My dad had hidden my NES behind his recliner. He even went so far as to do the ol' "Heyyy, what's that over there" thing to me.

My Nintendo.

Had I remembered the game I specifically set aside, none of this would have worked. It makes no sense. I don't believe in miracles in the religious sense, but from that day forward, I believed in miracles of joy. And my parents slipping up and putting that game under the tree where I could have easily peeked, followed by me not only finding the present but singling it out, then somehow forgetting about it on Christmas morning so my parents could pull that off, was a miracle. Pure and simple.

It was the best Christmas of my life.

If you're wondering what the game was, it was *Kung Fu*, the Nintendo version of the arcade game *Kung Fu*

Master that my dad and I constantly played at Jimmy's. It was so great.

Christmas 1988. You had to be there.

The following Christmas, the animated television show *The Simpsons* would premier with their holiday special, *Simpsons Roasting on an Open Fire*, followed by their own series, spawning from *The Tracey Ulman Show*. From the first few seconds of watching it at Roxy's house with our parents and his sister (who laughed at the opening title screen), I knew it was something special. Still, I didn't know how much it would inspire and mold me into who I am today. Created by Oregon native Matt Groening, *The Simpsons* is still producing new episodes at the time of this writing, some thirty-four years after that Christmas special aired.

Oh, and if you're wondering if Roxy got an NES that Christmas, too, he did. Like I said, best Christmas ever.

The second most memorable Christmas was in 1990, just a few months after Bebe's murder. The mood was much more somber. A dark cloud had cast itself over my neighborhood, probably over the whole town, but I had no way of knowing.

The morning was freezing. We've only gotten snow in Bakersfield once in my lifetime, and that wasn't until 1999, but on that morning, we got the next best thing. We got ice and frost. It had rained earlier the night before, then the temp hit 25 overnight. In the morning, the sidewalks, streets, and lawns were completely frozen over.

This was the Rollerblade Christmas, as I fondly call it.

Roxy and I each got a pair (Lightning TRS for both of us), as did Xavier (Macro Blades for him), who joined us that morning, along with another friend I'll introduce soon. We laced up and attempted to blade around the neighborhood on ice. It's one of the fondest memories I have of my childhood and nothing eventful happened, just four jackasses risking injury for fun. It was the turning point of healing after Bebe.

The skate mega-company arrived in a big way in

1990, although the inline skate itself had been around since the 1800s. It took a 19-year-old kid from a Minneapolis suburb to stumble across an old catalog featuring the skates to light the spark that started the fire of one of the '90s most popular products. Rollerblades hit in 1988, and by the time we got ours that Christmas morning, it was a half-a-billion-dollar industry.

Planned initially as helping hockey players during the off-season, Roxy's dad had a pair before any of us – he was an amateur hockey player and loved those damn things, but they weren't cool then, so we paid no attention.

Unwrapping those skates that morning felt like a new hope - a fresh start after the overall terribleness the entire little town had felt since that Fourth of July.

A young girl was murdered, but a small group of kids were able to find some happiness by falling on ice. The media had stopped shoving microphones in our faces by then, and we were finally back to just being kids, although I'm not sure how long it lasted. Looking back, it feels like the second half of 1990 had the potential to be the end of our innocence, like we were forced to grow up faster than necessary. Bebe's murder had robbed all of us of something, I'm sure of that, but I'm glad it didn't take everything. I was proud of our resilience.

I wonder how we felt at the time. Could we feel our lives slowly being returned to us? We had lived under a cloud for almost six months, so maybe that's why that Christmas sticks out so much. Perhaps our real gift was getting our childhood back for a precious few more years.

"Anyway," Mom said after our finger-crossing that Bebe would turn up safe and sound, "hopefully, she's just at a friend's house."

"Yeah, no kidding," my dad said from his recliner, the footrest so far up that he was almost completely horizontal, as he (somehow) watched the Dodger pre-game show on KTLA, the volume turned back down to a much more manageable level since dumbass Neil fart-walked his way out of the room. "I bet she got pissed at her parents."

"Probably," I said.

"If you do something stupid like run away when you're mad at us," my dad said, "we won't come looking for you. You know where the food is."

"Gary!" my mom said, fully aware he was joking. That's all it took to move on from the missing girl and my idiot brother.

For that day, at least.

After I left the living room, I walked down the hallway and entered Neil's room unannounced.

"Haven't you heard of knocking, you human turnip?!" Neil yelled at me before pegging me in the face with one of his pillows. He was wearing gigantic headphones over his ears and looking at a cassette tape insert. I had no idea what band it was, but I could almost guarantee it sucked. His music always sounded like the videos would feature unicorns shooting laser beams out of their buttholes while flying over rainbows or some shit. It was so lame.

"I did knock, you dumb fuckin' CHUD," I lied. Once all parents were out of earshot, us kids let the expletives fly! "Maybe if you turned your dumb dancing-Hobbit music down, you would have heard me." I picked up the pillow and asked, "Why the hell is this so crunchy?!"

"Give that back to me, you little skidmark!" Neil yelled, way too over the top, considering he's the one that threw it at me in the first place.

I chucked it back, nailing him right in the side of his head and spinning his headphones around.

"Gawd! So let me get this straight. You knocked, and I didn't answer, so you just came in, anyway?"

I shrugged. Neil sighed.

"Well," he said, "what the hell do you want?"

I walked farther into his room and sat on the end of his bed. This seemed to enrage Neil, but he somehow managed to maintain his cool. He was still wearing his shades, after all. It smelled like the store Hot Topic would smell later on in the mid-90s – some weird mix of incense, plastic, and straight-up nastiness. Gone was the lotion smell I was used to and, honestly, preferred.

"That girl," I said.

"What girl?"

"The one that's missing," I said. "You know. Town Bicycle."

The music still blared from his headphones, even though they were wrapped around his neck. "Ohhh, that girl. Bebe-Lynn. What about her?"

I stalled for a few seconds before finally saying, "She's really dead?"

Neil, smiling, said, "Totally!" He seemed to be getting a kick out of this, though I didn't really understand why at the time. This wasn't a movie; this wasn't even some exploding space shuttle - this was a person we knew in real life.

"How... do you know, though?" I was genuinely curious and distinctly remember getting a pit in my stomach.

"I'm a smart fella, lil' bro."

"That's not... I mean, did you see her?"

"Did I see her?" Neil said, finally turning his crappy, butthole-unicorn music down. "Yeah, dude, I saw her every day at school for like two years before I graduated."

This fool barely graduated. And when I say barely, I'm talkin' the teachers probably gave him a d-minus just so they wouldn't have to deal with him a second time. It's what I suspect happened in every grade he went through. It seemed like a miracle that he was never held back, but when you think about it, who would want him for two years in a row?

"That's not what I meant," I said, gulping loudly; that pit getting bigger and more unmanageable, my mouth getting dryer and dryer by the second. I regretted going in there.

"Oh," Neil said, "you mean did I see her disgusting, maggot-infested rotting corpse?"

I nodded, my mouth too dry to squeak out a single word.

"Nah."

I took a deep breath, saliva began to fill my mouth again, but the pit remained. I managed to ask how he knew she was dead.

"Look, kid," he said, scooching down the bed and sitting next to me, which was weird. "People just don't go missing for no reason. She didn't have a car or a bike, so it's not like she took off somewhere, and she didn't even have a job or money because her family is probably poor or some shit. So where would she even be able to go? She was chained here. Just like you. No escape! Ever!"

Apparently, my brother had been taking overacting classes from my mother and Ms. Franks. I shrugged off his dramatics and asked, "What if she's lost?"

"Lost?" Neil laughed. "Here? This town is like tiny, dude, and she's lived here her entire life. Just like us. How the hell would she get lost? Dumbass. Would you get lost here?"

"N-no... I suppose not," I said, trying to gather my thoughts. "But, if she's dead...how did she die? And where is her body?"

"Bro," Neil said, slinging his arm around my shoulders, "you know she was probably at Jimmy's or whatever to meet some older dude or somethin'. Guy probably got what he wanted from her then killed her. Dumped her ass in a ditch or something. Happens all the time, my man. Sad but true."

"It does? I thought shit like that only happened in those made-for-TV movies." I wasn't that naïve, I knew most of those terrible Sunday night movies were based on true stories, but I didn't know what else to say, and, despite the pit in my stomach turning into a cauldron for poo, I didn't want this conversation to end just yet.

Neil arched his eyebrows like Magnum P.I. and said, "Yep!"

"What was it that the guy...wanted?"

I knew damn well what the guy wanted. I wasn't an idiot. Maybe I didn't know exactly what sex was, but I knew it involved girls, and I knew it involved boners, which I felt I was an expert on by that point in my life. I was a boner machine, same with Roxy, same with Xavier. We would even sometimes compare our boners in some weird contest of... actually, I have no idea. We were only ten, so they were certainly nothing to brag about.

Kids today have it easy. Porn is never more than a few clicks away and can be carried safely and discreetly in your pocket. But back then, shit was rough!

There were a few nudie channels on cable, but you had to subscribe to them, which none of our families did. Instead of simply not showing up while scrolling like blocked channels do these days, the nudies were scrambled, causing every adult who scrolled past them to click the remote extra fast to save the embarrassment of even acknowledging those channels existed.

But when the parents weren't around, that jumbled tits' n ass channel was the most watched program on television for boys my age. We would gather around the TV, as close as we could get in the hopes of glimpsing a brief nipple, a flash of ass, literally anything. How many knees we mistook as tits is probably laughable, but at the time, it was the greatest thing ever. And if the boner gods happened to be smiling down upon us that day, we might even hear a moan.

Watch out! Hoo-boy! I'm convinced this was the most exciting moment in the lives of a pre-pubescent boy in the late 80s.

If a parent happened to come home unannounced, whoever was in charge of the remote could quickly hit the Flashback button. The TV would flip to more wholesome entertainment, like the cheesy, syndicated game show *Funhouse*, starring JD Roth and Tiny. Totally family-approved. Nothing weird goin' on here, Mom and Dad. Just some kids watching a little TV with a crayon in our pockets.

As far as I knew, the adults were none the wiser, but I could be wrong. We just assumed adults were idiots, but that didn't mean they actually were.

But still, at that age, our nudity was limited to horror

movies, which is probably why we were such big fans of them. Still, we longed to see a fully nude woman, like in those magazines behind the register at the mini-mart. One day we would get our hands on one. We had to!

"Ask Mom and Dad," Neil said, laughing, knowing full well I would never dream of broaching that subject with our parents. *Uh yeah, hey Mom, hey Dad, groovy, yeah, I was wondering if you could tell me about sex. I am really interested, and there isn't anyone else in the whole wide world I want to hear about it from more than you guys.*

Said no kid ever!

I pressed on with Neil. "Do you know where she is, then?"

"You know that huge, wooded area on the other side of The Tube?"

"Duh."

"Well, if you go deeper into the woods, way deeper, that's where she is."

I smelled bullshit, but there was still a chance it was true. "How come they haven't found her yet, then?"

"Because it's a secret, dumbass. You don't hide a body out there and then tell everyone about it. Jesus. Nobody talks about it."

"We're talking about it."

"Get a load of this kid!" My brother leaned in even closer to me, I could smell the disgusting cigarettes on his breath, and he whispered, "That's because I know I can trust you. Right?"

I nodded. "Yeah. Of course, Neil. You can trust me. But I thought all the bodies were in the sump..."

"No way. The sump is way too obvious. You're such a child."

And that was that. I got up and exited the room.

Roxy came over a few hours later, and we took our bikes down to the park to hang out like we usually did on Saturday afternoons, this time with a goal in mind. Xavier joined us on the ride down. It was always nice when he was with us. I missed him, even though I very clearly had a new best friend, and I'm sure he did too at his private school.

"Did you see the new neighbors?" Xavier asked as his bike pulled even with ours.

"Which ones?" Roxy asked.

"The ones that moved in around the corner from me."

"Oh yeah! No, why, did you?"

"Yeah. I think they're black."

Black people in our neighborhood were a rarity. As far as I knew, only a small handful of black kids were at our grade school, though more would start rolling in later.

"Right on," I said. "Wanna go check it out?"

"Heck yeah!" Xavier said, and we swiftly turned the corner, already abandoning our hunt for the supposed dead girl.

We pulled up, dropped our bikes like the Frog Brothers in *The Lost Boys*, and stared at the house. The SOLD sign was still there, but there wasn't a person in sight.

"They were there this morning," Xavier said. "There were five of them."

"Five of them?" Roxy said.

"Yeah, dude. A mom, a dad, two boys, and a girl. One boy was like a toddler, though, and the other one looked like our age. The girl was older. Probably junior high school."

"Was she hot?" Roxy and I said in unison.

"Probably. Looked pretty hot, but I was far away. It may require closer inspection. I'm the man for the job."

We both laughed at him.

"Whatever," Xavier said. A sick burn, indeed.

"We'll come back later," Roxy said, picking up his bike from the gutter. "You wanna go to the pool?"

So much for finding Bebe. A pathetic effort at best.

"I don't even have my suit," Xavier said.

"Dude, I could spit on your house from here. Besides, we don't have ours either. We're not going to swim, dude. We're going to scope chicks! Grant, you in?"

"I thought we were going to the park to..."

"We can go to the park any day. It's Saturday afternoon. That pool is gonna be poppin' off. Come on, I bet Daphne will be there."

Daphne Monroe. The girl of my dreams. Cheerleader at our school. Daughter of the town sheriff. And my neighbor.

I've never been able to say more than four words to her at a time. It was embarrassing, I know, but there was nothing I could do about it. The closest I got was the previous school year during computer lab. I was sitting there playing a round of *Where in the World is Carmen San Diego* when my machine completely crashed. I told the teacher, and she pointed to an empty seat right next to...you guessed it. Daphne. I walked over there as slowly as possible and sat. She smiled at me and said, "Hey, Grant." This was the closest I had ever been to her, like our elbows would literally touch when she moved the mouse around. Roxy noticed and was fanning his arms at me, trying to get me to talk to her.

I saw Roxy mouth, "Say something, stupid!"

I was panicking. What could I say? The obvious response would have been to say hi back, but I wasn't thinking correctly.

A solid two minutes had gone by since she talked to me, and I sat there, frozen. I stared at her until she turned to look at me again, and I said, "I like Sprite, also."

I wanted to die.

Why did I say that? First off, she didn't say she liked Sprite to begin with, so why did I say also? Second, there wasn't a Sprite anywhere nearby, so again, why?!

What an epic disaster.

She nodded, looked confused, giggled, and said, "Yeah, I guess it's pretty good," then she returned to her game.

But Roxy was right. There was an excellent chance she would be at the pool, and I would love to get some redemption. Literally, anything I said would be cooler than 'I like Sprite, also.' I didn't even like Sprite! It tastes like lemony pee-pee! I had no idea what I was talking about and wanted to cry. The only positive was I couldn't do any worse next time. Up was the only way to go from there, so watch out Daphne Monroe, Grant is on the prowl!

"*Ohhhh, I love you, Daphne,*" Xavier said, mocking me, which was ballsy, considering the only girl I'd ever seen him talk to was his mom. But it was true what he said. Maybe I was too young to know what true love was, but at the time, no one could have convinced me otherwise.

"Dude," Roxy said, "she might be wearing a bikini. You know the Monroes don't have a pool, and it's a very hot day. I bet she's dying to jump into that nice, cool water and maybe even frolic! And you can be there. Watching her frolic. Where else would you rather be, dude? Tell me, where?"

The truth was, there was no other place I'd rather be than there, especially if that situation Roxy made up turned out to be true. "I'm in."

"To the pool!" Xavier yelled, lifting his bike and taking off toward the community center. When we arrived, the parking lot was filled with cars, and the sidewalk was littered with bikes. There was an excellent chance Daphne would be there. I was getting nervous.

When we walked in, I scanned the crowd and didn't see her. My heart sank. That day was totally going to be the day I talked to her. I just knew it. Oh well, it would have to wait.

Daphne may not have been there, but several girls I knew, like Chelsey Cady, Sharon Little, Devin Kerns, and Nicole Leathers, were huddled in the far corner, talking and giggling about who knows what. I waved, but no one saw me.

Xavier leaned over and whispered in my ear, "Check out the babes!"

The 'babes' were high school girls in skimpy bikinis, and boy, was there plenty for our viewing pleasure that day. The downside, however, was they seemed to all be talking to high school guys, each of them shirtless and tanned, none of which seemed to be bothered about the missing Bebe.

"Son of a mother!" Roxy mumbled. "We need tans, bros."

Xavier was the darkest of the three of us, and that's only because his grandfather was from Mexico. The fact of the matter was we were all just scrawny little white boys, and girls simply would not pay us any attention.

"Got any suntan lotion?" Roxy asked me.

"I'm not sure. I know we have sunblock; my mom makes me put it on every time I go swimming. Bull Frog. It's neon!"

"Yeah," Roxy mumbled. He had to put it on too. "I know."

"Xavier?"

"We don't have a pool, and my parents aren't really the laying out type."

I had an idea. "You know what? My idiot brother has some lotion under his mattress."

"Suntan lotion?" Roxy asked, pep in his voice.

"Probably! What other lotion would he have?"

"True! Can you get it?"

"We can definitely sneak in and steal it if he's not home."

"Let's ride!"

We gathered our bikes and headed back to my house. My brother's stupid Trans-Am wasn't parked in the driveway, so we really lucked out. We walked into the house, and Roxy and Xavier quickly moved into the living room to distract my parents with way-too-friendly chitchat. They couldn't have been more obvious.

No matter, though. With lotion in hand, I was in and out of my brother's bedroom in thirty seconds. I quickly ran to the bathroom and flushed the toilet, then walked back out, cool as a cucumber, with the lotion shoved down the back of my shorts.

"Whew," I said, "much better. I had to pee so bad I could taste it. Okay, we can go again."

My parents were none the wiser. We said goodbye

and headed right back out the door we came in.

In those glorious olden days, kids would come and go as they pleased. Parents didn't helicopter over you, making sure you were constantly safe. Some days you left the house in the morning and didn't return until well after nightfall. Some kids had curfews, like when the streetlights came on, but not us. We were free to roam as we pleased, which is perhaps why Bebe missing for only a day wasn't too startling to people.

That would all change less than twenty-four hours later, but right then, life was good. We headed back down to the pool, crashed our bikes into a wall, and headed in like we owned the place. Roxy tore off his shirt like a wrestler entering the ring at *Halloween Havoc*, twirled it around his head a few times before launching it randomly onto the concrete. Xavier and I followed suit. We sure felt like hot shit, despite not catching a single glance from any member of the opposite sex, although Booger-Eating Danny saw us and waved. Damn-it.

No matter, though. That would all change once we got sweet tans like all these high school dudes seemed to have. We scoped out three plastic loungers on the far side of the pool and sauntered over to them like we were the coolest kids in school, our pale bodies glistening in the sunlight, blinding anyone unlucky enough to look in our direction as we passed.

The oil was still tucked in my shorts, so I removed it and held it up like it was the holy grail.

"I don't think that's suntan oil, dude," Roxy said, grabbing it from my hands.

I grabbed it back and said, "What's the difference? Oil is oil."

"Says it's for babies."

"It's not for babies. It's just called baby oil. Like, that's the brand. It'll work."

"Yeah," Xavier said excitedly, "it'll work!"

I squeezed out a palmful and rubbed it on my dorky little body, face included, then passed it to Roxy, who did the same thing and passed it to Xavier. We took a moment to gaze at each other. We sparkled. Even our shorts had become covered in the oil, somehow. Apparently, a little baby oil goes a long way. No worries, though. The chicks were sure to notice us now! How could they not?! We looked like Arnold in *Commando* or the Ultimate Warrior. This was gonna be awesome.

Roxy went to lay down on the lounger, glancing around the pool one last time before taking a seat, hoping to build some hype for his soon-to-be incredible bod, but as soon as his skin made contact with that cheap plastic, he lost all control, sliding straight off, twisting in midair before landing face first on the concrete. "Fuckin' shit!" he yelled! His face had left a perfect oily impression on the ground.

In normal situations, I would have died laughing, but there was no time. I was past the point of no return, Xavier too. We were committed to sitting, and there was nothing we could do about it. I slipped right through the plastic slats, as smoothly as a hot knife through butter (pardon the cliché), my ass hitting the hard ground, my legs hoisted up by my nose. I heard Xavier yell, followed closely by a thud, but I couldn't see what had happened to him. I struggled to get up, but it was no use. The oil was everywhere. I could see Roxy, now flat on his back like a flipped turtle, struggling like mad to no avail.

The sounds of laughter coming at us in all directions was like a donkey kick straight to the nuts. All those hot high school girls, all those tanned and cool high school boys, parents, grandparents, little children, even that dork Danny, they all laughed at us. Roxy yelling the obscenity to end all obscenities had drawn everyone's attention.

At that moment, we were the most popular kids at the pool. Only, we would have given anything not to be. We were panicked, unsure if we would ever survive this situation. My motivation to get out of there was heightened with each failed attempt to get up because I knew, I just knew, that Daphne would be arriving soon. If she saw me like this, that was it. It would be all over.

There's no coming back from it.

We could survive the laughter from a bunch of older kids, and we could possibly survive endless retelling of the events to people who missed it, but there was no way I could survive if Daphne saw me like this, fighting with a cheap plastic lounger while looking like hot glazed ham.

I had to get up!

My hands were useless. Trying to grip the side of the chair was like trying to grasp melting ice. My only chance was to fling my legs outward, like a crab, and try to get my feet to contact the ground.

I looked back up just in time to see Roxy fall again. To my left, Xavier was face down, not moving. He had given up. Tapped out. Called it quits. He would die here, his mind seemingly made up.

My left foot touched something, but it wasn't the ground. I think it was Xavier's chair. With all the force I could muster up from the thought of Daphne walking in and seeing this, I pushed. Over and over until I eventually applied enough pressure to hoist myself out of the plastic beartrap I was stuck in.

Ever so gently, I rolled to my side, then slid both legs around and set my feet flat on the ground. It would be risky, but I had to try and stand. I was focused. The laughter didn't bother me anymore; it could have died down entirely for all I knew.

I was in the zone.

You know when you sit on the toilet too long, then you have to stand back up, but your legs are completely dead, and you kinda get up and stumble around like a newborn cow, desperately trying to not break a leg or roll an ankle?

That's what I did.

It wasn't pretty, but it worked. I was vertical!

Roxy had managed to roll back onto his stomach and was in the process of getting to his knees.

"Xavier."

His head rolled to look at me.

"Come on, dude. We've gotta get the hell out of here."

"It…" Xavier said quietly. "It didn't work."

"No, dude. It sure didn't."

Roxy had gotten up, but we both remained completely still, like our feet were bolted to the ground or like we had on those magnetic prison boots from *Face/Off*.

"We gotta get the hell outta here, dude."

Xavier managed to pull himself onto the lounger, then slid like a snake right back off and onto the ground with a moist splat. We couldn't wait for him, and any attempt at us pulling him up would end in all three of us back down. We had to leave him. We had no choice. The nearest exit was twenty feet away; the back gate led out to a small park area and the basketball courts.

We took one step, and both almost fell. It was going to be more complicated than we thought. Another step, another success, but just barely.

Xavier had begun sliding himself across the cement on his belly. It wasn't pretty, and he was leaving a little snail trail, but he was making better time than us. We took another step, and Xavier pulled ahead of us.

Another step.

We hit his stupid oil-slick trail, and both went down on our asses hard. We yelled obscenities, the worst we could think of, some that didn't even make sense. We were desperate and needed out of there pronto.

We followed Xavier's lead and scooted ourselves out. We looked like we were breakdancing our way to refuge. The funny thing about all this was that we could not stop laughing once we started sliding and rolling our way to safety.

The laughing could help soften the blow of the humiliation we were suffering by at least forcing the crowd to laugh with us instead of at us.

Xavier reached the metal gate door, reached up, and tried to grip the handle. It took three tries, but it finally pulled down far enough to disengage the lock. He pushed the door open and slithered out. Roxy and I followed. Once we hit the dirt, it was much easier to stand.

Roxy slammed the door behind us.

We made it.

We could still hear some laughter, but we didn't care. We were out. And Daphne didn't see. I could breathe a sigh of relief.

Whew!

A group of boys was hanging out under a tree about twenty feet ahead of us. We ducked behind some dumpsters to not draw any more ridicule. Eventually, we calmed down, although we would still bust out in little giggle fits from time to time.

After about ten minutes we felt the coast was clear. All we heard from the pool were typical screams and non-mocking laughter. I peeked my head out from behind the large trashcan, checking if the coast was, indeed, clear. We still had to get on (and stay on!) our bicycles somehow, and we really didn't want an audience.

One of the boys up ahead I recognized as Daphne's older brother. He was in junior high. I was suddenly terrified that Daphne might arrive and see us covered in oil and dirt and grass like a trio of Swamp Thing wannabes. Could you imagine?

I called off our escape. I just couldn't chance it. Maybe Daphne was back here with her brother. Just because I didn't see her doesn't mean she wasn't there.

I told my friends to *shh*. I needed to listen. They didn't know what I was listening for, but they joined in intently all the same.

Jeremy Monroe, Daphne's brother, was talking to his friends. I struggled to make out the words at first, but like tuning in a radio station, his words became clearer the more I concentrated, and I heard him distinctly say the words' porno mag.'

I first learned what a porno mag was when my parents told me, much to my embarrassment, during an explanation of why they didn't want me listening to the Beastie Boys. On the Beastie's breakthrough track (which turned out to be a parody song of dumb frat boy music), *Fight for Your Right (To Party),* Mike D proclaims his dad threw away his best porno mag.

I was so dumb. After the explanation, I thought mag was a bad word. I remember seeing a MAD Magazine with a cover that proclaimed it America's Wackiest Mag! I was afraid my parents would soon ban me from MAD as well.

What an idiot.

To say my parents' ban backfired would be an understatement. The Beastie Boys turned out to be my all-time favorite band, and as I type this, right now, locked away in my office at the age of forty-three, I am wearing a Beastie Boys hoodie.

Back in the eighties, music was sold on little plastic squares with tape rolled inside, called cassette tapes. They were similar to VHS but smaller, and you would play them in a, you guessed it, tape deck. A major perk for broke kids in that era was that tapes were endlessly copyable, meaning if you had a dual tape deck, you could put one tape in one deck, then a blank tape, available at that time literally almost everywhere, in the other deck, and easily transfer the contents on the music tape to the blank tape, by only pressing PLAY and RECORD at the same time.

It was brilliant.

I remember telling my parents I desperately needed a tape called *Licensed to Ill* by this incredible new rap group, The Beastie Boys.

It was a hard no.

The same hard no I would get hit with less than a year later when I absolutely needed the tape from a new rock band formed from the ashes of hard rock groups L.A. Guns and Hollywood Rose, Guns' n Roses, another of my all-time favorites.

As for the Beastie Boys, with some begging (relentlessly), I was finally able to convince my parents I could have the *Fight for Your Right* single. (Back then, you were able to buy a tape or 45 record with one, or maybe two, songs on it, much like you can do now on iTunes or whatever, but way more awesome. These singles turned into loopholes for certain bands to get their music into the hands of the youth without the dreaded Parental Advisory logo by offering singles of hit songs, usually cleaned up for radio play, like 2 Live Crew's *Me So Horny* {which was somehow perfectly acceptable}, then sneaking a dirty track on the B-side {*City of Boom*}. GN'R's *Welcome to the Jungle* had *Mr. Brownstone* on the flip side, complete with F words and no advisory.)

Anyway, like I was saying, they agreed to the single, but wouldn't you know it, there was no single. You'd think a band that got its big break opening for Madonna and being universally hated by her crowds would at least be able to score a single. But as far as Bakersfield, CA, goes, there wasn't one to be found.

Luckily for me, one of the neighbors, who my dad always referred to as a jackass, happened to have the full album. He was in high school in 1986/87 when all this was going down, so I have no idea how I convinced him to come hang out and let me bum his tape. But he did.

He sat in our living room, sleeves ripped off his shirt, along with Xavier and me, as I set up the song for recording. My parents were in the kitchen watching, with odd looks on their faces. No idea where my brother was, as usual.

Jackass Neighbor, whose name was Billy, said, and I'll never forget it, "Come on, Mom and Dad, quit being such wet blankets and give it a chance."

My parents, former hippies, not wanting to be wet blankets and probably in shock that this little idiot would talk to them like that, agreed to give it a chance. It went exactly as well as you'd expect, and when all was said and done, I was lucky I was able to record even the one song.

No matter, though, Billy being the rebel he is, made me a full tape and gave it to me the next day. Three months later, Billy and his family moved away. I did a google search of him last week to prepare for this segment and was saddened to learn he was killed just a few weeks after moving away. The story I found said a drunk driver smashed into the back of his parent's car while they were down in Yucca Valley. Honestly, I had no idea and feel bad about it. Billy was a cool guy, and my dad only called him a jackass because he was a typical, obnoxious high school kid.

If there is an afterlife, maybe Billy could see how much his small, kind little act changed my life, and that might bring him a spark of joy. Who knows.

In high school, I drifted away from my friends a bit; like many childhood friendships go, different people fall in with different groups. I fell in with afterschool drama nerds, which left me pretty much friendless for the first two years at that new school.

I would ease my loneliness by carrying around my Diskman and constantly listening to the Beasties. At the time, their fourth full-length album, *Ill Communication*, had just come out hot on the heels of *Check Your Head*, and I couldn't get enough. I would fill my free time down at World Records, a local record store in the shopping center across the street from my neighborhood that specialized in imports and hard-to-find albums. I would collect as many imported B-Boys disks as I could get my hands on, and there were a lot, each one featuring new remixes of old songs, live versions, demo tracks, etc.

Out of the hundreds of concerts I've attended in my life, I could only see the Beasties once, during the *Hello Nasty Tour*, September 11th, 1998, at the Great Western Forum in Inglewood. It was spectacular.

In 2009, for my very first Father's Day present, my wife got me two tickets to see them at the Hollywood Bowl on September 24th of that year. Less than one month later, on July 19th, Adam Yauch, in a video with fellow Beastie Adam Horowitz, announced the tour would be canceled – Yauch had a cancerous tumor in his left salivary gland, and he would need to have surgery. He was optimistic, as usual, and said since the cancer was localized, it wouldn't affect his vocal cords and that he would see us all again soon.

I wasn't even sad or disappointed about missing the show. I only needed him to get better. He was there for me through so much, I had to be there for him, as silly as it sounds.

It was the last time I ever saw him alive.

Adam Yauch died on May 4th, 2012, at just forty-seven years of age. He was the first (and only so far) celebrity death that really took the wind out of my sails. When I found out, my wife and I were driving into Hollywood to watch *The Avengers* at the El Capitan. I had to pull over.

Long live the Beasties, and RIP MCA!

"Yeah," Jeremy said, "My old man's got a mad amount of them. I've seen 'em! Tits-o-Rama! Cooter-a-plenty!"

Xavier's ears perked up, "Did he say Sheriff Monroe has a bunch of porno?!"

"Did he say tits and cooter?!" Roxy said, also way more attentive now.

"And 'o Rama!" I added.

"So much beaver, dudes, I promise," Jeremy said, eliciting squeals from his little gang of perverts.

Roxy turned to me, his hands up by his face with pure excitement, and quietly yelled, "Muff!"

"No way," one of Jeremy's buddies said, "prove it!"

"Prove it? You want me to prove it?"

"Hell yeah, we do, dipstick, don't bogart 'em! Share, man! Sharing is caring!"

Jeremy looked offended but took the challenge seriously. "Fine, lameoids, I'll prove it. Meet me at Jimmy's tonight, and I'll show you."

"You're on," another boy said as they gathered up their bikes and took off.

"Holy shit," I whispered, "we have to go to Jimmy's tonight!"

"He's not going to let us see them, you know," Xavier said. "They're in junior high, dude. No chance."

"Can we break into their house?" Roxy asked, practically salivating at the thought of finally seeing the ever-elusive female crotch. Our previous attempts to see one was thwarted by adults who didn't want us kids to have a good time. We were resigned to hoping for a half-second clip of a moan and possibly a nipple that was probably a knee.

Our most recent attempt to get our hands on a mag happened the weekend prior. There was a mini-mart up the street and around the corner (they had the best little deli there, too), and behind the counter, and behind cardboard blockers, were the magazines, only their titles visible – Playboy, Hustler, Penthouse, Asian Fever, Beaver Hunt, Swank, Juggs, Perfect 10, and so much more. An entire rack dedicated to these little paperback miracles. And they could be ours if we could just reach over the counter far enough to snag them.

We needed a distraction, though. This is where our horny little idiotic brains kicked into high gear. While eating a Tootsie Roll Pop, I discovered my wrapper had the little Indian (indigenous, but everyone in the 80s was a moron) kid with the bow and arrow. Next to said bow and arrow, a STAR! Now, everyone in the world knew that if you got a wrapper with a star next to the bow and arrow, that entitled you to a free Tootsie Pop.

The plan we came up with was for me and Roxy to approach the mini-mart clerk with our winning wrapper, explaining how we were now entitled to a free sucker, while Xavier, the tallest of the bunch (now the shortest), would reach over and grab any magazines he could get his hands on and quickly stuff them down his shorts.

We were well prepared. I was convinced that in order to get this free Tootsie Pop, there would be a lot of red tape the clerk would have to go through, allowing Xavier ample time to get what we needed. So sure our plan would work, Xavier wore the shorts his mom bought him to 'grow into' so there would be a ton of room, probably enough room for one of each magazine.

It was going to work.

It had to.

Xavier walked into the store first, real smooth-like, and made his way to the deli, which wasn't even open yet. He would busy himself looking at items he was pretending to be considering buying. Shortly after, Roxy and I strutted in, totally normal, high on life, nothin' to see here, just a couple of kids out having a great time on a beautiful sunny summer day. We headed straight to the register, the wrapper in my hand, totally cool. I started to feel my heart thump in my chest. I heard Roxy gulp.

It's going to work, I thought over and over again.

It's going to work.

It's going to work.

"Top o' the morning to you, kind sir," Roxy said – just two happy-go-lucky kids.

The clerk didn't respond. My hands started to sweat as I saw Xavier make his way down the counter toward the magazines. Brilliantly, I took a step to the left, making the clerk follow me, thus turning his back to Xavier. Roxy followed.

We had this.

I handed the clerk my wrapper, smiled large, and didn't manage to say a single word. I wanted to glance at Xavier but couldn't risk losing the clerk's attention. Finally, I managed, "You'll notice, sir, that this wrapper has a star on it. I believe we are entitled to a free Tootsie Pop. We will gladly wait here while you do the necessary paperwork required for us to obtain said free Tootsie Pop."

Roxy nodded his head and said, "Word to your mother."

The clerk took the wrapper, studied it for a second or two, then said, "Get the fuck out of here, perverts!" He had stealthily grabbed a broom and swung it at Xavier's reaching hand. "If I ever catch you in here again, I'm calling your parents!"

We ran like the wind and never set foot in that place again, sacrificing countless delicious ham-and-cheese subs in the future.

So, remembering how badly our plan to rob the store had been, robbing the sheriff's house didn't seem like such a great idea.

"There has to be a way," Xavier said, looking at me, "he lives two doors down from you, dude. We can figure this out."

True, the sheriff, and Daphne, lived just two houses away, but that didn't make breaking into his home and stealing his porno stash any easier. I'm not sure where Xavier was going with that, but I just shrugged.

"I don't see it happening. Our best bet is to go to Jimmy's tonight and see if we can talk him into letting us see... or even having one."

"We'll need money," Roxy said. "Bribery usually always works."

"Great idea," I said before quickly realizing none of us actually had money, at least not the kind of money it would take to bribe someone, unless he really wanted a few tokens.

All this action distracted us from another significant problem. We were half-naked and covered in baby oil and dirt. Our only way out was going back through the pool area to get our bikes, which would be impossible to ride anyway due to how slippery we were. Still, we had no other option; just being out here on the grass, we were becoming a bug graveyard. Hundreds, it seemed, of bugs were stuck to our glistening pale skin, some dead, some desperate for death, and it would only get worse the longer we stayed.

"We have no choice," Xavier said, trying to wipe as much oil from his body as possible, which was none; the best he could do was relocate it. "We have to cross."

"Stick to the back wall," I said. "Play it cool. Don't go too fast or we'll fall."

"10-4, good buddy," Roxy said with a salute before peeking through a crack at the gate. "Let's do– shit."

"What?" I said.

"Look."

I pushed my face as far as I could into the crack, closed my left eye, and leered through. "Shit!" Guess who just showed up. Daphne. In a bikini. Walking with Ariel McCormick, also in a bikini, and heading directly for the path we had to take. "Abort, abort!"

"Mother eff!" Xavier said, "looks like you're on your

own, Grant!"

"You can't leave me."

"Well, we can't stay here."

"I'm not going," Roxy said, who, at that moment, I realized had a thing for Ariel. His face was bright red, possibly due to the massive sunburn we were getting but primarily because of his bashfulness around Ariel.

"Look," I said. "My mom is showing a house right across the street. It's empty. We can take the long way around. If we can make it over there, maybe we can get in the backyard and clean ourselves up a bit then come back and get our bikes. And shirts"

"Forget the shirts, my dude. Let's just get the bikes and book it!" Roxy said, starting to panic.

I said, "I can't forget the shirt, dude. It's a brand new Jimmy'Z. It cost my mom twenty-three dollars at Wavelengths! If I don't come home with it, she's going to paint the walls red with my insides!"

"It's gone, dude! We can't go back in there. Look, Daphne is there!"

"And Ariel," Xavier added.

"Yeah," Roxy said, "and Ariel. Look dude, I've got a new Stüssy shirt that looks similar. It's yours. Your mom will never know!"

"My mom knows everything!"

"Dudes!" Xavier yelled, trying to shut us up. "Look… there's no way to get out unless we walk all the way around the park, past all those dudes playing basketball, and gosh knows who else. We're sure to get beaten up. And I don't know about you guys, but I don't really want to get beaten up by a bunch of jocks."

"Come on," Roxy pleaded, "their punches will slide right off us. We won't even feel 'em!"

"Fine, if you want to get beaten up, have at it. I'm not going to, though. So, what'll it be?"

We thought about it for a moment.

"Shit." Xavier had had enough. "I'm going through the pool area. I don't care about those girls. I'll play it cool. You chickenshits coming or not?"

Roxy and I both shook our heads, tightlipped, and eyes wide.

"Fine. Catch ya on the other side, losers!"

We remained silent while Xavier walked towards the gate, leaving oily footprints in the dirt. He was really going to do it. What balls!

The gate was metal, so no one could see him lurking on the other side, which worked in his favor, because it seemed to take him a few seconds to gather enough courage to reach for the long, silver handle, pull it down, and walk back into the area we were just laughed out of less than fifteen minutes prior.

"Don't do it," Roxy warned, but Xavier completely ignored him.

Xavier reached out his hand, grabbed the door handle, and...slipped.

Forward!

His hand slipped right off that handle, causing him to lurch forward, his chin opening the gate on his way down. The crash from the door drew everyone's attention just in time for them all to see Xavier fall flat on his face.

"Mother fudge!" Xavier yelled, desperately trying to get back to his feet, like trying to balance on a Slip 'n Slide. Roxy and I raced to his aide, grabbed him, and tried to desperately stay out of sight as we struggled to pull his shiny ass back into the park so the door could close and put this entire incident out of its misery.

I caught another glimpse of Daphne just as the gate was closing on me. She looked so fine! I'd like to think I smiled at her or maybe winked, but I know damn well I probably just stared at her slack-jawed until she was out of view.

With the gate door now closed, Roxy grabbed a nearby stone and, in yet another pathetic effort, tried to wedge it under the frame to prevent anyone from coming out. We all crawled through the dirt and sat against the opposite side of the wall where Daphne and Ariel were gabbing about New Kids on the Block. We sat and listened for a few minutes, trying to calm ourselves down from the hysteria we just partook in.

From the other side of the wall, the topic changed from boybands to daredevil activities. Daphne asked Ariel, "Do you think you could jump from the roof into the pool."

"No doy!" Ariel said, "like, not only that, like, I could do a flip."

"So could I, and, like, a twist."

"Like, I bet you couldn't do a handstand on the diving board and then like vault yourself into a flip into the water."

"I bet you couldn't..." This went on for the entirety of us sitting there, each 'bet you' getting more and more absurd. We just sat, covered in dirt and oil and dead bugs and who knows what else and listened, smiling.

I would have given anything to walk back in there and finally say a coherent sentence to her, but I just couldn't do it. That poor Jimmy'Z shirt would probably be lost forever. I don't recall ever going back and grabbing it, although I suppose I could have. The shirt was no longer my top priority. Talking to Daphne was.

Instead of doing either of those things, we sat in that hot afternoon sun, our sweaty, slippery backs pressed against the stucco wall, our knees up by our chests, and took it all in. I removed an oil-stained pouch of Big League Chew from my back pocket and offered the guys a pinch. It could have been the best day of our lives, and we didn't know. We didn't care. When you're that age, you think you'll feel like that forever, like nothing could ever come along and steal that pure joy, and it's so easy to take it for granted.

By the time we were ready to make our way across the street, our embarrassment didn't seem to matter anymore. We still didn't want to risk cutting across the pool again, instead opting to walk past the basketball players who didn't even notice us. We crossed the street and made our way to the empty house my mom was trying to sell and tried to use the spicket on the side yard to wash ourselves off, but there was no water. Instead, we used a neighbor's, then made our way back to our bikes. We needed to get home and get ready for the night, and we really needed shirts.

If things go well, some sweet, sweet porno will be in our future!

Xavier was the first to break, then Roxy, and I peddled the rest of the way home alone. As I passed Daphne's house, her dad, Sheriff Monroe, was getting into his official cruiser. He saw me and waved. I waved back shyly, quietly saying, "I love your daughter, Sheriff."

In the eighties and nineties, the arcade was the coolest place in town. It welcomed all races, creeds, sexes, whatever, and rarely anything bad happened there. If it did, it would be someone losing their temper over getting their ass beat at *Street Fighter* or whatever other head-to-head game they happened to be playing. But for the most part, it was the friendliest place you could possibly be, and most parents realized that, which is why so many kids were allowed to hang out there unsupervised.

There were a lot of other places around Bakersfield where people could hang out. There was an entire shopping center worth of fun and excitement over on White Lane, several miles from our house. There you could play miniature golf (and video games) at the Green Valley Golf Course, get lost in a gigantic maze at the Maze Craze, or go down the waterslides at Wet and Wild. I loved those places. Many happy days were spent there, but the one thing separating those places from Jimmy's was that we could get to Jimmy's by ourselves. We didn't have to rely on our parents to take us.

This made Jimmy's feel like it was ours, just like the pool was ours, and the Stockdale Six movie theater was ours. They were all within reach and gave us just enough freedom to make us think we were getting away with something.

Above: The original Jimmy's sign.
Below: All the original neon
from inside the arcade.

I looked up at the glowing yellow neon sign.

Jimmy's.

Written in one of those half-cursive, half-printed fonts, positioned at an upward angle over the block lettering of Arcade. Even over all the noise, outside and in, I could hear the relaxing, soft hum of the lights.

According to my brother, Jimmy's was the last place Bebe-Lynn was seen. He said Bebe had left here with a boy and hadn't been seen since. So, who was the boy? Why haven't we heard anything about him? I may not have known every person in the arcade by name, but I certainly recognized almost everyone. I was tempted to ask an employee if they had any new information but chickened out.

Instead, Roxy, Xavier, myself, and a boy from my school named Ronny sat on the curb playing a MASH Cootie Catcher game made from a piece of paper Ronny had in his pocket.

It's a common misconception that only girls play this dumb game. Guys played it too. We were living examples. Although, the only reason we were playing was because we were perhaps a bit too eager to get to the arcade and ended up arriving before Jeremy and his buddies. I didn't want to waste the small number of tokens I had left (I blew through a week's worth the previous night trying to beat that stupid *Teenage Mutant Ninja Turtle* game, but I could never beat Shredder! Son of a bitch! Games like that were designed to eat quarters. They could get away with only having six levels if they made the last two levels nearly impossible.), so MASH it was.

Now, I liked Ronny just fine, but he was known for stretching the truth a bit. In fact, he was a dirty, downright lying sonofabitch. At his birthday party back in January, I gifted him an Orbi, which was basically a rubber ball with two long streamers attached to it. You would twirl it around and then launch it the length of a football field. Roxy gifted him a Pogo Ball. Ronny claimed his dad invented both, despite the former being a Hasbro product, the latter from a company called License to Play.

His dad worked for neither.

That was far from the only, or worst, lie he told. This one just has always stuck out to me for some reason. Most of the others were more forgettable, or so far out there they were almost laughable, like when he said he worked on the upcoming Teenage Mutant Ninja Turtle movie that would be coming out in a few months. When we went to see it, you'll never guess whose name was not in the credits.

But yeah, his dad inventing the toys always stuck with me because it seemed so sad and desperate. As far as we knew, Ronny's father was nowhere to be seen. I had no idea where he was, but Ronny always talked him up. Of course, I now understand why it made me feel so bad, but I was thoroughly confused then. Later, my dad would explain that Ronny and his mother didn't have a lot of money, and maybe Ronny stretched the truth because he was afraid you won't like him. "That key he wears around his neck means that he goes home to an empty house every day. He doesn't have a dad, and his mom struggles to make ends meet. Understand?"

I nodded. I knew what a latchkey kid was. There were several at school, and I never really gave it a second thought. In fact, the very next year, when my mom got her teaching credentials, I came home to a gloriously empty house all the time. It was great!

"Good." I remember my dad saying, "But please remember, not having money does not diminish someone's worth."

That stuck with me throughout life, too, even though, at the time, I probably didn't fully understand what he meant. Still though, Ronny was a decent dude, despite the constant lying.

"Tell me when to stop, Grant!" Ronny was sitting on the curb, his hands stuffed inside this origami-like folded paper, opening and closing it faster and faster until I finally told him to stop.

"You ready for the results?" he asked me.

I shrugged. "Ready as I'll ever be."

Ronny informed me that I was destined to live in a shack... With Naomi Butler!

Barf-city, man.

"Come on! I don't want to go with Naomi Butler! Was this rigged?"

Oh, Naomi Butler.

About a year prior, my dad had taken Roxy and me to the mall on a Saturday afternoon. As I mentioned earlier, our city's mall is called the Valley Plaza. It was developed by The Hahn Company from San Diego in partnership with John Brock Sr. – the owner of the now defunct Brocks department store, and opened in 1967 with three anchor stores: Brocks, of course, Sears, and The Broadway.

In 1986, the mall started to expand amidst the current boom of malls worldwide. Teenagers couldn't seem to get enough, and developers took notice. New malls and new expansions began popping up all over the world. By 1987, our little Valley Plaza had two new wings and two new anchor stores with JC Penny and May Company, along with one more new section that was becoming the most essential addition – The Food Court!

The idea was to keep customers shopping for as long as possible, so providing food that wasn't traditional dining or a buffet, like Wyatt's, was a no-brainer.

Our food court is called The Oasis, and I was literally just there yesterday. When it opened, there was Sbarro, Orange Julius, Hot Dog on a Stick, Schlotzky's Deli, Taco Bell, a bunch of shit I never bothered with, and our all-time favorite, Tommy Burger!

On this trip to the mall, my dad had parked at The Oasis, and we had lunch at Tommy's before we went into the actual mall, probably to shop at the Dick and Fart Store we loved so much called Spencer's.

On our way back to the car, as we were cutting through The Oasis, which was insanely crowded by this point, Roxy and I spotted poor Naomi Butler off in the distance at a table, minding her own business.

Instead of acting like fully functioning human beings,

Roxy and I hit the deck! In the middle of the food court, two ten-year-old boys crawled across the tile like it was some sort of army training exercise.

My dad looked at us in total shock and asked, "What the hell are you idiots doing?"

"Naomi!" Roxy yelled way too loud. "Twelve o'clock"

"Who's Naomi?" my dad asked, still bewildered by the shocking turn the day had taken.

"She's barf city!" Roxy said, pulling on my dad's shorts to get him to hide with us. "If you make eye contact with her, you'll crap your pants!"

"It's true, Dad. It happened to Skip McVey! He was just walking along one day and Naomi came up and said hi and then, plop, squirt, right in his pants!"

"Totally true story!" Roxy said, still panicked.

"That sounds like bullshit," Dad said, looking down at us.

"Get down, Dad, get down."

"Yeah," Dad said, "I'm not doing that. In fact…" Dad raised his arm and yelled, "Hi, Naomi!"

Naomi, still a good hundred feet away, turned, looked at my dad with a confused expression, then waved back.

"My idiot kids just wanted to say hi. They're down here on the floor!"

Betrayed! By my own father!

We had no choice but to get to our feet, our faces so red they looked like they were about to explode. We just stood there, unable to move, unable to speak, and it felt like every single person in the mall was staring at us.

My dad leaned in between us and whispered, "Don't ever judge someone based on their looks. Especially a woman. What the hell is wrong with you two jackasses?"

I could have died.

I remember this as I'm sitting on the curb outside Jimmy's doing the exact same thing – still judging people by their looks, like I'm really anything to write home about, with my dorky shorts and unkempt shaggy hair. Boys really are idiots.

"You'll drive a Datsun pickup and have fourteen

kids!" Ronny added.

"Fourteen kids?! Why the hell was that even an option?"

Ronny laughed. "Why not?"

Roxy and Xavier joined in the laugh fest, Roxy saying, "Can I be your Maid of Dishonor?"

Apparently, this was the funniest joke ever told to everyone but me. I didn't even bother telling him that maids of honor were for girls. Instead, I threatened to walk over to the pay phone, call Melissa McCutty and tell her how much Roxy loooooooved her.

"You wouldn't!" Roxy said, the laughter leaving with a quickness.

"Oh, I would. And I will." I stood up and made a show of digging in my pocket for a quarter.

"Dude, she brings a toothbrush to school!"

"Yeah, that should make her breath nice when you two are smooching."

This next part is going to be hard to write because of how cringe it is. But it happened, and it happened right there at that exact time, so it needs to be told.

Seemingly out of nowhere, Ronny interrupts this conversation by saying, "My dick hair sure does itch."

We all looked at him like his face was melting.

"Huh?" Xavier said.

"My dick hair. It's itchy. Doesn't your dick hair itch?"

Now, I was no expert on dick hair, but I was almost certain that the actual dick didn't grow hair. I thought the hair grew around it, hence the name bush, and not fur-banana or something. Still though, this was shocking news. Did Ronny have dick hair? Was dick hair a thing? Did mature wieners really look like David Naughton in *An American Werewolf in London*?

Nothing about the scrambled-up porno, or my dad having no shame walking from the shower to wherever he was going dead-ass nekkid, would lead me to believe this is true.

I mean, he could have been lying, like he usually did, but what if he wasn't. I couldn't afford to call his bluff.

Not now, anyway. For a boy my age at the time, this seemed like a huge step forward in life. Was I being left behind?

I knew for a fact that neither Roxy nor Xavier had any either because not two weeks ago, we had another contest during our jumbled nudity session. That didn't stop Roxy from saying, "Oh yeah, sometimes it itches. But sometimes it doesn't itch."

Xavier started itching his dick. "Yeah," he said, "sometimes, but not always."

Peer pressure is a bitch. "Yeah," I said, mirroring Xavier's statement, "sometimes but not always."

Jesus, how embarrassing. I told you it was cringe! I may as well have said I could fly and shoot lightning from my nostrils; it would have been just as convincing.

Fuckin' Ronny.

"Yeah," Ronny said, for the fourth Yeah in a row, "sometimes when I'm walking too, my dingaling gets stuck in my butt crack. That ever happen to you guys?"

Oh, give me a break! Now I knew he was full of shit! This guy had the same amount of hair in his shorts as my Cabbage Patch Doll had and probably the same size johnson!

Still though, Ronny made a show of attempting to remove his wiener from his butt. Pathetic.

Roxy said, "Sometimes I step on mine. It's crazy."

Silence. Pure silence.

Then, "Don't worry, Grant," Ronny says, patting me on the shoulder, "It'll happen for you one day."

Son of a bitch, lying ass mother....

Desperate to change the topic, I asked, "What do you think Daphne is doing right now?"

Roxy said, "Probably jumping from the second story onto their sofa while doing backflips or something. Those girls are insane."

They didn't have a second story, but I didn't bother correcting him. I took a deep breath, imagining those girls playing around in Daphne's living room. How awesome would it be if I was there? "I saw Sheriff Monroe leaving when we were riding home earlier. The odds are good that Jeremy will be able to get some of those mags."

"Oh yeah?!" Roxy and Xavier say together.

"What mags?" Ronny asked.

"MAD mags," I said way too fast. I didn't want that fool ruining our chances!

"Oh," Ronny said, "That's for kids. I prefer Penthouse."

"You have Penthouse?!" Roxy screams, unable to set aside all the other bullshit Ronny has spouted and recognize this as the blatant lie it was.

"Oh yeah," Ronny said, "my dad has tons. He lets me use them."

Right. The invisible dad who lets Ronny use his tits and ass magazines just out of the kindness of his heart.

Sure, Ronny. Whatever you say.

"Shit, look!" Roxy said, pointing down the road towards Jeremy riding his bike straight for us. "Showtime!"

"Just be cool, guys," I said, my arms up like I was trying to calm an angry bull by showing it I was no threat. "We have to think this through."

"What are you guys talking about," Ronny asked, oblivious to our real motive for being there.

"Nothin," Xavier said, his eyes locked on Jeremy while trying to shoo Ronny away. "Go uh, go away, you're bothering us."

Jeremy pushed his bike into a rack, chained it up, and headed inside. Slung over his right shoulder was a backpack...

"Dude, I bet he brought like fifty of them!" Roxy said, unable to remain still, the excitement almost too much to bear.

"Fifty of what?" Ronny asked, squeezing his body between us, trying to catch a glimpse of whatever it was we were looking at.

"Jesus, Ronny," Xavier said. "Load up another MASH or something. Shit."

"Yeah, alright, I can do that. But I'm putting Betsy

Flagel on your girl list."

"I don't give a shit about Betsy Flagel; you can put Ms. Franks on there for all I care. It's not real."

"Who is Ms. Franks?" Ronny asked.

We ignored him.

"Come on," I said, "he's in. Let's rock 'n roll!"

We tried to regain our composure as best we could, then stepped into the arcade, totally cool, just here to play some games and hang out, nothing more. Oh, what's that, good buddy? You have a porno mag? Would you mind if I partook in viewing it with you?

Walking into Jimmy's was like stepping off a spaceship onto a new, far-off, alien planet. Nothing from the real world meshed with the interior. You were bombarded with flashing lights, buzzers, dings, pings, explosions, laughter, and yelling. The smells ranged from incredible to putrid, with the mix of delicious arcade food (nachos, three-foot-long licorice ropes, Nerds, cherry soda) and sweaty kids packed into a building like sardines in a tin. It was the best smell in the world, and I often search Etsy candle shops looking for an arcade smell that can come close. I've yet to find one, but I'll keep looking. I feel the missing ingredient in those candles is always the B.O. It's vital!

If you're reading this, Etsy candle makers, I'm giving you crucial information here.

Anyway, it was a Saturday night in the middle of summer, so the place was almost wall-to-wall. We had to snake our way through the mass of kids toward where we thought Jeremy would be. I didn't see any of his friends, but then again, I didn't see much of anything. All the teenagers I was pressed up against were much bigger than me, and they blocked my view.

"That fine girl's ass just touched my hand!" Roxy yelled to us. "Holy shit!"

I looked to see who he was talking about, only to discover she was not fine, but she did have an ass, and I couldn't help but feel a little jealous.

We finally made our way to an open area between the

pinball machines and took a moment for reconnaissance. The snack bar was packed, but there was no Jeremy. Nor was he near the area set up for the larger games, such as *Off-Road* or *Mad Dog McCree*, or down Pinball Alley.

"He has to be in the back," Xavier said, looking down the far aisle of games. "I don't see him down here at all."

"Let's head to the party area."

The back of Jimmy's featured a few tables, usually designated for birthday parties, but mostly they were occupied by girls drinking soda and talking about boys or dieting.

The gods must have been smiling upon us that night because after weaving our way through another mass of people, we saw him standing at the *Dragon's Lair 2* cabinet, his backpack at his feet while he focused intently on that lousy game I could never figure out.

"Holy shit, dude!" I said, knowing I could get into that bag without him ever knowing. If he had even half as many magazines as I thought he had, he would never miss one or two.

A plan was formed. This one would definitely work better than our previous plan at the convenience store. Xavier and Roxy (we had successfully ditched Ronny by this point) were to stand next to Jeremy and engage in a (fake) private conversation to hopefully divert his attention from the game. If his concentration stayed on the game, I would stroll by, casually bend down as if to tie my shoe, unzip his backpack, slip one or two magazines out, and quickly shove them in my pants, then I would make my immediate departure. We would meet up at the Sail Thru burger joint across the street. We couldn't risk staying close by, just in case. Plus, we needed privacy, which is a stupid thing to desire at the most happenin' fast food place in town, but hey, like I've said countless times, we were massive idiots.

This one would work! There wasn't a doubt in my mind. But we had to act fast. Once Jeremy's friends arrived, I was convinced he would ditch that shitty video game and get down to business.

———

We put the plan in motion.

Roxy and Xavier made their way down that long center aisle while I went wide along the far east wall where all the older games like *Q-Bert* and *BurgerTime* were. When I got to my post, I waited for my squad to be in position.

Behind me, at the tables, I could hear a group of high school girls talking. One of them said, "Yeah, well, she was boning every guy in town!"

This got my attention.

"Like, seriously," she continued, "I heard she was getting with half of the B.C. football team."

B.C., or Bakersfield College, is our local community college.

I turned towards them. A brunette with waffled hair said, "Probably at the same time!"

The girls laughed. It all seemed so cruel.

"I'm glad she's gone," the first girl said.

"Yeah, and never coming back," the brunette laughed. "Like, leave some boys for us, slut!" More laughter.

"Yeah, for real, she definitely got what she deserved."

A crimped-hair blonde said, "Good riddance, Bebe-Lynn. Fuck. You."

Those last two words were said in the most valley girl accent I had ever heard, and they made me a little sick to my stomach. I wanted to say something to them so badly. I wanted to take another step towards them, slam my fists down on the table, and yell at them to shut the fuck up! I wanted them to look at me with their dumb mouths wide open while I stared them down. Mostly I wanted them to realize that Bebe-Lynn was a human being who probably needed our help, and here we were, sitting around in an arcade while she was out there.

I wanted to say that, but of course, I said nothing. I pretended like I didn't hear anything, then turned back around just as Roxy and Xavier came into view. I watched them intently as they took up the position next to Jeremy, who didn't give them the time of day.

That was good.

The girls behind me had already been forgotten. I was in the zone. I knew what needed to be done, and damn-it, I was going to do it!

It was way too loud to hear what the guys were talking about, but Xavier gave me the signal (crossed fingers behind his back), and it was my time to move. I took the few steps necessary to get myself within arm's reach of the backpack, then knelt down, my back to the backpack, and fiddled with my shoe for a second before being knocked flat on my ass by another flock of teenage girls not paying one bit of attention.

"Oh my gaawwddd," the girl who knocked me down said, "Jolt Cola tastes like my dog's piss! And she has a yeast infection!" I will never forget those words. What a wonderfully bizarre thing to say. The universe is 13.8 billion years old, and I managed to somehow be alive at the exact time when this girl in the stonewashed overalls compared Jolt Cola to a dog with a yeast infection's whiz. I was a lucky fella!

I didn't have time to contemplate what it all meant because I saw Roxy leap into the air, his hands grabbing the side of his head in pure panic, sure we were busted, but Jeremy didn't seem to notice. I had to act fast. I unzipped his backpack, grabbed two, maybe three, magazines, rolled to my back, stuffed them down the front of my pants, looking like a drunk break-dancer (or Roxy at the pool earlier that day), then shot back up and moved as quickly as I could to the rear entrance. I could hear Roxy and Xavier cheering me on, even over all the other ruckuses.

Jeremy must have been so confused if he even noticed.

I remember crashing into the *Double Dragon* cabinet, then doing a ridiculous spin move before regaining my balance and blasting through the door. Outside, I ran across the parking lot and entered Sail Thru, which was almost as crowded as Jimmy's. The place was always popular due to having, hands down, the best soda fountain in town, but since adding a second restaurant, Taco Taco, to their building, the place had turned into a money-making factory. Have you ever seen teenagers around cheeseburgers and tacos?! And those sodas! I don't know what made them so good, but my gosh, once you had a Sail Thru Coke, no other Coke would do.

I surveyed the room, looking desperately for an empty table, preferably a booth, but I wasn't going to be picky.

There was nothing.

The white tiled walls and glass paver room dividers made the whole place almost unbearably bright. We needed dark! This was not the place for us!

I turned to leave just as Roxy and Xavier came storming in, huge grins plastered across their faces.

"You did it, dude!" Xavier said, high-fiving me.

"Shit, this place is packed," Roxy said after nearly being knocked off his feet by a couple of dumb jocks. Once they were safely past and not paying any attention to him, Roxy squared up and said, "What?!" It was kind of pathetic, but then again, so were we and almost everything we did, so it fit well.

"We have to go outside," I said. "Way too many people in here, and it's bright as shit. We can't be caught with this stuff."

"I agree."

Roxy, still staring down the jocks that didn't even realize they ran into him, had to be dragged out. "They're lucky," he said once we were in the parking lot.

Lucky indeed. Sure thing.

"Come on," Xavier said, "let's just hide behind some cars. Over there, by the lights."

I nodded, and we all headed off, hiding behind a sick red Camaro with black rear-window louvers, the cool-looking slats a lot of sports and muscle cars had back then. My dad's car was almost identical. I checked the rearview to make sure it wasn't his, just in case. There was no hula-girl air freshener hanging from the mirror, so we were safe.

We all sat on the asphalt; Xavier and Roxy were both

so giddy they were literally laughing with excitement. With a grand flourish, I pulled the magazines from my pants and dropped them in the center of our little circle.

The smiles faded rapidly.

"What the fuck is this shit," Xavier said, picking up a copy of Harper's Bazaar.

Roxy yelled, "Nooooooo!" as the next magazine was revealed to be Woman's World. "These are mom magazines! Why?!"

"Dude," I said, in shock, "I did exactly as planned."

"Why the hell is Jeremy walking around with mom magazines?!" Xavier said, clearly pissed.

Roxy hopped to his feet, his hands clenched into fists so tightly I could see them turning red. "This makes me so angry! So angry! So angry I could just hit this fucking car!"

And hit the car he did, for some reason. He wound up and threw a right hook right at this sweet-looking Camaro, causing the alarm to start wailing and forcing us to leave our mom magazines and dash clumsily (I know one of the guys fell, but I'm not sure which) into the night and back to Jimmy's.

I was going to confront Jeremy and make him answer for this travesty.

Unfortunately, I never got the chance because his friends beat me to it. Once we made our way back to the rear of Jimmy's, Jeremy was there, standing around one of the tables with his friends.

"Dudes," Jeremy said, addressing his idiot friends, "my dad keeps them locked in a gun safe! I had no way of getting them."

"So instead, you bring us this gigantic panty bullshit?!" one of his friends yelled angrily while smashing his fist on the table next to a Sears Catalog. "I can't use this shit! This woman looks like my mom!"

Roxy looked at me and silently lipped, "Gun safe" to us.

Sigh.

Even if we could somehow weasel our way into the

sheriff's house under false pretenses, there is no way we could ever get into a gun safe. It seemed like this dream had officially been shattered, just like all our other attempts.

Damn-it.

"Dudes," Jeremy said, pleading in his voice, "I'm not lying! I swear to God. I've seen them. The girls had boobs out to here, I promise!" He made a show of holding his arms out as far as they would go to really drive home the point of how big the boobs were in these phantom magazines.

"Whatever, dude," one of them said, his head held down. He looked almost as depressed as we did.

"I swear," Jeremy said again, his voice cracking this time. "Cross my heart and hope to die stick a thousand needles in my eye! Give me another chance. I swear, I'll get 'em next time."

"Sure, man," the other friend said. "Whatever you say. Come on, guys."

The friends all left, leaving Jeremy standing alone at the table. "I swear, guys! He has a ton! And the girls get hotter and hotter with every turn of the page! Guys!" Then quieter, "Shit." He sighed as he grabbed the catalog, tossed it into the closest trashcan, and squeezed past us, not giving us a second thought.

The three of us all sighed in unison, our shoulders slumping.

I gathered up all the energy I had left in me and said, "Come on."

We left out the rear exit and walked around to the front of Jimmy's. More people were spilling in, all laughing and having a great time. Not us, though.

We were sure tonight was the night. But alas, it wasn't meant to be. We walked past a group of teen girls, and one of them said to us, "Like Jesus Christ, did someone like just run over your dog?"

Her friends all laughed.

We did not.

The girls walked into Jimmy's to continue their night

of fun.

We rode our bikes home silently that night, foiled yet again by the cruelty of adolescence. Those beautiful little porno mags were beginning to feel as out of reach as the farthest star.

When it was time for Xavier to break off, we all stopped and stood on the street momentarily, still upset but perhaps a little less now.

"Don't worry, guys," I said, "It'll happen. In the meantime, I still have all those Jason movies. I mean, part five has a lot of tits. And I mean a lot! And I know it doesn't even have Jason in it, and Roy is a pretty lame copycat, but they totally make up for it with bazooms!"

"I know," Xavier said, frowning, "but it's just not the same. They don't show...everything."

"If I don't see a muff soon," Roxy said, his hands back into fists, his arms so stiff and tense they're slowly rising from his side, "I'm gonna go crazy here!"

"Calm down, dude," I said, putting my hand on his shoulder. "It'll happen. I promise."

"But I need it to happen now. I'm makin' Hilary's Cabbage Patch Dolls hump each other, here! I'm so desperate I'm stackin' Pepsi cans just to see the word sex!"

In 1990, Pepsi introduced a can with a neon design all over it. Sure enough, if you stacked two cans on top of each other and lined it up correctly, the neon, in a downward angle, spelled SEX. It was all the rage for boys my age. My dad saved two cans because even he thought it was funny. Ten years after he died, those two cans are still on a shelf in the garage.

"I know, man," I said. "Me too."

"Just look at this!" Roxy pointed down to the little bulge in his pants. "I got a boner from my bike and thinking about Pepsi cans. That's how desperate I am now!"

"I've got this drawing I did of April O'Neil humping some turtles," I said, realizing how lame it was before I even finished the sentence. Besides, I had already shown

Roxy, and honestly, the drawing was embarrassing because I didn't know how the hell sex even worked. I thought sperm looked like goldfish, so I drew it as such.

"I might have to take you up on that," Roxy said, getting back on his bike. "Looks like you're my date tonight, Ms. Bike."

"My idiot brother said Bebe-Lynn was the town bicycle, so maybe that's kinda what it feels like. Maybe we should take another ride around the block."

We laughed, realizing how stupid we sounded, then eventually said our goodbyes and went home.

I ended that night lying flat on my bed, my weird see-through phone sitting next to me. In my hand, Daphne's phone number.

Back when Daphne's dad was campaigning for sheriff, he canvassed the neighborhood handing out little business card-type things with his picture on them, along with his home phone number. He would tell everyone in the community, and who knows where else, that "Your problems will be my problems" and that we were to call him if we had any concerns where a sheriff candidate could possibly help.

I remember my dad laughing and saying that Mr. Monroe would be regretting that decision by the end of the week.

I guess Dad was wrong because when Monroe was elected, he went back around to all the houses in our neighborhood, thanking us for electing him, and giving us a new card, this one with his home phone and sheriff's department phone numbers on it, right next to a picture of his smiling face.

The newer card is stuck to the fridge with a magnet. The old card, with just his personal number, had been in my nightstand drawer, just waiting for me to use it.

That night, I sat on my bed and held her number in my hand, looking closely at it. I had moved my ridiculous-looking x-ray phone and set it directly in front of me. I could pick up the receiver, dial the number staring me in the face, and I could talk to Daphne.

Right then, I could do it.

I didn't even have to ask her out or try to be smooth. Hell, I could have made a joke about what happened at the pool earlier just to break the ice.

Anything!

I just needed to pick up the phone and dial the number.

Just do it, Grant.

Just pick up the phone, dial that number, and... ah, who were you kidding?

The thought of calling her mortified me. Past girl-calling trauma had permanently damaged me, and I wasn't even really involved. I was doing a 'favor' for a friend, and it went horribly wrong.

One of my other best friends at the time was a dude named Brandon Hall. He lived over at the farthest side of Quailwood on Chukkar Lane and had a massive crush on this cute brunette girl named Angela. He wanted to ask Angela to be his "date" for the Skate-a-Thon but was too chicken to ask. I, however, had no real desire to go anywhere with Angela, so I said I would make the call and ask. No problem.

After about an hour of convincing him to let me, I finally made the call. Angela's mom answered, and it surprised me for some dumbass reason. It took me a few seconds to regain control, tell Mom who I was, and ask to speak to her daughter. The phone went silent for a few seconds before a girl picked up. Katy O'Rourke, not Angela.

"Hey, Grant! It's Katy."

This was a drastic departure from what was supposed to happen, and I totally panicked. "Um, hi."

"What are you doing?"

"Um... Is this... Angela's... house?" Damn, I'm smooth! (A very similar situation arose a year later, with Katy taking over another phone call I had made. By this time, I was in sixth grade and was feeling pretty suave, so after a brief and unexpected talk with Katy, I asked {very sheepishly} if she wanted to 'go with me.' She said sure, and for the whole afternoon at home, I was king of the world, shooting hoops in my backyard like I was the coolest kid in town. At school the next day, I was too chicken to even look at her, and she had one of her friends run over to me at lunch to inform me that I had been dumped. So yeah, I was never a lady's man.)

"Yeah!" Katy said, "This is her number, silly! We're hanging out. Her mom said you were on the phone, so I wanted to say hi."

I was friends with Katy's brother Trey, so I knew her pretty well. Still, this felt like being thrown into a fire, and I was woefully unprepared for such a detour. "Oh, um... Was just going to...(gulp!) ask...um... Angela a, ya know... question."

I wanted to die.

"Oh yeah? What were you gonna ask her?"

From the background, I could hear Angela ask, "He's gonna ask me something?"

Katy responded to her friend, and they went back and forth for a few seconds. Then, to me, she said, "She wants to know what you were going to ask."

"Oh, uh... You, uh, know my friend Brandon...Um, cute little guy, small handwriting, sits behind me in class? Um, he was um, wondering if um, Angela wanted to go the uh, Skate-a-Thon, um, with him..."

"Ohhhh!" Katy said, giggling. "Hold on!"

The line went quiet again. I could imagine Katy holding the phone tight against her body to block out any sound. The wait was pure agony for poor Brandon and me. When someone finally came back on the line, it wasn't Katy. It was Angela. I took this as an excellent sign so I held the phone out so Brandon could hear. He was beaming!

"Hi, Grant."

"Hi."

"Tell Brandon no because I like other guys, okay, and like I have a boyfriend...that like doesn't go to our school and stuff, ya know."

Oof!

This was the hospital scene in *E.T.*

This was Atreyu's horse drowning in *Neverending Story*.

This was the cartoon shoe getting dropped in the Dip in *Roger Rabbit*.

Brandon looked like he was about to collapse. I think I said okay, and possibly bye, to Angela, but I'm not sure. I heard Katy say bye to me in the background, but I was in the middle of hanging the phone up.

Crash and burn.

Not only does she like other guys, but she also pretended to have a boyfriend...just to get out of going to a school event they were both going to be attending anyway.

If I was nervous to talk to girls before this, I was petrified now. What if I called Daphne and asked her out, and she made up a boyfriend? I would never recover. I don't think my poor heart could take it. I didn't know how Brandon was staying vertical. He bobbed around like a stunned boxer as he made his way across the living room, eventually collapsing on the sofa, face down.

What the hell do you say to a guy in this position? I certainly couldn't think of anything. All I could come up with was, "Wanna go to the Skate-A-Thon with me?"

Brandon, with his face buried deep in the white leather of his parent's couch, mumbled, "I'd like that, yeah."

And that was that.

Brutal

Nope.

No way.

I couldn't face that sort of rejection.

I set my phone back on the nightstand, slid Daphne's number under my pillow, and laid down, staring at the ceiling for what seemed like forever, almost mad at myself for being such a wimp.

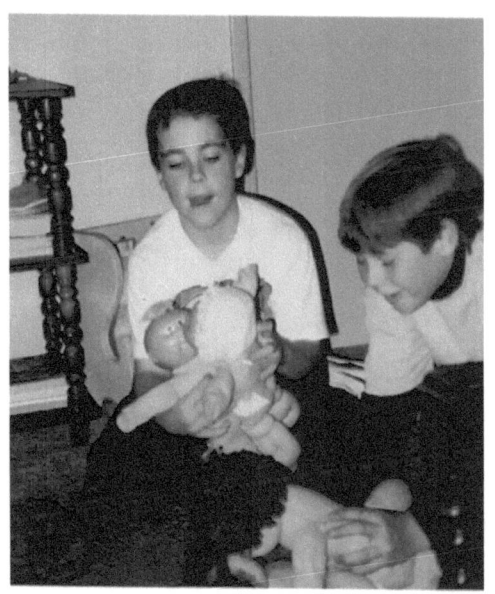

Above: Perverts
Below: Perfect angels

"Dude, they're never going to play a video." Roxy is sitting upside down on his sofa, I'm in his dad's old blue recliner. According to my stupid Swatch Watch with the Swatch Protector, we've been staring at the Video Jukebox Channel for well over an hour now, watching mindlessly as potential video choices flashed across the screen.

Please allow me to explain for those of you lucky enough to not have wasted countless hours in front of a television desperately waiting for an N.W.A. or Too $hort video to play.

In 1985, a fellow by the name of Steve Peters launched a music video television station in Miami. The idea was simple; take the basic premise of an actual jukebox and apply it to videos. In theory, it sounded great. It allowed videos to be played that typically wouldn't be played (or were literally banned) on the far more mainstream MTV. This was a time when rap music featured violence, drug dealing, and tables full of Uzis and other weapons, all for the sake of 'keepin' it real.' MTV said thanks but no thanks and demanded these rappers clean up their act, resulting in horribly lame videos shot with fish-eye lenses and dancing.

But did the Video Jukebox Channel care about what MTV wouldn't allow?

Hell no, it didn't!

Do you want to see *By the Time I Get to Arizona* by Public Enemy? You got it!

How about *100 Miles and Runnin'* by N.W.A.? Jukebox has got you!

Ice-T's *I'm Your Pusher*? No prob, Bob!

But there was a catch!

Unless someone called the 900 number and paid to have a video play, the channel would relentlessly scroll through all the videos you *could* watch. Sometimes it wasn't so bad, with numerous videos in a row. Others, like that particular day, were pure torture. But for whatever reason, we just could not make ourselves turn it off.

We placed requests in the past, but once our parents got the dreaded phone bill, we were forced to stop. Back in the eighties and early '90s, almost everything had a 900 (or 976) number. Remember earlier in the book when I mentioned that America's favorite child murderer Freddy Krueger had one (1-900-909-FRED)? Well, there were others. Lots and lots of others.

Need your fortune read over the phone? Call Miss Cleo. She had a different number for every city her commercial played. (Nothing fishy about that!)

Big wrestling fan? Call up Captain Lou at 1-900-660-4LOU.

Have an overwhelming desire to talk to a cartoon character? Call He-Man at 1-900-909-2233.

Were you in love with Corey Haim and Corey Feldman? Give them a call at 1-900-909-3700.

Grandpa Munster? 1-900-909-4300.

Want some jackass to insult you? 1-900-2-INSULT will connect you to, you guessed it, Dial-An-Insult.

Want to talk to a fucking rubber hand puppet? Call up Freddie Freaker at 1-900-490-FREAK!

Feel like having a good cry, but you're a spoiled white kid in eighty-dollar Reebok Pumps that lives in a nice neighborhood and has nothing to complain about? Call up the Crying Hotline at 1-900-740-3500 to hear a story that will "make you cry."

I wish I was making these up. Even more, I wish I didn't remember all these useless phone numbers.

I've been saving the best for last. You see, there was another kind of 900 number back then... any guesses?

You got it.

The phone sex lines.

They would advertise primarily at night, but sometimes the commercials would find themselves smack dab in the middle of primetime family programming, causing awkward glances around the room.

Before our awful convenience store porno-grab failure, we had our goals set on placing calls to these "hot chicks."

101

The problem?

That pesky phone bill.

While calling Freddy Krueger was funny enough for my parents to sluff off, and the Video Jukebox, while a waste of money, could be played off as us kids just being idiots and not realizing it cost money, that excuse would not fly with the phone sex lines. That would most definitely lead to some severe consequences and perhaps some conversations I would rather die than partake in.

So how could two kids successfully call these numbers without their parents ever seeing the bill?

I'll tell you how.

Now... I must warn you that there are a few stories coming up that don't make me and Roxy look too great. I mean, we didn't commit murder or anything, but we were definitely a bit conniving and, I don't know, maybe we committed fraud, and perhaps there might be a couple counts of petty theft in there, but please remember that we were just horny kids doing what we had to do. Just like we did with the Nintendo, we completed our missions without an ounce of shame, which I suppose is a perk of being young and carefree. And stupid.

So, I guess my point is, don't judge us by our past discretions. (lol – teehee- awkward glance)

Anyway, like I said, we were on a mission. A phone sex mission. And after many hours contemplating how we could pull this off, it finally came to us during P.E. one beautiful Spring afternoon just a few months prior.

For some reason, we were bussed over to the junior high for swimming lessons (even though there was literally a pool a hundred yards from the school) and some weird "test" where you would take off your shirt and bend forward, and the teacher would check the curvature of your spine.

Apparently, this hot-headed, red-faced madman of a gym teacher was fully capable of detecting scoliosis. We had to do that once a year from grade five through eight. The bright side was when we went, we'd get to not only leave school but we'd also get a swimming lesson, which was mostly just jacking around in a pool.

This was where we got our idea.

So, we're all lined up on the edge of the pool, waiting for the teacher to tell us to jump in so he can see if we do it properly. Instead of having us all jump in at once, he would go down the line, tap your shoulder, and in you would go. It was all boys that day, so any anxiety about being shirtless in front of girls was removed, replaced by the anxieties of being shirtless in front of a bunch of dick-head boys.

That day, however, Roxy and I were the dickheads.

The teacher was not our regular gym teacher; this guy was about three feet tall and four feet wide with a head like a cinder block. He was terrifying, and he always looked on the verge of exploding. His entire body looked so...clinched. Veins popped out of his neck and ran down to his shoulders like tree roots. His face looked as if he had been holding his breath for fifteen minutes and refused to give up. I don't know what we did to make him seem to hate us all, but I really didn't want to find out. I also don't know how he got away with talking to us like he did. (This would be the first of two stark-raving lunatics we would encounter in the span of about three months. More on the other one later.)

I was standing between Roxy and a kid named Lico Garcia (who, at Camp KEEP the following year, had Poison Oak pointed out to him by a counselor, then managed to trip and fall directly into the same poison oak mere seconds later.) At the very end of the line, the first to get picked to jump in was a little fat kid named Brian Seager. Brian wasn't in my class, so I only knew him from the playground, and even then, he didn't really play with us. If you're a fan of *The Simpsons*, think of Martin Prince, the chubby little smart kid in Bart's class.

So, the gym teacher, Mr. Funk (seriously), walked down the line of students and stopped right behind Brian. We were all grab-assing and not paying much attention. That must have really rubbed the Funk the wrong way because he snapped his gigantic firewood neck around like an owl and screamed, absolutely screamed, at us to all shut up!

When a man of that much girth tells you to shut up, you better shut up. So we did. This didn't work out well for poor jiggly Brian, who was probably desperately uncomfortable to begin with, shyly trying to cover his little boy bosoms, as he had become the focus of everyone's attention.

Madman Funk tapped Brian on the shoulder, signaling him to jump in. Brian stood there, trembling. Funk tapped him again, this time more like a jab, which just made Brian tremble more.

"Jump!" Funk said (yelled). "What are you waiting for?!" A vein the size of a garden hose was weaving across his forehead. "Jump!"

Fearing no way out, Jiggly Brian removed his hands from over his boobs and plugged his nose, then jumped.

He hit the water and went straight down. Kid sunk like a fucking rock. We couldn't believe it. Straight to the bottom. I didn't even know humans could sink like that without concrete shoes, but somehow, he managed. We stood there and watched as his body hit the bottom and just...stayed.

No movement, no panic, nothing. Just a pale, chubby body at the bottom of a pool. Still, we watched. I swear it felt like minutes.

Funk went crazy. "Are you kidding me?!?! Use your legs!"

The commands fell on deaf ears.

Still, we watched.

Not even so much as an air bubble escaped him. Now, normal people would be mortified by this; they would jump in and try to help.

But fifth graders are not normal people.

Fifth graders find things like this hilarious, and watching Funk look like he was about to blast off into space made it even better.

So, we watched.

And we laughed.

Typing this now, I literally just ran my hand through my hair, thinking how terrible we were, but nothing I can do about it now... but laugh.

And I am... damn it.

Brian had been down there for what could have been an hour by now. Finally, Funk decides that yelling like a lunatic will not cause Brian to surface, so he rips off his shirt like Hulk Hogan, says an incredibly impressive potpourri of profanity, then jumps in and rescues the portly little human cannonball.

Funk's verbal tirade continued so smoothly when his face came back up, I'm convinced he was cursing even underwater, which somehow made this all funnier. Because we certainly didn't stop laughing.

Due to that day's unfortunate circumstances, we were ordered to return to the locker room and get our clothes back on. There would be no swimming today ("Goddammit!" Funk was yelling, over and over.)

After we were all dressed and back on the bus, Roxy and I decided that we would befriend poor Brian.

Before you think what a nice gesture it was on our part, let me continue.

We put in a solid week of work becoming Brian's friend before we subtly dropped the hint that we should all have a sleepover at his house. Of course, he went for it. Why wouldn't he? The fuck else was he gonna do?

So that Friday night, Sharon, Roxy's mom, dropped us off at Brian's house; we said our goodbyes to her and then ran up to the door.

Brian lived on the far side of the neighborhood, where the houses were bigger than the rest, and the backyards were an acre. The backyards butted up against the street with The Tube under it.

We spent most of the evening in the game room, Roxy and I hogging the Nintendo, playing countless games of *Jordan vs. Bird*.

Ugh, this is so cringe, and I apologize in advance.

After mooching free pizza and soda all night, and after his parents had gone to bed, we waited for Mr.

Sandman to take little Brian off to sleepy-poo, then we made our move.

Scribbled on a piece of paper, even though it was permanently etched into our brains, was the number for one of those late-night commercial phone-sex lines. I still remember it. 1-900-704-KISS.

Like ninjas on a mission, we stealthily sneaked from the game room, through the kitchen, and into the living room, where the Seager's phone was just waiting for us to become men. Trying our best not to laugh and blow the whole plan, I picked up the receiver as slowly and quietly as possible while Roxy pressed the numbers as gently as one would touch a bubble, not wanting it to pop.

When it started ringing, I thought we both might have heart attacks. We had pulled it off. We had a plan, we put in the work, and it was about to pay off. We would make the call, return to the game room and pretend to sleep. When the bill came, Brian would deny it with the sort of believable authenticity only the genuinely innocent can get away with. If our names were brought up, Brian would certainly defend us because we were going to maintain the friendship for another month, making sure he would help clear our names. The best-case scenario would be Mr. Seager catching the blame, and honestly, what did we care? They had a house with a huge backyard, they could afford $3.99 a minute.

We were kneeling behind the sofa, huddled around the phone receiver, when the line picked up. Before a single word was spoken, we rolled onto our backs excitedly.

"Hello?" I said quietly.

Silence.

"Is anyone there?" Roxy asked.

Still nothing.

"Um, is-"

A recording began to play, the smooth velvety voice of Bambi, or possibly Tiffany, thanking us for calling. She was talking so slowly and softly it was almost aggravating. Like, come on, get this message over with, and let us talk to the chicks! The real chicks!

The recording played on.

Thank...

You....

For...

Calling the...

Sexy...

Play...

Hot...

Line...

We're so...

Glad...

You...

Decided...

To...

"Jesus Christ, woman, spit it out!" Roxy said, a little too loud, causing us to take cover again, this time pulling a quilt off the sofa and covering ourselves.

Play...

With...

"Us!" I yelled. "We get it!"

Us.

"Shit, dude, come on!"

Before...

We...

Connect you...

To...

The...

HOTTEST SINGLES...

"Come on!"

We...

Must...

Remind...

You...

"Just remind us and shut up!"

That...

This...

Call...

Costs...

"Three ninety-nine a minute! We know! Let's move it, lady!"

Three...

Ninety...

...

...

...

Nine...

Per...

Sexy...

Fun...

Filled...

Minute...

With his hands balled into fists again, Roxy says through gritted teeth, "I'm gonna lose it here, dude! I can feel it happening. I'm gonna explode!"

Please...

Hold...

While...

We...

...

...

Connect...

You...

To the...

Next...

Available...

Nympho...

Then fucking Hall & Oates started playing! I shit you not. We were paying $3.99 a minute to listen to *Maneater*, some bullshit song my parents liked. Meanwhile, Roxy looked like the front of his face was going to come flying off.

I wasn't doing much better. I had an overwhelming urge to take the phone receiver and smash it against the floor until it broke into a hundred pieces.

Still, Hall & Oates played.

We were halfway through Kim Carnes's *Bette Davis Eyes* when we started to suspect that we had been scammed. We didn't have much time to ponder because we heard a door open upstairs.

Roxy threw the quilt off, and we saw the upstairs light was on. I quickly hung up the phone while Roxy did a half-assed job of folding the blanket and returning it to its proper spot; then, we ran to the kitchen, diving behind the center island just as the living room light kicked on.

"Hello?" Brian's dad said in a groggy tone that suggested he was still half asleep, and this was not his idea.

"Boys?"

We remained as quiet and still as possible, hoping he wouldn't go check on us in the game room. We had no way to sneak back in without opening the door, which we felt would be pretty stinkin' obvious. So, we waited.

If we were smart, we could have just acted like we were hanging out in the kitchen, unable to sleep and perhaps a bit thirsty, but like I've said many times before, we were idiots.

The path of most resistance was a path we traveled often.

"There's nobody down here," Brian's dad said before flipping the light off.

"Whew!" Roxy said, wiping fake sweat from his brow.

"Shit," I said, still highly irritated, "what a fucking scam!"

"Yeah, really, at least Freddie Freaker told us a funny story. That dumb broad didn't tell us jackshit!"

"Yeah! I'm so pissed, dude. Like, so pissed. All this work and for what?! Nothin', that's what!"

"Let's just go home."

"We're stuck, dude. Game over, man. Game over. We can leave in the morning."

"They're still gonna get charged for that," Roxy said, his mood improving with the thought of someone other than us being stuck with that bill. It made me laugh. Then he laughed. Then we headed back to the game room, where we helped ourselves to some money in Brian's piggy bank and then giggled ourselves to sleep.

To this day, I have no idea what happened with the bill. We never heard a word about it, leading us to form the conclusion that Brian's dad was a secret phone sex addict, and he didn't even notice the extra call.

No idea if that's true or not, but it sure was funny to us.

We never hung out with Brian again, instead choosing to waste our lazy afternoons staring at the Video Jukebox Channel, desperately waiting for a video.

Any video.

When *Mentarosa* by Mellow Man Ace finally (finally!) played, we felt that our morning had not been wasted after all.

When the video ended, it went right back to scrolling songs, leading us to wonder who in their right mind decided to spend almost four dollars on *Mentarosa*.

Oh well.

"What do you want to do today?"

"I dunno," I said. "I'm sick of just sitting here, though. Wanna skate?"

Skate was another term we used rather loosely. Both of us had "big" skateboards, which were an upgrade from the little Penny and Nash boards we started with, but neither of us could actually skate. I mean, we could stand on the board and maybe even go forward, but as far as tricks go, that was a major nope.

We recognized that once we got to junior high and especially high school, skating would be something that the cool kids did, and did well, so we had to practice, but when you can't even successfully ride over a pebble without being flung to the asphalt while your board rapidly retreats in the opposite direction, it really seems to crush your spirits.

"Um," Roxy said, "not really."

"Wanna go be nosey to the new family?"

"Now there's an idea I can get behind!"

Roxy turned himself right side up, and we headed to his garage where our bikes were parked, then took off down the street to the recently sold house around the corner, where Xavier had said a black family moved.

When we arrived, there was nothing to see. There were no cars in the driveway or signs of life anywhere, but seeing as this was all we had planned for the day, we decided to ring the doorbell. It turned out to be a great decision.

A black guy with the coolest Jheri curl I'd ever seen answered the door, looked at us staring up at him, and said, "Can I help you, fellas?"

"Hi!" I said, perhaps a bit too enthusiastically. I had to remind myself we weren't here to bullshit our way into mooching off these people somehow.

"Hi," the man responded with equal enthusiasm, which we both found pretty funny.

"We live..." I vaguely pointed in a direction that could have possibly been by where I lived, then shrugged, "over there somewhere. We saw you guys moved in."

"That's very observant of you two."

"So," I said, "do you, like, have a kid our age or something?"

"We're bored," Roxy said, too loud.

The man laughed and said, "Get a load of you guys. You guys are alright. Yeah, sure, I've got a boy about your age. What are ya, ten, eleven?"

"Almost eleven," Roxy said.

"Well, fellas, you're in luck. Can I first ask your names?"

"I'm Grant. This is my best bud, Roxy."

"Well, nice to meet you, Grant and Roxy. I've got a boy your age named Marcus, but we call him Mookie."

"Like the Met?" I asked. Being a massive baseball fan and card collector, I knew that Mookie Wilson was currently due to retire with the Toronto Blue Jays at the end of the season, but for all his fans across the country, he would forever be a Met, hero of the 1986 World Series where he was hitting just a .115 average and somehow, someway, drove in a run in the ninth inning of game four of the NLCS against the Houston Astros, sending the game into extra innings and giving the Mets an eventual win.

That hit set him on fire, and by the time the tenth inning of Game Six of the World Series came around a week or so later, Mookie was batting a .273 average.

The Boston Red Sox had scored two in the top of the tenth, giving them a 5-3 lead heading into the bottom of the inning. It was do or die for the Mets at that point. After New Yorkers Wally Blackman and Keith Hernandez were retired, leaving two outs on the scoreboard, the Sox reliever, a guy named Calvin Schiraldi, gave up three singles in a row, causing the Mets to gain a little ground, now only down by one.

Schiraldi was pulled and replaced with Bob Stanley, and guess who was coming up to bat.

The red-hot Mookie Wilson!

Vin Scully was on the call. My dad and I were gathered around the television, watching intently. Lifelong Dodger fans we both were, we still had love for the Mets. It was hard to dislike a team that featured, along with Mookie and Keith, Daryll Strawberry, Gary Carter, and Dwight Gooden. In fact, as I type this, my old Mets hat hangs on a hook in the corner of my office.

Stanley throws the first pitch, and Mookie fouls it off. Mookie pulls ahead of the count 2-1 when he fouls off another one, bringing the count even. Three more fouls followed before Stanley threw one wild, allowing Kevin Mitchell to score from third and Ray Knight to move to second! The crowd goes batshit insane! Tie game. Mookie could end it all with one swing. Streamers are floating down behind Mookie as he retakes the batter's box.

With so much enthusiasm in his voice, Vin says it would be impossible not to get caught up in the excitement, "5-5 in a delirious tenth inning!"

Stanley throws. Mookie pops it up out in foul territory, out of reach. It lands safely.

Another pitch. Another foul, this time down the third-base line.

The stadium is at a fever pitch. My parents and I were on our feet.

Then it happened. On the tenth pitch, Mookie swings, doesn't make great contact and hits a little chopper down the first-base line directly at Bill Buckner.

Easy out.

Only, Buckner tries to rush the play, anxious to get this inning over with, the pressure, surely, off the chart, and he doesn't get his glove down all the way. The ball rolls right between his legs, and if you thought the stadium was loud before, you hadn't heard anything yet! Mookie practically hops to first, his hands waving through the night sky, while Ray Knight scores from second, ending the game in, quite possibly, the most unpredictable way.

It wouldn't be until two years later, on October 15th, 1988, that we would get that level of excitement again. Game one of the World Series, when Kirk Gibson, with both legs injured, is put in to pinch hit for the Dodgers in the bottom of the ninth inning with two outs. He couldn't run. All he could do was try and hit the ball as hard and as far as his bruised and battered body could manage. It was all we could hope for. Anything less would mean lights out. He literally hobbled to the plate.

We just needed a hit to stay alive.

Come on, Kirk! Just give us a hit.

What he did for us was unimaginable. With two strikes, Gibson drove a fastball from Oakland A's pitcher Dennis Eckersley into the right field stands, in what was later voted as The Greatest Moment in L.A. Sports History.

Vin was on the call.

Me, my mom, my dad, and even my brother, were all gathered around the television. Whoever said baseball can't be magical hasn't been paying attention.

Bill Buckner, whose error caused the Met's game-winning run, was haunted and harassed over the play until the day he died of Lewy body dementia on May 27th, 2019, at the age of just 69. He never let it go, and he was never able to escape it.

"You know it," Mookie's dad said. "You guys Met's fans?"

"Mostly Dodgers, but you know, hard not to love the Amazin' Mets."

"Yeah, you guys are okay. Let me go get the boy. Hold on."

Mookie's dad, who I would later find out is named Leroy, retreated into the house. A few minutes later, a kid our age came to the door. I don't remember what we said, but it doesn't matter. Within four minutes, Mookie was out the door and hanging out with us.

"Let's go to my house," I said, hopping on my bike as Mookie dragged his out of the garage.

"Where is it?"

"Just right around the corner. Two seconds."

"Cool."

We rode down the middle of the street, turned the corner as fast as we could, and sprinted towards my house when a voice called out to us. We hit the brakes hard when we saw it was a foxy girl.

We circled back and rode towards her. She was older, probably in her twenties, with her long brown hair pulled back into a ponytail. She was carrying a stack of papers.

"Thanks for stopping," she said, and we nodded silently. "My name is, um, Skye Sanders. You haven't seen my sister by any chance, have you?"

She handed us each a paper from the stack. A photocopied Bebe-Lynn Sanders stared back at us with her wide smile, so full of life. "She never came home, and we haven't been able to find her anywhere."

Even to this day, I can still see the sadness in that poor girl's eyes as she talked to us. I said, "My mom...said she saw her on Friday morning."

"Yeah," she said, scrunching her nose up a bit, then, "Friday morning seems to be the last time anyone saw her in the neighborhood. Would you mind if I talked to your mom?"

"No, you can talk to her, for sure. I'm Grant, that's Roxy, and that's Mookie."

She reached her free hand out and shook ours.

"I live close. You can just follow us."

We hopped off our bikes and walked them the rest of the way, Skye by our side.

"Let me go tell my mom you're here, okay."

"For sure," she said with a forced smile.

Roxy, Mookie, and I walked into my house and headed straight for the living room. My dad was sitting on the floor in front of the coffee table, fiddling with an old Cuckoo clock my mom loved but hadn't worked in at least five years. He was listening to *The Breakup Song* by Greg Kihn Band on the radio and singing along.

He didn't hear us come in.

We let him finish the chorus (*Ah-ah-ah, ah-ah-ah-ah, aaah, they don't write 'em like that anymore*) before we made ourselves known. He laughed, then scooted over to turn the music down.

"Hey, fellas. Caught me singin', huh?"

"Just for a second."

"They really don't write 'em like that anymore, ya know."

Roxy mimicked the chorus, "Ah-ah-ah, ah-ah-ah-ah, aaah."

"See? Roxy knows what's happenin'!"

"Uh, hey, Dad. This is our new friend Mookie."

Mookie smiled and waved.

"Nice to meet ya, Mookie! Hold on." My dad got to his feet and walked over to shake Mookie's hand. "So, you live around here?"

"Yes, sir, we moved in around the corner."

"Oh geez, don't call me sir. These two just call me dad, or you can call me Gary."

"Cool."

My dad gave us kind of a funny look and then said, "Rox, your mom is here, too. Something not great is going on, I think."

"We have someone outside that wants to talk to Mom, too."

"Huh? Who?"

"Um. I think she's Bebe's sister."

"Uh oh. Okay, turn that stereo off. I'll go get her."

The stereo in question was a massive piece of furniture about four feet tall and five feet wide. Like the TVs at the time, it weighed no less than seven-hundred pounds.

When Skye entered the room, we all just stared at her. We didn't know what else to do. My dad told her to hold on for a second, then went onto the patio to get my mom. We all stood silently until my mom and Roxy's mom entered.

"Hi, sweetie," my mom said, patting me on the head. I remained quiet. It was easy to judge the seriousness of this situation.

"Come on, guys," my dad said, "let's get out of the way."

We followed him out of the living room through the kitchen and into my bedroom. "I don't know what's going on in there, but it's better if you guys are out of the way."

We nodded, and my dad closed the door as he went out. We kept that door closed for about half a second before we snuck back out and down the hallway. From what I could see, Skye had taken a seat at the kitchen table, where I assumed our moms were.

Dad pulled up a chair and joined them.

"Your little boy," Skye said, "he told me you may have seen my sister the day she left."

I tried not to be offended by the little boy comment, but I don't think it worked.

"I did," Mom said, "but there was nothing out of the ordinary. I was showing the house across the street from the community center and saw her walking by."

Skye waited a moment before speaking again. "What made you notice her if you don't mind me asking?"

"I... I don't know. She was just walking by. I assumed she was heading for the pool."

"Was she dressed for the pool?"

"No. She had a bag, though. I suppose it could have had pool stuff in it. Or she could have been wearing her suit under her clothes. I think she was wearing little jean shorts and maybe a tank top. She had sunglasses on, though. I remember that. Those Thomas Magnum kind."

"Yeah, that's what other people have said too, but I just can't find anyone who actually talked to her that day. I believe when you saw her, she was headed to Video Network. There is a rental copy of *Who's Harry Crumb?* in her bedroom."

"You checked Video Network, of course."

Skye nodded. "Yeah. She definitely rented it. The computer showed it was rented Friday morning at 10:05 from our parents' account."

"So that checks out. It was about 9 when I saw her."

"Did she... look upset or worried? I mean, I know she went and rented a movie, but...."

"I'm so sorry, sweetie. I just saw her walking. I didn't think anything of it at the time. I was worried about selling that stupid house."

"I'm sorry," Skye said, obviously trying to hold back tears. "I don't know what I'm doing here. I'm totally flying blind. My parents are out doing the same thing, and we're all just lost. It's been two days, and there hasn't been a sign of her anywhere since Friday night."

Skye reached her hands across the table. I saw my mom's and Roxy's mom's hands reach out and grab them. My dad stood up and returned shortly with a box of Kleenex. Skye remained embraced with the moms.

"You said nobody had seen her since Friday night," Dad said. "It wasn't Friday morning, then?"

Skye sniffled, then said, "That's what we thought, but now we have a couple of kids telling us they saw her walking near Jimmy's Arcade Friday night. Wearing jeans and a yellow collared shirt and drinking a soda. So she had to have returned home from the time you saw her, obviously because the movie was there and because she had changed. I have no idea how long she was home before she headed out, though. I'm in school all day at Cal State, and both my parents were working until six that night, so we didn't know. She usually leaves us a note when she goes out, but not always, because, ya know, typical ditzy teenager. But, even if she had left a note, what would it have said? *At Jimmy's as usual?* Wouldn't be much help." She tried to laugh, but it just made my heart sink. The three of us boys all exchanged glances with each other, having no idea what to say or do in a situation like this.

As for Mookie, it was a hell of an introduction to our squad.

Roxy's mom said, "The boys were at Jimmy's on Friday night. I've already asked them, but it wouldn't hurt to ask again. Roxyhoney?!"

The three of us skittered back to my room, loudly opened the door, and pretended to walk out.

Roxy yelled down the hall, "Yeah, mom?"

"Come here for a second, would ya?"

"Yep."

We joined everyone in the living room, and Roxy's mom asked if we remembered seeing Bebe at Jimmy's on Friday night. She told us to think really, really hard.

My mom, noticing Mookie, said, "Hi, sweetie, I'm sorry."

Mookie smiled and said, "It's okay. I'm Mookie."

Roxy's mom smiled and said, "Hi, Mookie."

"It's great to meet you," my mom said. Then, back to me, "Where was your brother on Friday night? Any idea?"

"No, I never know where he is. I don't think he hangs out at Jimmy's, though. He hangs out with those idiots that always rev their dumb car engines."

"At Andres?" Mom asked. Andres was another famous burger joint in town. I nodded in the affirmative.

"Sail Thru is right across from Jimmy's. Any chance he could have been there?"

I shrugged. The whole area was basically for high school and under, so I doubt my brother would be there, but who knows with that guy.

"Yeah," Mom said, "but it's worth a shot." To Skye, "When my other son gets home, I'll see if he knows anything. I assume you've talked to Sheriff Monroe. He just lives two doors down."

"Yeah, we've talked to him. He's working on finding out if she met with anyone or something. I don't know. Sheriff Monroe said they were looking for witnesses who may have seen her with someone she could have left with. At least that way, they could track that person down or maybe, he said, work on a ...um...when someone draws a picture from someone describing... I don't know...."

"A composite sketch," my dad said.

"Yeah. Last I heard, that's what they were looking for. She had to have talked to someone. It doesn't make any sense that she would go to Jimmy's alone."

"Unless she was meeting someone there," Dad said.

I remember Neil telling me that Bebe was meeting an older guy there then took off with him, but he has absolutely no way of knowing that and he was probably full of shit, as usual.

Skye nodded. "Yeah. So... It's an official missing persons case now, but I don't know if that's a good thing or a bad thing. Please take a flier, though. It's got my parent's number on there if you hear anything. Or call Sheriff-"

"We have his number," I said, perhaps a bit too enthusiastically. Jesus, Grant. Tact. Quickly over-correcting, I add, "He, um, handed out cards. We have one on...the fridge..."

Everyone stared at me like I was standing in a pile of dog crap. My mom rescued me by saying, "He's right. We have his number on the fridge. And I promise, if we hear anything, we will call you and the Sheriff."

"Thank you so much," Skye said, getting to her feet. "Literally anything. No information is too trivial."

Our moms nodded, then walked Skye to the door. My dad holds us back. To me, he said, "Any idea where your brother is?"

"Nope, no idea."

"That guy, I swear to god."

The moms returned to make an announcement. "So," my mom said, "until this girl is found, we don't want you kids to leave the street. And we will need you home by the time the streetlights come on."

We moaned and complained with displeasure.

"We mean it," Roxy's mom said. "You guys are more than welcome to spend the night at our house-"

"Or here," my mom added.

"Yeah, or here, but we absolutely do not want you out at night. Mookie, I'm sorry we had to meet under such odd circumstances, but you are welcome to stay over as well. Who do you live with?"

"My mom and dad and sister and brother."

"Okay," Mom said, "do you mind if I go talk to them. We would like to introduce ourselves and really get this situation under control."

Aw, man!

"Yeah," Mookie said, "that's cool. And I'd love to sleep over. I've never slept over before, and we haven't even gotten my bed delivered yet."

"Oh, did you just move in?"

"Yeah, to the house around the corner."

It was faint, but I could see my mom's shoulders slump. She was hoping to sell that house. "Okay, we can all go over there in a bit if you don't mind."

"I don't mind."

He may not have minded, but Roxy and I sure did. Was there anything more uncool than having your moms meet your new friend's parents on literally the same day he became your friend? It makes us look like such losers, but unfortunately, we had no choice, so off we went, walking down the street with the moms. Please, please, please don't let Daphne be outside or look out her window.

Above: A typical meal with Grant, Roxy, & Hilary.
Below: My old man with Hilary, me, & Roxy.

Bebe's Missing Flyer - given to
me by her sister, Skye (1990)

I wish there was a funny story to tell you about regarding this whole ordeal, but the moms met Mookie's parents, explained the situation, and that was about it. Mookie's parents looked a little rattled by the Bebe Incident, but they seemed to trust our moms enough to let Mookie spend the night, which was another perk of the time period. Nobody trusts anybody these days, and for good reason.

So yeah, nothing to report there except that we would be having a sleepover, which was always awesome. Sleepovers in the 80s and early '90s were an entirely different breed of fun compared to what they've become since cell phones and social media took over.

I asked a couple of girls earlier today about their experiences with sleepovers around this timeframe and got wildly different answers from what us boys were used to; things like giving each other make-overs and playing dumb games like Truth or Dare and something called Light as a Feather, Stiff as a Board, or summoning pretend demons with a Ouija board.

That could be fun, I guess, but the slumber parties I was used to were much more low-energy. When we conned our way into Brian's house to spend the night during the Phone Sex Caper, all we did was order pizza and take over his Nintendo. That's fine and dandy, but it was missing a very crucial element for what I deemed a successful sleepover. That being a trip to the Video Store!

If you're younger than me and reading this book, there's a pretty good chance that you have no idea what a video store even is. And that sucks. Because the video store was the happiest place on Earth and a vital piece of the identity of the time.

The Video Store.

Summer 1975 – Kassel, Germany. A man named Eckhart Baum, an avid collector of reel-to-reel and Super 8 films, came up with the idea to start renting out pieces of his collection after repeatedly loaning out copies to his friends. It was a hit, and by the end of 1977, a man named George Atkinson opened the first professionally managed rental store in America. Hotels, restaurants, convention centers, etc., would go to George to rent out projectors and a selection of public domain film reels and Super 8's.

In 1976, JVC introduced the very first VCR in Japan, followed quickly by RCA launching their unit in the United States. Both companies made their new product available to the public, but for what purpose? Sure, these new fancy electronics looked fantastic, and the potential to bring Hollywood home seemed terrific at the time, but where would you get these movies to watch? The movie studios were pretty apathetic about the whole thing, not seeing it as much of a threat to cinema-going because these new gizmos were priced far out of the average consumer's range, so why even bother.

20th Century Fox was the lone studio that recognized the potential, quickly striking a deal with Andre Blay, the owner, and founder of Magnetic Video, a video cassette manufacturer, to license him fifty of the studio's titles for sale on a tape that could be played on these new luxury items. They would be called a Video Home System, and movies such as *The French Connection, Patton, Butch Cassidy, and the Sundance Kid*, and many more, could be purchased and viewed at home for the low, low price of just fifty dollars a pop!

With a price like that in the seventies, you can see why studios didn't feel threatened.

Was the Video Home System, or VHS as it was being called, set up for failure? It sure seemed so.

That didn't stop Japanese company Sony from hopping on the bandwagon and making their own cassettes called Betamax, which were smaller than VHS so they would seem even more advanced. In fact, the Max was added to the name Beta just to give a subtle nudge to the consumer that Beta was the way to go.

It doesn't get much better than Betamax! (I was always Team VHS!)

So what the hell was the point of two competing systems that only offered products to a small percentage of the world's elite?

———

20th Century Fox didn't care – they threw Betamax into their agreement with Magnetic Video. Why the hell not? What did they care?

So what do you do with tons of copies of *M*A*S*H** on VHS and Betamax?

You sit around and wait for everything to come crumbling down.

Yeah, the idea of Hollywood at Home was dead on arrival.

The thought of a typical American family purchasing video cassettes for fifty dollars apiece, on top of already having spent hundreds on their video cassette recorders (VCR), was absurd. Like so many other ambitious endeavors, this product was doomed to be a flop.

Until...

In walks the previously mentioned George Atkinson, a small shop owner from Los Angeles who was renting out his public domain titles in an unnamed store on Wilshire Ave. George took the money he had made and parlayed it into buying copies of every title 20th Century Fox offered on both VHS and Betamax, so he could offer them to his customers for...RENTAL!

It was a hit!

Hollywood started taking notice, and they were not happy.

Universal and Disney launched a lawsuit against Sony in the case called Sony Corp. of America v. Universal City Studios Inc in an effort to ban any and all sales of VCRs and the new VHS and Betamax cassette tapes, claiming these devices were created with the sole intent of stealing copyrighted material, via what they called Time Shifting, which was basically recording a show or movie off of a live television broadcast for viewing at a later time. The studio argued that the products had no other purpose; thus, they should be banned, and anyone using these products would be committing copyright infringement. If successful, this would have killed the entire video store industry just as it was really starting to heat up!

The case was eventually ruled in favor of Sony because what did the court system care about something that was viewed as a non-issue, citing Fair Use for any material the studios chose to broadcast that could potentially be recorded.

But the studio quickly fired off an appeal.

The case went to the supreme court in 1981. It appeared that Universal and Disney were going to win – they had the majority vote needed – and that the beloved VCR was destined to be nothing more than a memory because by the time the case was winding down, nearly three years later, VCRs had proven to be quite popular. They were not only for the elite like so many people had assumed. Now, typical American families had rallied around the product. A VCR was now in nearly fifty percent of the homes in America, which, just a few years earlier, seemed beyond impossible!

Now, there really was a case for copyright infringement, just as Universal and Disney had warned the first time around, and it had swayed the opinions of the judges presiding over the case.

The final votes were tallied...

It was all over.

5-4 in favor to overturn.

VHS is dead. Long live VHS.

Another victory for the two biggest movie studios in existence over the Average Joes of the world.

The ruling was overturned, and the sale of VCRs and cassette tapes was no more.

Until...

January 17, 1984. You'll never guess who barged into that supreme court and argued his case in favor of the VCR! None other than Fred (Mr.) Rogers!

Arguing an appeal, Fred Rogers said:

"I have always felt with the advent of this new technology that allows people to tape (Mr. Roger's) Neighborhood off-the-air, they then become much more active in the programming of their family's television life. Very frankly, I am opposed to people being programmed by others.

My whole approach in broadcasting has always been, 'You are an important person just the way you are. You can make healthy decisions.' I just feel that anything that allows a person to be more active in the control of his or her life in a healthy way is important."

He testified that he had "absolutely no objection to home taping for noncommercial use." He stressed how important such recordings could be for parents to tape his show, and any others they chose, to be shown to their children at the appropriate times.

Arguing the other side was the eye-bulging lunatic and head of the Motion Picture Association of America, Jack Valenti, ranting and raving about the "savages and ravages" of the VCR while saying it is "to American film producers as the Boston Strangler is to a woman home alone."

Deranged Fucking Lunatic Jack Valenti

v

Mr. Rogers

It's a tough choice, I know, but you have to pick one. Who ya goin' with here?

Who has had enough of this madness?

I'll tell ya who had had enough. Judge Sandra Day O'Connor, that's who! She stood up, gavel in hand, and said, "Yo, fuck this shit, bruh! I'm rollin' with Mr. Rogers!" (Actual quote may have varied.)

And that was that. The overturn was overturned, and VHS and Betamax were back, baby! Go grab yourself a VCR and let the parties begin!

Now, the only battle would be – Are you a VHS person or a Betamax person?! Because this was a very real rivalry back then.

This was iPhone vs. Android.

HD-DVD vs. Blu-Ray.

Netflix vs. Physical Media.

It was big, and it was awesome, and in the end, VHS won. America won. The world won.

Video Stores were popping up everywhere shortly

after the decision, and my dear readers, aside from the arcade, there was no better place for a kid to be in the 80s and 90s than the video store.

Even drug stores got in on the action. Grocery stores too. They all wanted a piece of the sweet, sweet, pie! In fact, it was at an Albertson's grocery store that my mom pointed out to little six-year-old Grant a movie. She said, "I think you'll like it. It's a scary one. The guy has knives for fingers."

Now she says things to me like, "I don't know where you got this obsession with horror movies." Seriously. The woman who showed me *The Howling* at age two can't piece together where my love of horror came from. 'Tis a mystery!

Anyway, the point is the video rental store was born!

All hail Mr. Rogers and Sandra Day O'Connor! True American heroes! (Also, the other four judges that were on the right side the entire time... whatever the hell their names are.)

That exciting bit of legal history is part of what brought us to the Video Store on a Sunday night in the midst of a town on the verge of panic.

Our video store of choice, although I loved them all, especially the Mom and Pop Shops that are all but extinct now, was Video Network, located just across the street from Quailwood in the same shopping center as the Miller's Outpost (that we shoplifted blind), and the Albertsons I just mentioned.

As soon as you walked through those double doors, all your stress would vanish. You were now in a fantasy land where nothing from the outside world mattered.

A little more than a year after Bebe, I was frequenting Video Network so often, the employees began giving me jobs to do, and I loved it. At first, I usually was there alone, so if I wasn't with friends, I was there, which probably made my parents happy to have a few moments to themselves. Especially if my dad was at work, I'm sure my mom loved the peace and quiet because dumbass Neil had finally moved into a shitty apartment with like nine other idiots, none of which had a job, so I'm not sure how that worked out. After Bebe, it seemed, Neil only came home to mooch food... that is, until his entire living-on-his-own plan came tumbling down, and he was forced to move back in with our parents for the rest of eternity, something my mom only agreed to as long as Neil promised to go on the gameshow *Shop 'Til You Drop* with her. Neil begrudgingly agreed, and in October of 1992, they finally got on. Poor Neil humiliated himself running up and down that fake mall, but it paid off. They won a table full of crap and a trip to Hawaii.

The way you rented a movie at Video Network was like this; the older movies were just in regular slipcases, but for the new releases, the cases would be displayed on a shelf, and another case, a clamshell with the actual cassette in it, would be placed behind. That's how you knew the movie was 'in stock' or not. You'd take the case with the video in it up to the register, rent it, then bring it back when you were done by dropping it in a little drop box. My job was to return all those dropped movies to the shelves after they were checked in.

I was obsessed.

After a while, Brandon started coming with me. We'd work at least ten times harder and faster than the barely-conscious teenage rejects getting paid to work there, but we didn't care.

This is actually one of two very fond memories I have with Brandon. Later, after graduating from high school, he and I, and several others, would stay up all night playing the Nintendo 64 classic *Goldeneye*, also known as the greatest video game ever made. In fact, if I had a time machine, aside from going back to the heyday of Jimmy's, I would return to '97/'98, gathered around Brandon's TV, blasting each other with Rocket Launchers in the Temple.

By 1999, we had started going our own ways. Some guys got their own place, some got jobs, girlfriends, whatever, but for that one year of endless *Goldeneye*, everything was... perfect.

Back at Video Network one warm Spring night, I was

desperate to rent *Child's Play 2*. I had already seen it, but it was new on VHS (and by this time, buying a VHS copy of a movie was pure insanity, costing around a hundred bucks a piece), and I wanted to watch it again. It was my new favorite movie and was due to be returned that night.

It was a Friday, and my parents and I had gone out to dinner at Rusty's Pizza in the same shopping center, then walked over here to rent a movie. They picked out the one they wanted (some Melanie Griffith clunker called *Pacific Heights*) and waited around with me, hoping *Child's Play 2* would finally be returned.

The hours went by, forcing my parents to leave me there alone at around 9pm, sitting on the metal railings next to the checkout counter. "Come home when you get it," Dad had said as they walked out, unable to wait another minute.

Back then, you could leave an eleven-year-old alone in a shopping center with little-to-no worries.

I sat there.

And sat there.

And sat there, until the store closed. Whoever rented *Child's Play 2* had made it clear they would not be returning it on time and would incur the late charge the store deemed appropriate for such a flagrant violation of their rules.

I walked home heartbroken.

The following day, I got the call. The movie had been returned, and they were holding it at the counter for me!

Pure magic, that old video store was, I tell ya!

Over the years, especially in junior high and high school, when I started spending more time for myself, I would go to these video stores and head straight for the horror section. They had 'em all. With the boom of VHS and home recording equipment such as camcorders, horror took on a life of its own and soon had its very own sub-category - VHS Horror. Movies shot by idiots on their own recording gear often featuring massive amounts of boobs, terrible sound work, and glorious, glorious gore.

I couldn't get enough.

I was up to a three-movie-a-day habit for several years. I didn't care what I watched, I just wanted to watch more. I would go into those glorious horror sections, studying the covers intently, before deciding which ones to take home with me.

I wish I could describe the feeling, but I think you just had to be there to truly understand.

It was 100% pure, uncut, bliss.

Roxy and I headed straight for the horror section. When we were together, we always tried to pick out the movies that looked the worst so we could crack jokes. This time was different, though, after Mookie said, "We don't watch many scary movies at our place. Not with a mom and sister who get scared over spiders in the house."

Any other time, it wouldn't have mattered which movies we picked out. But not this time. This time was different. On top of it being Mookie's first real sleepover, the only horror movies he had seen were the made-for-TV *Salem's Lot*, and *Mommie Dearest* (which is complete lame sauce!). So we took this as a challenge and knew we needed to find the perfect movies.

I love those old Video Stores. Video Network eventually became the more corporate Video City and lost its soul, the horror section being reduced to one little corner. I started frequenting the Mom and Pop places more and more because I knew they were passionate about the movies they rented, whereas Blockbuster, which somehow gets way more credit than it deserves, and others like it were simply corporations founded on the basic principles of greed, offering nine-thousand copies of trash like *Independence Day* or *Batman Forever*, and sacrificing the movies that built the entire movie renting industry.

At the smaller places, if you wanted a standee (the big cardboard displays for movies) or a promotional poster, you wrote your name on a Post-it Note and slapped that shit right on the back of it, declaring DIBS! If you even so much as asked for something at

Blockbuster, you'd be told no and laughed at. (One girl seriously laughed at me, no joke.)

Fuck Blockbuster.

(RIP Video Network, Video Zone, USA Video, Family Video, Atlas Video, Madman Video, America Video, and so many more.)

I remember we picked out four movies, more than we could ever watch in one night, especially since we knew we wouldn't even start them until *America's Funniest Home Videos* (RIP Bob Saget) and *America's Funniest People* ended. But that didn't matter. They were all absolute bangers and the perfect introduction to Mookie, even though we only got to watch two - first up was the original 1978 classic *Halloween,* followed by 1982's *Friday the 13th Part 3.* We didn't get around to watching *The Slumber Party Massacre* and *Sorority House Massacre* – two totally different movies, I *assure* you.

Instead of just sleeping in sleeping bags on my living room floor, Roxy and I would often set up tents in the backyard and sleep there. It was like having your own private apartment, and we adored it. We had set up my dad's old Army tent this particular time. It was kept in a chest out in the garage and sometimes housed black widows, but we didn't care. The tent was awesome and had that authentic tent smell that I can't even begin to describe. Must, maybe? A dash of dank. Mold possibly? It didn't matter.

When we got back from the video store, before we started the festivities, we pulled that old trunk from the garage out to the backyard, unrolled the tent, and drove the spikes into the ground.

"I've never slept in a tent before," Mookie said, connecting two of the poles together.

"Tents are awesome!" I said, rolling out the tarp we would be sleeping on.

"You guys do this all the time?"

"Yeah, pretty much. In the summer, it's too hot to come out here when the sun is still up, though, unless you're just playing and stuff. But to sleep, it's too hot, so we usually don't roll out here until like midnight."

"Have you guys been like, camping out in the woods before?"

Roxy and I both laughed.

Yes. Yes, we had.

"Yeah, we're Boy Scouts," Roxy said. "You should join when school starts back up."

"Yeah?" Mookie said. "What do you do?"

"Well," I said, "um, you go camping and stuff. And go to meetings."

Roxy said, "You learn how to survive out in the woods, just in case something happens."

"Yeah, and you help people and stuff. There are like, um, I don't know what they're called, like you volunteer at places that need help."

"And Pinewood Derby!"

"Heck yeah! Pinewood Derby!"

"What's that?" Mookie asked.

"Dude," I said, "you build these little wooden car things, right, and you kinda carve them out of a block of wood and paint them and get 'em lookin' all fresh to death and slap some plastic wheels on, then there is a big event where you race them down a big track."

"Yeah, but you need to weigh them down with weights because they're so light, so that's where the skill comes in. On top of the design you come up with, you have to provide enough weight in just the right spots to really make it move."

"That sounds awesome!"

"It is! And you get pocketknives, too, and different badges for your uniform for different tasks you complete. You have to join!"

"Sounds awesome!" Mookie said with a smile. "And you can go camping."

"Yeah," Roxy said, "sometimes it's just little overnight camping trips, but our dads go sometimes too, and your dad can totally come if he wants."

"We never got to go camping. My dad called where we

used to live an Asphalt Jungle, which is like a regular jungle, but the exact opposite."

"Well, he can come now!" I said, already excited about the prospects of all of us on a trip.

"Rad!"

"Yeah," Roxy said, "and sometimes you get to go camping alone, too, for more than just a night."

I laughed. "Yeah, dude. We just got back from a big trip last month."

"It was our first overnight with no parents."

"There were adults there, but like, not our parents."

It's incredible how many things happened during this one summer. We had, in fact, just gotten back from a weeklong camping trip to a place up north named Camp Kern. Now, here's the funny thing. Camp Kern could have been forty-five minutes out of town, or it could have been eight hours out of town. I really have no idea. I can easily look it up and find out, but it seems more fun for me not to know.

There was some major excitement and anticipation for this trip, not just for Rox and me but probably for our parents, too. Five days without us probably seemed like a dream vacation in the Bahamas to them. Back then, Roxy's parents had a Chevrolet Celebrity station wagon that we loved because it featured a third row of seats that faced out the back window. I have no idea of the safety measures that would have prevented our knees from being the first line of defense against a car rear-ending us, but we didn't care at that age.

"We call way way back!" was a common phrase we would yell when going anywhere in the station wagon, especially when Roxy's sister had a friend with her. We needed that way way back, damn it, and we usually got it. I can't imagine Hilary or her friends giving a rat's ass about where they sat. Something tells me they weren't nearly as interested in harassing other drivers as we were.

Both our moms and dads dropped us off at Camp Kern and waited for us to load onto the barge that would take us across the lake to the campsite. Once we were out of sight, I'm sure the champagne corks were popped, but whatever.

As far as I remember, this was our first time away from everyone. We were entirely on our own (so to speak) and couldn't have been happier.

As soon as the barge docked and we unloaded, we were shown to our cabins. Nothing special, just little wooden housing units with nothing but bunk beds in them. Roxy and I called the bunk in the far-left corner, then dumped our bags on them to claim 'em.

After everyone got settled, we were forced to do our safety training. The first course of action was to make sure someone would not die if they happened to find themselves in the middle of the lake somehow. And wouldn't ya know it, just like two months prior at the junior high with Madman Funk, we all had to line up along one of the docks and jump in, one at a time, and make sure we didn't sink like a stone like poor Brian did.

At least this time, there was an adult already in the water, waiting to rescue us should anything happen. Unfortunately, there was no repeat of what happened prior. Everyone in the scouts knew perfectly well how to swim, so the whole exercise was over in less than twenty minutes. The water, despite the heat outside, was ice cold. I would've loved to have avoided that goddamn lake for the rest of the week, but well, that didn't happen.

After the safety exercises were done, we all got dressed. We were told to gather around the campfire in twenty minutes. There were probably about fifty scouts there in total, ranging in age from ten (us and a few others from our troop) to upper high school, and we were broken up into smaller groups.

Rox and I got dressed and decided to hit the bathroom for the first time before we had to meet up with everyone. I know you're thinking, it took you guys that long to use the bathroom? Well, we both pissed in the lake during the safety meeting, so yeah, we were good until then.

We took the short walk to the bathrooms and strolled

inside expecting just another typical, totally boring bathroom, like at school.

Roxy entered first, and his screams of pure horror told me there would be nothing normal about this bathroom!

"Dude, what the - Ahhhhhh!!!!"

Screams! Like frightened little girls!

I was surprised we didn't hear a flock of birds outside scramble to fly away as quickly as their little wings could carry them.

Before us, there were no stalls. There were no private cubicles where a puny little boy of ten could sit and take a dump in private. What there was... was a long wooden bench with holes cut out.

Friends, I cannot stress this enough.

There was a BENCH... with HOLES CUT OUT!

"Holy shit, dude, holy shit!" Roxy said in a panic.

I was on the verge of a nervous breakdown. "This is a joke, dude. This is a joke."

We both looked around, desperate to find any evidence that this was some sort of hazing for the new kids. Nothing.

This was it.

"What the..." Roxy said quietly, moving slowly towards the bench.

"What the fuck is that, dude?!"

"It's a... It's a... POOPY!!!"

Right there, on the third hole, was a fresh, brown turd shaped like a shark's fin. We roiled in horror, our backs both hitting the far wall. We didn't dare take another step forward. We couldn't tell if the shark's fin shittle was on the outer rim of the hole or if the turd was so goddamn big it was a surface breaker. And honestly, we didn't care.

"We gotta go, dude, we gotta go!" I said, grabbing Roxy by the t-shirt. "Come on, dude, we can't be here!"

"Sweet mother of God, why?!"

I began stepping backward toward the door, never losing my grip on Roxy's shirt. "We can't go to the bathroom here. I can't gaze into another man's eyes while I'm trying to push out a dump!"

"I know, dude. I know. We'll figure something out. Come on, let's get the hell out of here!"

"Yeah," Roxy said, eyes wide and afraid, "I think you're right." We each took a deep breath and then ran! We bolted from that torture trap and didn't stop until we were completely out of breath (which honestly wasn't that far because we were in horrible shape, weak, and pretty much all-around pathetic.)

"Holy shit, dude."

"Dude," Roxy said, "we can't go to the bathroom here."

"Literally never! We're just gonna have to hold it until we get home."

"Pinkie?"

I held out my right pinkie, and Roxy hooked his around it. "Pinkie."

"I'm glad I pissed in the lake earlier."

"You and me both. Remember when Wesley said he found a warm spot in the water?"

We both laughed and laughed and laughed, then began our trek back to camp. We must have been a few minutes late because when we got there, our camp leader, a mountain of a man named Bill Leblanc, or as we would come to call him, Wild Bill, had already begun talking to the group.

Remember earlier when I said Mr. Funk was one of two stark-raving lunatics we would encounter in the span of a couple months?

Well, meet Wild Bill Leblanc. His son Jason was in high school and in the cabin next to ours. At first glance, Bill seemed totally harmless, maybe even fun in that John Candy-in-*Camp Candy* kind of way. That first night, gathered around the campfire, he proudly asked, "Anyone wanna hear a loud fart?" then ripped one so goddamn loud I thought the ground was going to split open and swallow us all. Everyone laughed, including a few little giggles from Roxy and me, but we exchanged a nervous glance shortly after. Was the shark fin Bill's? It was possible. Everything seemed less funny when we remembered our predicament.

I don't remember what dinner was that first night, so it probably wasn't as mind-blowingly horrible as the other meals were because, my god, the other meals were inedible. Roxy and I spent the next morning at the Kern Mart, a little booth set up at the far side of the camp that thankfully sold food that was edible. Even more thankfully, our parents had given us cash to spend. Otherwise, we would have been eff you see kayed!

The only thing we bought that second day was Reese's Pieces. A lot of them. We returned to our cabin, sat on the edge of our bunk bed, and fed all the excess to squirrels. We later would joke about how many squirrels we probably killed due to our apathy towards any and every event the camp had planned. We skipped almost everything, instead opting to sit in the cabin and feed squirrels until they exploded.

The one and only event we decided to participate in came on the third day when we were told shotguns would be involved. Score, we're in!

Skeet shooting took place over the lake, and these scoutmasters would happily hand over loaded shotguns to a bunch of shitty punk kids, Roxy and me included. Now, we didn't know much about guns. We were action-movie obsessed, so we had seen Arnold blow away no less than nine billion bad guys by this time. We were confident we could fire this massive weapon with no problems.

"Careful," one of the troopers said to me. "It's got a kick."

I gave him a dirty look. Don't tell me what to do! I know it all! "Pull!"

The clay disks shot out over the water, and I took aim and pulled the trigger. The shotgun flew out of my hand as I was thrown back onto my ass. Panic ensued as the live weapon hit the ground.

"Shit," Roxy said to me as I rubbed my shoulder. "My turn!"

___

138

With zero hesitation, the troopers loaded another shell into the gun and handed it to Roxy. "Pull!"

He landed right next to me.

"I told you!"

"Son of a bitch hurts!"

"You wanna go again?" a trooper asked us as we struggled to get to our feet.

We didn't say a word.

We walked back to the Kern Mart, our shoulders throbbing, and restocked on candy as a reward for our pain.

By the next day, our poor little tummies were really starting to rumble, having only eaten the bare minimum of camp food and a shit ton of candy. Some turds were brewing with no chance for escape. Outside our opened cabin door, a squirrel barfed and then keeled over.

We were jealous.

That day's event involved rowing a canoe over to the island in the middle of the lake for some fun adventures. Sounds great, right?

Hang on.

We were broken up into canoe groups, and Roxy and I were stoked to be together (like we would've listened anyway if we weren't.)

So, we all walk down to the water's edge, gather in our groups, and drop our canoes into the lake. Our group consisted of me and Roxy, the little twerp nerd kid Wesley that we peed on in the water that first day, and another little nerd named Frank Piancky, who whined and complained so goddamn much he earned the nickname Cranky Franky Piancky. The four of us combined probably weighed about two-hundred pounds.

We were all sitting in the canoe, and a trooper on the dock was handing us our oars when here comes Wild Bill, all three-hundred and fifty pounds of him, heading right for us. "I'm with you guys!" he said as he stepped down into our little yellow deathtrap and took a seat facing us.

A trooper on the other side of the dock yelled, "We'll see you all over there!" Kids cheered as the canoes began filing out into the water.

"Okay," Bill said, "let's go!"

The trooper that handed us our oars gave our boat a little shove away from the dock. We were on our own.

"Okay," Bill said, "row."

We tried. I promise we tried. Roxy was at the opposite end of Bill, so far up in the air his oar didn't even skim the top of the water.

"Holy shit," I said, "it's like we're on a teeter-totter."

Bill started yelling, "Row! Come on!" Franky and Wesley, the closest to Bill, had their oars so goddamn deep in the water it would be impossible for them to move 'em, the pressure being way too great for two wimpy little kids. Wesley turned to look at me, pure horror on his face. He fought back the tears as he struggled to pull on that oar with all his might. It just wouldn't move. We were outmatched.

"Jesus Christ," Bill yelled, "what the hell is wrong with you?!"

Franky was panicking up front, repeating, "It's too heavy, it's too heavy," over and over.

"COME ON!!! I thought you were men!!!" Bill's face looked like it would pop like an overfilled water balloon!

Speaking of water, it started flooding into Bill's end of the canoe. "Jesus Christ," Bill yelled again. "Paddle!!! Paddle! You're embarrassing yourselves!!!"

Roxy leaned over the boat, getting his oar into the water to try and help. I did the same. "Come on, guys," I yelled, "pull!"

"Dude, we're going in a circle," Roxy yelled.

Poor Wesley had enough. His oar dropped into the water, and he began to cry.

"Pussies!" Bill yelled. "How did I get stuck with pussies?!"

"We're ten years old, dude!" I yelled.

"You outweigh all four of us," Roxy added. "What the hell do you expect?!"

Water had reached my shoes. We were going down. We were barely ten feet from the dock but about to be shipwrecked.

All the other canoes were almost to the island, and here we were, goin' down hard!

"I can't goddamn believe this shit!" Bill yelled as water flooded over his knees. "Sorriest sacks of shit I've ever seen!"

The boat started to wobble. There was no saving it. We were done for. Bill fell out, causing the canoe to slam down with such force it tossed poor Roxy out.

"Fucking freezing!" Roxy yelled, his head bobbing just above the surface.

I reached out to grab his hand, but it was no use. I looked around. Wesley was dog-paddling his way back to shore. Franky's head dipped below the water. He was as good as dead.

The canoe went down with me in it. The lake felt like it was filled with ice cubes, somehow even colder than it was the first day.

I swam over to Roxy, my teeth chattering. "H-Holy s-shit, dude! W-What the f-f-f-fuck was that?!"

"That g-g-guy is a f-f-f-fucking maniac!"

We looked at Bill off in the distance. Instead of helping us, he swam his fat ass back to shore and collapsed on the sand like a beached whale, leaving us all to fend for ourselves. He eventually rolled himself up and began to walk away.

We could hear him yelling obscenities the entire time until he was out of sight.

Shortly after, the barge came and got us and took us to the island for about twenty minutes of (wet and cold) fun. We didn't feel much like having fun, so we sat on a hot rock directly in the sun and quoted funny lines from *Spaceballs* until it was time to go back.

By Friday, when it was time to go home, Roxy and I had successfully avoided pooping the entire week. We did, however, piss on the side of Bill's cabin a bunch, one time behind the Kern Mart and once when we were out in the woods alone surrounded by squirrels. That time, we would pinch the tips of our wieners to build up pressure, then fire off short bursts of whiz at the little rodents running around. It was the most fun we had.

By the time our moms came to pick us up, our poor little stomachs were clinched so tight we could hardly stand up straight. We just wanted to go home, drop these deuces, and return to our everyday lives.

That's how we learned the hard way about constipation.

Mookie is rolling, laughing at our stupid story. "That sounds amazing!"

"For sure," I said. "You have to sign up."

"Oh, I'm gonna!"

We all laid our sleeping bags out and traded stupid stories until we eventually drifted off to sleep.

Can you spot Grant and Roxy?

The next morning, after peeing in the flowerbeds like we always did during a backyard campout ("You guys just pee in your yard like this?" Mookie had asked, seemingly shocked), we walked into the house to look for food when we saw my parents gathered around the TV. It was 10am, and Sheriff Monroe was on the screen addressing the town.

"Come here, guys," Dad said, "you should watch this."

Sheriff Monroe was standing at his podium. A small crowd was gathered around him. He cleared his throat, leaned forward towards the microphones, and began to speak.

"Hello, everyone," Monroe said. "Thanks for coming down on such short notice."

"Neil!" my mom shouted, "get out here, please!"

I heard Neil yell, "Huh?!" from his bedroom.

"Get out here, please!"

A shirtless Neil came sauntering in from the hallway. Honestly, I was surprised he was even awake.

"Watch," Mom said.

Monroe said, "Bebe-Lynn Sanders has been missing since Friday, June 29th. We waited for her to return safely all weekend, but we still have no information on where she is. There have been no sightings, no phone calls to her friends or parents. Nothing. We are desperate to find her. This is a beautiful young woman with a bright future ahead of her. We need to find her.

"When I was elected, and even before I was elected, I made sure every single person in my district had my card. I said you could call me day or night if you were ever in desperate need of me, and I meant it.

"But now it is me who desperately needs you."

Monroe took a step away from the mics and cleared his throat again.

He continued, "We need to find this girl. We need to return her home where she belongs."

I glanced at Neil, but he didn't notice. He was actually paying attention. I was shocked.

Monroe said, "If there is anyone out there with any knowledge of Bebe-Lynn Sanders' whereabouts, please contact me. Even if it's just a rumor, contact me. Even if you think it's some useless piece of information, I am begging you to call me. No matter how small you may think it is, it could help. I pray there is someone out there that knows something."

I looked at Neil again; this time he noticed. He shook his head quickly.

"So," Monroe said, "let me run down what we have. On Friday Morning, Bebe-Lynn was seen by several residents, and nothing appeared out of the ordinary. She was wearing shorts and a crop top, along with some aviator sunglasses. Her hair was pulled back into a ponytail. She rented a movie at Video Network around 10am, then eventually returned home.

"She was spotted later outside of Jimmy's Arcade, this time wearing pants.

"The people who saw her outside of Jimmy's said she was standing along the wall on the north side of the building. Witnesses said she looked like she was waiting for a friend. If this is true, we need to find this friend. All of Bebe's regular friends have been talked to and accounted for, so we're apparently looking for a mystery person.

"If you recall seeing Bebe-Lynn meeting with someone on Friday night, please, please," his voice cracked. "Please contact me at home or at the sheriff's department. If I'm not at either one, dispatch can get ahold of me.

"If we don't hear anything today, tomorrow, I'm afraid we may have to resort to more drastic measures. I'll discuss those when the time comes. For now, I am putting my full faith in you, the fine people of Bakersfield, to help us out with this case. Please. If you don't have my number, I am in the book. Do not hesitate to call."

He stepped back from the microphones and let a woman take his place. She was fighting back the tears. Her resemblance to Bebe-Lynn and Skye was very noticeable. She spoke softly.

"My name is Becky Sanders, Bebe's mother. Thank you all for coming out. Bebe, if you're out there... We need you to come home.

"Okay?

"If you're in trouble, we can work it out. If you're hurt, we can come get you. Just, please... Come. Home."

A man, presumably Bebe's father, wrapped his arm around Becky and pulled her away. Sheriff Monroe retook the center stage.

"Thank you again for coming out. We have photos of Bebe-Lynn for you all to take. They have all the appropriate phone numbers on them. Bebe, if you're out there... It's time to come home. Please... someone... We need your help."

Monroe backed away from the mics again, this time for good. The camera lingered on him for a few moments before the local news returned, KGET anchorman Gaylen Young giving a recap of what we just heard.

It took us a few seconds to snap out of it, but when we did, all eyes were on Neil.

"I don't know shit."

"Neil," Dad said, "if you know something, you have to tell us."

"I swear to God, I don't know anything."

"You didn't see her on Friday night?"

"Of course not. I was just blowing smoke earlier. I heard the rumors about her, but I didn't see her the night she went missing. I was miles away at Andre's!"

"Calm down, Son, we believe you. We all just want this girl found. The longer she's missing, the more on edge this town is going to get. We're not used to stuff like this."

"Dad. Mom. I swear to God, I don't know anything."

"Of course not, Neil," mom said, wrapping her arm around Neil's waist. "Alright, guys, well, same as before, nobody leaves the street without us."

Can't say we didn't see that one coming. We all nodded.

"Mookie honey, do you need to call your parents?"

"Phones not set up yet."

"Then let's all walk you home just so you can check in. You're more than welcome to stay, but your parents need to-"

A knock on the door. My mom let go of Neil and answered it. Mookie's mom Samantha was standing there.

"Hi, mom!" Mookie said, walking to her and giving her a hug.

"Hi, baby. Hi everyone. We just saw the news. We don't have a phone yet, so I wanted to run over and make sure everyone was okay."

My mom laughed, "We were just on our way to see you guys. Come on in."

Mookie's mom sat on the sofa. My mom took a seat in her weird, uncomfortable wicker chair and said, "This is all so new to us. We're not used to anything like this happening. I mean, I'm sure she'll come home, but for now, it is mighty worrisome."

"It is. I totally agree. Obviously, we never saw the girl before, but that doesn't make the worry any less."

"We've told the boys they have to stay close until Bebe-Lynn comes home. You never know what's out there."

"Is Mookie being a pest? He's a little loud sometimes."

"Oh goodness, loudness doesn't bother me at all. And he's been a perfect angel. He is welcome to stay over here as long as he wants, but everyone will have to stick close."

"You don't mind?"

"Not at all."

"I'm sure Mookie appreciates that. We haven't even finished moving in. Half our stuff got delayed in transit, so everyone slept on the floor last night. We don't even have our TV. We happened to see the news when Leroy was fiddling with his old black and white set, desperate for some sports or something."

The ladies laughed, and we left the room. There was no point in us being there. We walked to the kitchen to scavenge for food. This is where my mom's secret lies.

Once we opened a cabinet door, Mookie was able to see the inside - covered with Tom Selleck cutouts. And it wasn't just that one cabinet. It was literally every cabinet in the house. There must have been hundreds of pictures taped up, cut from magazines, TV Guides, newspaper listings, anything.

Just tons of them. The cabinet Mookie opened had a full-page picture of Tom dressed in his Indiana Jones gear, complete with hat and whip. "That's not Indiana Jones," Mookie said.

Somehow my mom heard. "Mookie honey, Tom Selleck was the original Indiana Jones."

"He was?" Mookie asked before I could warn him not to.

Here comes mom. "Yeah! See, you know *Magnum P.I.*?"

Mookie nodded. *Magnum* had only ended two years prior, so even kids without Selleck-obsessed moms knew what it was.

"Well, my boyfriend Tom there had shot the pilot for *Magnum P.I.* and-"

"He shot a pilot?"

"Not like, bang bang, a pilot is what you call the first episode of a...Forget it. Anyway, he had filmed one episode of *Magnum* and then screen-tested for Indiana Jones. Steven Spielberg and George Lucas loved him. I mean, how could they not... that smile... That perfect mustache and tall, chiseled frame... those dimples...." Mom drifted off for a few moments before remembering she was in the middle of a conversation. She started exactly where she left off without missing a beat. "...and offered him the role. The problem was CBS, who was doing *Magnum*, wouldn't let Tom Selleck do the movie, so he was stuck doing the show instead, and Harrison Ford took over the role. It's okay, I do love me some *Magnum P.I.*"

We all looked at my mom like her hair was on fire.

Mom noticed, shook her head in frustration, and said, "Just...find some food." Then she waved her hands and was gone, back to the living room to talk to Samantha. Mookie just looked at us and shrugged. What else could he do?

We found some hotdogs in the fridge, threw them into buns, wrapped them in paper towels, and then tossed them into the microwave for fifty-five seconds. It was as good a lunch as any. We took them, along with a couple of Squeez-Its, to the front yard and ate them while sitting on the curb. It didn't take long for the boredom to set in.

Roxy found a pen in the gutter and mindlessly doodled on his shoes.

I noticed and said, "Does that say Cool Roxy Roxy?"

"Huh?" Roxy said. "Oh yeah, I guess."

"What the hell does Cool Roxy Roxy mean?"

He sighed. "I dunno, dude."

"That's gonna be on there forever."

He licked his finger and tried rubbing it off. No luck. "Damn it."

"I'm never going to let you live this down. Those are brand-new David Robinsons! And you ruined them."

Fun side note: I never let him live it down. Every present I give him for holidays or whatever is labeled COOL ROXY ROXY.

"I'm so bored," Roxy whined.

"Wanna walk to Miller's Outpost and steal some more fake earrings?"

There was a Miller's Outpost in the shopping center directly across from our neighborhood that we used to rob blind. In fact, I think everyone robbed them blind. That's probably why they're not in business anymore. They practically begged kids to shoplift from them. They would place tons of pocket-sized goods right out in the open, then hire stoned teenagers as employees that could not give a shit less about anything going on, allowing us, and everyone else, to do shopping sprees.

Our latest snatch had been magnetic stud earrings. Thankfully our parents wouldn't let us get real earrings, but we showed them by rolling up with quite possibly the lamest product of 1990. They lasted less than a day before the magnet gave out, and the earring was lost, forcing us to go steal more.

Good thing we didn't pay money for that shit, right?

"No," Roxy said, "those things sucked."

"They really did."

"Hey, look," Mookie said, pointing up the street where a group of girls was walking towards us.

I recognized one of the girls as Skye, Bebe's sister. She was still holding those missing posters as she and her friends walked up to a house down the street and rang the doorbell. A few seconds later, they walked back down to the sidewalk and over to the next house.

"I hope they find her," I said.

"Yeah, no kidding," Mookie said. "Where do you think she is?"

"My idiot brother said she's dead and hidden out in the field on the other side of The Tube, but honestly, I think he's just a lying jackoff. If you gave that guy twenty I.Q. points, he'd have an I.Q. of exactly twenty."

Roxy said, "Hopefully these girls will have as good of luck as we had when we went door to door."

I laughed. How could I not? What a couple of scheming idiots we were.

"What's so funny?" Mookie asked.

Remember earlier in the book when I said I was going to tell a couple of stories that didn't make me and Roxy look too great?

Yeah?

Well, this is another one.

Please don't judge us by our past actions. We were desperate kids on a desperate mission. Magnetic earrings ain't got nothin' on this savage bit of conning.

So, late the year prior, probably November 1989, it was announced that Vanilla Ice was coming to town and would perform at the Civic Auditorium! Don't laugh. This was huge news! His album *To the Extreme* had been released a few months prior and was about the coolest thing ever.

His first single, *Ice Ice Baby*, was not only a massive

success, but it was the first hip-hop track to reach number one on the Billboard Hot 100. Now, Roxy and I were already big rap fans, much to the dismay of our moms. It was one of the reasons we watched the damn Jukebox channel so much because they would play the shit MTV banned – like N.W.A., Boogie Down Productions, Ice T, and Body Count, you name it, Jukebox offered it, and we wanted it.

When I fell in love with the Beastie Boys and Run DMC, I looked into their influences and discovered rappers like Africa Bambaataa, Kurtis Blow, Schoolly D, and the Fat Boys (to be fair, I was already a fan of the Fat Boys due to their popular Freddy Krueger song and their song about their nuts, ingeniously titled *My Nuts!*), so I was already well into rap when The Iceman took it to number one. And maybe I should have realized how lame it was at the time, but it was undeniably catchy, and it still is, I'm not ashamed to say. (About fifteen years ago, when iPods were still a thing, my car was broken into and my iPod Classic was stolen. I was so pissed, but then I realized that the last song I was listening to was Vanilla's song *Havin' a Roni*. The thought of that thief turning on his stolen music player and hearing Vanilla Ice attempt to beatbox almost made the whole ordeal worth it.)

Needless to say, Roxy and I needed to go to this show. Neither of us had been to a concert for us before. I was dragged to a few 'Parent Bands' in the past, like Paul Revere and the Raiders, The Lovin' Spoonful, Tommy James and the Shondels, and other such lame bullshit like that... But The Iceman was for us!

The only thing in our way was tickets. The obvious choice was to simply ask our parents for them. Christmas was coming up, and the show wasn't until February anyway, so the timing was perfect.

My mom wasn't havin' it. Nope. Not at all. Rap was dangerous, apparently, and there was no way she was going to spend her hard-earned money on it. "If you want to go to that concert, you can earn the money to pay for it."

She said this knowing full well there was no way we could ever raise the twenty-plus dollars per ticket. She said it almost with a smile, which really rubbed me the wrong way. Like we couldn't come up with fifty bucks!

Chal-oonnngggeeee!

(Okay, I admit that *Chal-oonnngggeeee* joke is such a deep cut that maybe three people will get it, but I don't want it to be edited out, so allow me to explain. There is an episode of *The Cosby Show* where Cliff Huxtable, played by world-famous rapist Bill Cosby, is doing tap dancing battles with some dude named Howard B. Sims Sr. After each of Howard's routines, he would open his arms and say Challenge, but he said it literally as *Chal-oonnngggeeee*, even with a thick Bayou accent that suddenly appeared. I never understood why, but Roxy and I still find it funny, even to this day.)

Anyway. The gauntlet had been thrown. Roxy and I needed at least fifty bucks, plus possibly more for snacks and an Ice Man t-shirt.

But how?

We certainly didn't want to work for it. We were ten years old, who the hell would pay us to do anything?

We put our heads together and tried to figure out where our talents lay. The only thing at which we were both pretty good was the Oral Language Festival. While most kids our age did tired, old, prewritten speeches (usually poorly), we always wrote our own, and we always killed. We went to the finals every year, and rightfully so.

So good we were on stage that we used to perform at our school's talent shows. Now, the talent shows at Quailwood took the word talent to the bottom of the barrel. They were basically talent in name only. Most of these kids performing were laughable at best. So bad were these talent shows that every year more and more people would come just to laugh at the misery of pathetic kids trying.

To this day, my mom still laughs about a kid named Josh Biggers who did a breakdance routine that moved about as fast as a DMV line. He had cardboard laid down right next to a big silver boombox he had set up, and honestly, at the sight of this, I was pumped. I fully expected this little blonde kid to show us how it's done! What we got looked like a defective robot in slow motion. Have you ever tried to squeeze out chilled honey from a bottle? About that fast. No words can paint the appropriate picture of how amazingly awful this dance truly was. The audience, parents and teachers alike, were fighting back tears as the performance seemed to drag on for twenty minutes. I glanced through the crowd at my mom and saw her digging her nails into her arm to keep from laughing. Seven people excused themselves and left the auditorium.

Josh, if you're reading this, I'm sorry!

Anyway, our plan was maybe if we did some stand-up comedy routines, we would absolutely kill, and people would start paying to come see us perform. We wrote some material and family-friendly jokes and were all set to take the stage. No one in the history of the world had ever come up with an idea this good. The money was going to come rolling in by the truckload!

Before we even got a chance to go up, Trey O'Rourke, Katy-From-Earlier's brother, took the stage and did his own stand-up routine, complete with impressions of Pee-Wee Herman and Robin Leech.

It killed.

Unfortunately, it also killed our dreams!

We didn't even bother performing.

We needed a new idea, and fast. Those tickets were sure to sell out! (They didn't.)

Our backup idea consisted of us winning tickets. It wasn't a great plan, but it was better than nothing. The week before the 'Simpsons Christmas,' our major radio stations, KKXX and Q94 (we had another station, KUZZ, but it only played shitty country music that we hated.), would be giving away tickets! We listened nonstop for two straight days, one radio tuned to KKXX, the other to Q94, and when the time came to call, we dialed as fast as we could!

You'll never guess what happened!

We lost.

Like, not even close.

They didn't even pick up to tell us we lost. They just left us in limbo, listening to that sad, mocking ringtone over and over until we finally hung up.

The third plan was to try and sell our Garbage Pail Kids cards. We had a shit ton of them and knew they were totally worth some money, so we loaded up our backpacks and rode our bikes to Inner Sanctum Comics, which was close to Jimmy's, and asked the employee if he wanted to buy our stash. He said, and I quote, "No," then turned and walked away.

Foiled again!

Our fourth plan came in January (the week after Ronny's birthday party) when the school was doing its annual Jog-a-Thon to raise money for whatever schools need money for. We didn't care.

The way it worked was that each fifth and sixth grader would get a pledge sheet, and we were supposed to hit up friends and family and get them to sponsor us. People could pledge a flat rate or a certain amount per lap we ran. We would turn the sheets in to the school, do the run, then get our sheets handed back so we could go around to those same family and friends and collect the money.

I had an idea.

This is so cringe. I'm sorry.

Roxy and I would definitely go door to door, but we would do it with a little twist. We hopped on our bikes and headed down to Kinkos, where you could get a photocopy for half a penny (Seriously, half a cent!), and we ran off two extra copies of the pledge sheet. The employee didn't even bother to charge us the penny, choosing instead to call us little rat-bitches before returning to make out with this fried-haired girlfriend, but whatever.

We tried to stay and watch, but he picked up a hole punch and launched it straight at our heads. We ran out and tried peering in through the window, desperate to see even a grope, but it was useless.

Anyway. Ugh.

This is almost too cringe to type. Please keep in mind that we were only ten. I know I've said that before, but I can't overstate it enough.

So, after Kinkos, we split up, each taking one side of the street, going door to door, and saying our little spiel. If someone decided to sponsor us, they would fill out the sheet with the money they pledged, then we would move on to the next house, and if they decided to pledge, we would hand them a different pledge sheet, so after a long week of fleecing the entire neighborhood, we had a total of four filled-out pledge sheets between the both of us.

The scam: We would only turn in one sheet each, so when it was time to go around and collect all the money, the school would have no idea that we actually made twice as much dough as we said we did.

That money went straight into our pockets.

I had a similar idea during our candy bar sale fundraiser the year prior, but I was too chickenshit to pull it off. Turns out, I just didn't need the money badly enough. For the candy bar scam, we would go from house to house with a box filled with chocolate bars in white wrappers. They were long and skinny and cost two dollars. My idea was, "Hey, I'm gonna charge three dollars and keep the extra." But the more I thought of it, the more I couldn't make myself do it. Every fourth grader in school was slangin' chocolate in that neighborhood. It would have been way too easy for someone to figure out I was charging a dollar more than everyone else. So I put it on the back burner until I needed it.

Thus the Jog-A-Thon scam was born.

Sleazy little conning bastards, I know, but come on, that's a pretty good little scam for a couple moronic ten-year-olds! We cleared over a hundred bucks a pop on that little smoothie. We didn't even have to explain where we got the excess, either. We just spent it on whatever crap we wanted, like candy cigarettes and Fun Dips, and didn't tell anyone. All we had to explain was where we got the fifty bucks for the tickets, which would be easy.

We would lie. Again.

And it worked. Shockingly, I don't even remember what the lie was, but I'm sure it was something so goddamn stupid and unbelievable that my parents had no choice but to believe it. To a ten-year-old, lying comes as naturally as sleeping, but I carried my bullshitting skills all the way through high school graduation and beyond. (I remember once, in junior high, I had forgotten to do a creative writing assignment, so on the bus ride over, I wrote down the lyrics to Red Hot Chili Peppers' song *Sir Psycho Sexy*, changing out the word sexy with studly to avoid any potential criticism the former word may cause to a seventh-grade teacher. I got an A-!)

The kick in the nuts came after we convinced our parents we got the money honestly and were all set to buy the tickets. My mom, thinking we would never in a million years get the money, told me she didn't want me to go to the concert because, as I said before, rap was scary and dangerous, and we were sure to get shot. I couldn't believe it. Rap wasn't scary. She had just heard some bullshit on some dumb news station spreading propaganda! If The West Coast Rap All-Stars had come out with their one and only song, *Same Gang*, a year earlier, I bet that would have made my mom see the error of her ways and allowed me to go.

Actually, no, probably not. That would have made everything worse.

But come on! Vanilla could barely be considered rap!

Had it been an M.C. Hammer concert, she would have let me go with no qualms, so I wonder what she had against the Ice Man. Maybe it was because Hammer had his own Saturday Morning Cartoon show. How dangerous could a dude be who starred in a cartoon alongside talking shoes that gave him magical dancing powers?

Hammerman premiered just a few months prior and would be canceled a couple weeks later after just eleven episodes. So poor was the cartoon that it was animated at two frames per second, whereas the typical cartoon of that time was animated at anywhere between twelve to fifteen frames a second.

It was almost, quite literally, unwatchable. (The Yakov Smirnoff commercials that aired during the show were a hundred times better!)

After this, things really began going downhill for Hammer, so he turned gangsta, wore a bandana and dark shades, signed to Suge Knight's Death Row Records, and made a song about gigantic asses called *Pumps and a Bump*... Even after all that, my mom would still say, "Hammer is cool," and would have let me go to his show.

But man, she just didn't like Ice!

After throwing a fit for who knows how long, a compromise was made. It was quite possibly the worst compromise in the history of compromises.

We would be allowed to go... if... and only if... the moms went with us.

Ughhhhh!!!

After all that talk about her not giving her hard-earned money to Vanilla Ice, you know what she did? She gave her hard-earned money to Vanilla Ice!

But we got to go.

Our mommies walked into the show with us but were promptly ditched. Roxy and I bolted and headed to the floor to catch the show. As far as I knew, our moms stayed in their seats, which worked out well, allowing us to pretend we were there alone and impress all the hot chicks that were there. Turns out, no hot chicks gave a rat's ass about us, so we hung back and watched them dance while C&C Music Factory got the party started. Then Ice came out and opened with *Stop That Train*. Man oh man, it was awesome. At one point, he started humping the stage in what we thought was the illest dance move ever.

My mom still brings it up occasionally as leverage, saying something like, *I went to Vanilla Ice for you...* Like I begged her to take me or something. That's rich, mom! Nice try.

I will give my mom credit, though, because a year

later, when my dad was at work, she was forced to take me to see *Child's Play 3*. She had no idea what she was getting into. To say she hated the movie would be laughable – she despised it. She still brings that up monthly. She was a good sport, though, and I appreciated the hell out of it. After that, Dad was back in charge of the horror movies, even though by the time Jason went to hell, he had desperately wanted to tap out. He took Roxy and me to see that one at the Stockdale Six Theatres in August of '94 and offered the ticket seller twenty bucks to allow me and Rox to go in alone. It didn't work, and poor dad was forced to sit through what was sure to be *The Final Friday*. (Spoiler Alert: Despite its title, it was *not* the final Friday.)

"Kids! Kids!" We turned to look and saw miserable old Ms. Franks, gimped over at the waist and running our way with her stupid little bird legs and an ass like E.T.'s face. She was holding a cigarette that was no less than two feet long. I hoped she wouldn't faint when she saw Mookie.

"Haven't you heard, kids?! There is a girl missing! Go inside! Go inside!"

"Um, I live right here. Like, this is literally my driveway."

Ms. Franks put her hand over her heart like Fred Sanford thinking he was having a heart attack, and said, "Why! I never! Your mother will hear about this!" Then she stormed off the way she came.

"What the hell was that?" Mookie asked.

"Ugh, dude. That's Ms. Franks. She's the worst."

"Yeah," Roxy said, "she's the neighborhood busybody. Don't do anything bad around here 'cuz she's a lousy snitch, dude. Like, bad."

"Noted. Thanks. Why does she walk like a chicken?"

"Did you see her legs? They can't support her upper body!"

"Bawk bawk!"

"She looked like a California Raisin."

We didn't do much the rest of the afternoon besides lying on our backs on my front lawn. Back in those days, that was a perfectly acceptable way to spend an afternoon just gazing up at the clouds, talkin' trash with your buddies. People no longer have the patience for it, but we loved it. Mookie and Roxy's moms eventually left, but we stayed there.

When we finally decided to head back inside, my dad was sitting in his chair watching an episode of *Murder, She Wrote*. It must have been near the end because my dad looked right at us and said, "Ya know, Jessica would never solve a case if these murderers would just shut the fuck up!"

We about died laughing. It was so out of character for my dad, and that was the first time I heard him use the F Word. Even if we were working on something or attempting to fix something, his expletives were always PG-13. Sometimes even G. I heard him once change the term grab-assin' to grab-rumpin,' and I never let him live it down.

This was next level, though.

My dad realized what he said and had no choice but to try and play it off. "I mean, all these dumb murderers just practically confess for no reason. Just shut up!"

My dad loved *Murder, She Wrote*. In fact, he loved almost all detective shows, Mom too. They passed that on to me, as it is pretty much all I watch these days, aside from a handful of old sitcoms (and *The Simpsons*), and hell, I even made a career out of funny little rom-com detective novels that I adore, called *The Archie and Elise Mysteries*. You should read them! (Wink wink.)

The phone rang and was quickly answered by, I guessed, my mom in the bedroom. A few seconds later, here she came, telling us to turn on the news. There was a break in the case.

Murder, She Wrote had ended anyway, so Dad picked up his gigantic remote control and changed the channel. Sheriff Monroe was again standing at a podium. He cleared his throat and began to speak.

"First of all, I would like to thank each and every one of you that reached out to me and my department with tips and clues we could use. We listened to every single one, and I am happy to announce that, just a little over an hour ago, we sat down with a citizen of this town that saw a boy Bebe-Lynn Sanders left with on Friday night. Together with this person and our sketch artist, we were able to produce a composite sketch of this individual."

He held up a drawing of a boy that looked to be in his twenties, with long shaggy hair, a mustache, and what looked to be an earring (probably not a magnetic one stolen from Miller's Outpost) in his left year (at that time, wearing an earring in your right ear signified that you were 'gay.' At least that was the rumor. Cringe, I know, but still a popular thing in the '80s that should be mentioned.)

The picture, honestly, could have been of anyone. If the mustache wasn't so full, it could have been Neil, but everyone knows his mustache pales in comparison to even chocolate milk stains, so that let him off the hook.

Sheriff Monroe continued, "I need to stress that this individual is not a suspect. In fact, he is currently missing as well. If you recognize this man, please do not hesitate to contact us. From our eyewitness, the man seemed to be in his early twenties. He was last seen wearing tan shorts that hit about mid-thigh and a white t-shirt with a Maui & Sons logo displayed largely on the back. His hair is light brown and hangs to just above his shoulders. He has a mustache.

"If you know him, or know of him, or have ever just... seen him around town, please contact me or my department at 805-833-"

My mom cut in. "You guys haven't seen this boy anywhere, have you? At Jimmy's?"

"Every guy his age looks like that, Mom. Heck, it's probably Neil." (I used words like Heck around my parents so they'd know what a perfect angel I was.)

"Please, Grant," Dad said, "that boy in the photo has a real mustache, not that stupid little dirt lip your brother tries to pull off. Neil looks like a toddler that just ate a turd sandwich."

We laughed. Hard. My old man was a pretty funny dude.

"That's not the point," My mom said, trying to get us to stop giggling.

"I know, I know," I said. "It's not Neil, but we could go to Jimmy's right now and find thirty people that look just like that."

"Yeah," Dad said, "I can vouch for that. In fact, this might actually cause more trouble and chaos than it's worth. Ol' Monroe is gonna get a million calls about a million different people."

We realized we were missing some action on TV. Monroe was still talking.

"Every man I have available is dedicated to finding this person. He may be in danger, too. We don't know. That is why it's of the utmost importance that we locate him.

"Now... I hope it doesn't come to this, but it's my job to make the tough decisions, so if we have not located Bebe-Lynn or this Mystery Man by tomorrow afternoon, I have no choice but to begin organizing search parties. And again, I will need your help. We will start in the area she was last seen and canvas outward. I know this sounds like a bummer, but we can't just sit around and wait for her to return. We must be proactive, and if that means walking every inch of this town, then that's what we'll do.

"Please, if you know anything, give us a call. I will be back tomorrow morning with an update and further instructions. Please. Please call. Bebe-Lynn, if you're out there, it's time to come home. No questions asked. If you're in trouble, we'll help you. We all need you home.

"Thank you."

The three of us boys turned to my mom and asked if we could go.

"On a search party?! I don't think so."

"Sheriff Monroe said he needs all the men he can get."

I saw my mom glance at my dad. Dad shrugged. "He's right. I can go with them."

"Mom, this is literally what Boy Scouts do. We help. In fact, if we were in session right now, we'd probably have to go anyway. C'mon, mom."

"Yeah, Mom!" Roxy said.

"Yeah, Mom!" Mookie said.

Mom was silent momentarily before saying, "Fine, but you go with your father." She looked at Roxy, then Mookie, and said, "And there is no way I can grant permission to you two. You two need to take it up with your own mothers."

"Maybe I'll go, too," Neil said, seeming to appear in a puff of smoke, wearing his stupid British Knights shoes, a Big Johnson tanktop with the arm holes cut so goddamn big that his disgusting nipples with two sad little hairs around them were peeking out. I didn't even know he was home.

"Jesus, Neil," Dad said, "you're barely motivated enough to come to dinner, but you're going to spend an entire day, maybe several days, walking around town with a search party?"

Neil looked offended. "I'm motivated!"

His nipples seemed to be following me.

"By what, Neil?" Dad asked. "'Cuz I know it ain't learnin'."

"Psh!" Neil said. The ultimate comeback. Neil was full of them. "You don't even know!"

"And shave that mustache off. It looks like you fell asleep at a slumber party and someone drew stink lines above your lip."

"You don't even know what cool is, Dad! Gawd!" He turned and stood next to Mom, putting his arm around her shoulders. "At least Mom loves me."

"I didn't say I didn't love you, but I've seen you sit right here on this sofa and try to use the Force to get the remote to fly over to you. You think I don't notice these things, but I do. But hell, if you want to come on a search party and walk all over town, let's go."

"I didn't want to get up!" Neil yelled. "I was comfy!"

"Okay!" Dad yelled back, his arms flailing to really prove his point. "That's what I thought!"

"I'm gonna go!"

"Fine!"

"No yelling, guys," Mom said. "Come on."

"We're not yelling," Neil said. "Talking loudly, not yelling."

"Yeah," Dad said. "Talking loudly. Now get the hell out of here."

Neil and Dad both laughed. "Fine," Neil *talked loudly*.

"So go."

"I'm gone!"

"Adios."

That continued for a while before Neil finally accepted defeat and waddled back to his bedroom.

"Hopefully, we won't even need to go tomorrow," Dad said.

"Yeah," Mom said, "if they've got a picture of this guy now, someone in town will know who he is. They'll pick him up by morning."

"Unless he's down in a ditch with Bebe," I said, somehow even shocking myself.

"Grant!"

"I know. I'm sorry. But seriously, I've seen a lot of movies, and if she was out in some dark parking lot or something with another dude, that is pretty much prime bait for masked slashers. I don't want it to be true, but it's a real possibility."

"It's not a real possibility, Grant," Mom said, getting irritated with me. "Slashers aren't real. People don't walk around with hockey masks and chainsaws."

"You're mixing up two different-"

"Not the point. This girl is going to be found alive. I truly believe that."

"We want her to be alive, too," Mookie said.

"Thank you, Mookie," Mom said, patting him on the head. "You're my favorite. I don't know about these other two. Warped minds, they've got, caused by too many horror movies and Nintendo."

The rest of the night was spent playing *Ring King* on my NES before everyone had to go home. We would all anxiously be awaiting news from Sheriff Monroe the following morning.

I hardly slept that night. Bebe missing was really getting to me. I know what I said earlier about her being dead by Jason or Michael Myers or whoever, but I promise I was distraught. A pit had formed in my stomach, and I couldn't seem to ditch it. I wasn't even entirely sure why. I had never said a single word to Bebe, so why was I feeling so...down about it?

It couldn't have been just because she was so pretty. Why would that have mattered to me when I couldn't even talk to ten-year-old Daphne, who lived two doors down?

I had seen countless teenagers hacked to death in movies and usually cheered the killer. But this... I don't know. This was real, and I hated it.

When I finally fell asleep, I had a vivid dream that I still remember to this day, which is rare because even though my memory is excellent, I never remember dreams. But this one stuck with me.

Bebe was there, talking to a bunch of her friends just outside the side exit of Jimmy's, but I was an outsider looking in. It played out like a movie. Far off in the distance, a huge explosion leveled the skyline, followed by another explosion, and another, each one getting closer, each one demolishing everything in its radius. They kept coming, closer and closer, louder and louder, faster and faster, but Bebe didn't seem to notice. Her friends all took off running, leaving Bebe there, confused as to why all her friends had left. Then the blast hits close, and suddenly Bebe-Lynn Sanders is no more. Erased from the face of the Earth in half a second. I woke up covered in sweat and stayed up the rest of the night staring at the ceiling, wondering where she had gone.

The following day, just as promised, Sheriff Monroe was back on TV. He looked like he had been up all night, too.

"I come to you this morning with a shred of good news, but I'm afraid it might not be enough. We believe we have identified the male from our composite sketch. His name is Trip Windham, and he is a student at U.C. Santa Barbara. We have tried to contact him, but... he can't... We can't find him.

"We know he lives in an apartment near campus, but his roommate says he hasn't seen him in over a week. We're not sure what he was doing in town, but as of now, he is also a missing person. If anyone out there has any information on Trip, call us. We are desperate to speak to him. And same goes for him as it does for Bebe. If he is in trouble, we want to help. His roommate was able to fax us over a recent picture of Trip, so that could be of more use than the sketch. I will make sure the news stations have it, and it will be in tomorrow's issue of the Bakersfield Californian, along with several neighboring city's newspapers, including Santa Barbara.

"Now for more unfortunate news. We can't wait any longer. A search party must be formed. Today at 2pm, we will start in the shopping center Bebe was last seen in and begin canvassing out. Depending on the number of volunteers we get, we can map out areas that need to be searched. I'm calling on every citizen with time off today, every Boy Scout, every Girl Scout. Please come help. We need you.

"I hope to see you there."

"Well, shit," Dad said. "Can't say as though I was particularly looking forward to this."

And I couldn't say I was, either. After my dream last night, I honestly didn't even want to go anymore. But I was a Boy Scout, and it's a Boy Scout's duty.

"You better wear your scout uniform," Dad told me. "It's the only reason we're letting you go."

I nodded.

"Go call Roxy, see if he's still going."

"Okay."

I left the room and called Roxy. We agreed to meet at

my house at 1pm. He would wear his uniform, too, and I reminded him to bring his walking stick. When I hung up, that pit in my stomach returned with a vengeance. In fact, typing this right now, the pit is with me.

I just sat around the house, killing time until 1. It felt like an eternity before my dad finally told me to go get ready. "Don't wear those eighty-dollar shoes we bought you. Wear some crappy ones. Who knows where we'll end up today."

I nodded again and left to get ready, choosing to wear my Converse All-Stars, which at the time were about the cheapest "cool" shoe you could get. Now they're ridiculously overpriced, especially considering they're just a cheap piece of canvas stretched over a flat, uncomfortable piece of rubber.

I heard my dad out in the living room telling my mom he didn't want her to go. "There's no reason to go... I don't even know where we're going to end up... I'll keep an eye on them, don't worry... You two can canvas the neighborhood but stay together. At this point, I don't trust anyone."

"We're still going to the meeting," Mom said.

Dad nodded.

I heard a knock on the door, quickly finished tying my neckerchief, then ran out to the living room, where I was surprised to see Neil, fully clothed in short shorts and a Bear Whiz Beer t-shirt, standing next to my mom.

"Are you going?" I asked.

"Yeah, but I'm gonna stick with the moms. They might need some protection."

Mom laughed. "Oh, give me a break. We're sticking to the neighborhood."

"I know," Neil said with a smile, "I'm still going with you guys."

"We'd enjoy that. Thank you."

I don't know what happened to Neil overnight, but he somehow turned into a fully functioning twenty-year-old.

"Oh," I said, "well, right on." To Mom, I said, "Good luck with that."

Neil picked up a pen from the kitchen table and launched it at my face. It missed by a mile.

"Hey, hey!" Roxy said, entering the living room, also wearing his Boy Scout gear.

"Yo, Joe!" (I was not a big fan of the *G.I. Joe* cartoon show, but everyone in the world saw the 'lessons' at the end of each episode {Now I know! – And knowing is half the battle!})

Behind him was his dad, Dave, who always reminded me of a mix between Tom Jones and gameshow host Burt Convy. Apparently, he would be coming along, too. "Sharon will be over in about twenty minutes to pick you up. She's running just a tad bit late, and I wanted to get there early."

"No problem," Mom said. "We'll be ready. Neil is coming with us."

"Right on, Neil," Dave said, then to my mom, "keep an eye on him."

Neil rolled his eyes, and we all laughed, despite the joke not being funny. Just nervous laughter, I suppose.

"Alright then," Dad said, "you guys ready to rock?"

"Ready as we'll ever be," Dave said as Roxy and I exchanged a nervous little glance.

What if we found her?

What would we do?

How would we feel?

Just because we liked horror movies didn't mean we were ready to see a real live murder victim if, in fact, she was one.

When my grandpa died in 1988, I couldn't make myself get closer than about twenty feet from his coffin during his viewing, and when my dad died all those years later, even as an adult, I had no desire to see him dead.

This wasn't a space shuttle exploding on TV. This wasn't some dumbass little girl trapped in a well. And it certainly wasn't Jason Voorhees dicing up horny teenagers at Camp Crystal Lake.

This was real life, and I gotta tell ya, I wasn't impressed. But we were Boy Scouts. And, like I said before, it's a Boy Scout's Duty. So, we all loaded up into Dave's Chevrolet Celebrity Classic station wagon and hit the road.

"We gotta stop at Mookie's house, remember," I said.

"Okay," Dave said. I assumed Roxy had filled him in.

"Just turn right at the end of the street. He's right on the corner."

Dave turned right and pulled to the curb. Roxy and I jumped out of the rear hatch.

"Hold on," Dad said. "I better come with you."

We walked up to the door together, careful to avoid stepping on the grass (some people were very peculiar when it came to walking on their grass during that time period. You never know who would run out, shaking their fist and yelling at you, so until you knew for sure, you avoided that goddamn grass!)

My dad knocked on the door, and Leroy answered a few seconds later. "Well, hey there, Grant and Roxy. Don't you guys look dapper."

My dad reached out his hand and said, "I'm Gary. Grant's dad."

Leroy shook my dad's hand and introduced himself.

"I know this is a really awkward introduction," Dad said, "has Mookie filled you in on what's going on?"

"Yeah, we saw the news last night and this morning. Mookie seems like he really wants to help. Talkin' about how he's gonna be a Boy Scout next year."

"Yeah!" I said.

"And it's a Boy Scouts duty to help when help is needed," Roxy said, standing straight and holding up three-fingers in the Boy Scout salute.

"I respect that," Leroy said. "Only one problem. My wife."

"Ohhh," Dad said.

"Yeah, let me go talk to her real quick. Give me a minute?"

"You bet," Dad said as Leroy left us at the door. To us, Dad said, "Is Xavier coming?"

"Not sure," I said, "he might be there. He said he

didn't know if his parents would let him go."

Dad just shrugged. Leroy returned a few seconds later with Mookie at his side. He held up his two pointer fingers and said, "Would you all mind if I came with ya?"

"Yeah, you bet," Dad said again.

"Can't let the boy out of my sight. Wife's orders."

"I get it. Come on, Roxy's old man is driving."

My dad introduced Leroy to Dave, then loaded up the station wagon and hit the road. The drive was less than five minutes to Jimmy's. When we arrived, Dave parked the car, we unloaded, then joined the crowd that had already formed, despite us being almost thirty minutes early.

We didn't bother making our way to the front, it wasn't like Cinderella or Poison was up there about to crank out a few bangers, so we just hung to the back and waited. Our moms and Neil arrived about twenty minutes later, just before things really started to get moving.

I saw Xavier running over to us, his dad closely behind him. "I talked my parents into it," he said, out of breath.

We high-fived and introduced him to Mookie. When his dad arrived, we did the same for him. We didn't have time for chit-chat; the reverb from a microphone told us someone was about to talk.

It was hard to see since there wasn't a stage or anything, so we mostly just listened.

Sheriff Monroe thanked us all for coming out, and the crowd all nodded, some clapped for some dumbass reason, others, like us, remained silent.

"I know this isn't what you had planned for the Fourth of July holiday, but me, and Bebe's family, cannot thank you enough. We are still looking for the boy believed to be Trip Windham, so if anyone has any information in that regard, please come forward."

The crowd was silent, a few shook their heads. No luck there. Monroe continued, "I know how unpleasant this is...." He cleared his throat and took a few seconds before he spoke again. "Again, we are just looking for anything that can help us locate Bebe. Please be mindful of where you step. Please do not go out alone. The plan is to form a radius of four miles from this exact spot, including our... her neighborhood. My men and I will assign your group a specific area. Please check any and all places where a... where a clue may be found. We're looking for... dumpsters... and open fields, and grassy areas, behind buildings, just... anywhere. If you will be walking through a wooded area or an area with tall weeds or grass, I encourage you to use a stick as a guide, like a blind person would use. This can alert you to... well, something you may have walked on by and not noticed.

"So, I would like to get started as quickly as possible. We have a few sticks here that you can borrow, or you can find your own, or use a golf club or fishing pole. It doesn't matter. We have fliers with Bebe's face on them, along with all our phone numbers. Obviously, I will not be at home, so please call the station if you find anything to report. I will make sure someone is there at all times to answer.

"So, please, get your group together and come see us up front, and we'll give you instructions. Please do this in an orderly fashion so we can get this done as quickly as possible. Again, thank you for coming."

The eleven of us stayed together, waiting in line until we were given our assignment. It didn't take but a few minutes. My mom informed the deputy that we were going to break into two groups, and my mom volunteered to make the rounds of Quailwood. The deputy nodded, looked at a photocopy of a map and circled an area in red pen then handed it to my mom.

When it was our turn, I told the deputy (like a little kiss-ass twerp,) "We're Boy Scouts so we can handle more difficult areas."

"Oh, is that a fact," the deputy asked.

"It's a fact," I said with a big smile. God, pathetic.

"We should check the sump," Roxy said. "It's a big, like, weird area in our neighborhood that definitely needs to be checked."

170

"We have walking sticks we can use too. Always be prepared; that's our motto." (God Grant, shut up.)

The deputy nodded and then looked down at his map. "I know the sump. It's on our list. You guys can have it, but please be careful. There might be a couple other teams out there with you. It's a high-priority zone, so we don't want to miss anything. In fact, we've got a deputy headed over there in a few minutes to get the gate open. If you beat him out there, just wait a few minutes for him to arrive. We don't want anyone getting injured hopping a fence or anything."

My mom told Dad they were leaving and would see us back home. My dad wished them luck, and they left.

I turned my attention back to the deputy who had circled the sump area on a map and handed it to us. "Good luck. Please be careful."

"How's this for a welcome to the neighborhood?" Dad said to Leroy.

"Well..." Leroy said, "it's certainly unforgettable. I'll give you that much."

Dave said, "You guys ready?"

"Ready as we'll ever be, I suppose." Dad put his arm around my shoulders, and we walked back to Dave's station wagon. When he started the engine, the song *Season of the Witch* by Donovan had just started playing on the oldies station he was tuned to. It played for the exact amount of time it took to get us back to the sump. I remember feeling a little weird about that. Like, the song started when the car turned on, and ended right when the car turned off.

I can't hear that song without thinking of that car ride. It always struck me as eerie. It still does.

By the time we all unloaded from the car, another sheriff was just pulling up and parking behind us at the curb. When all was said and done, there were two deputies and four other teams to cover every inch of the sump, along with twenty or so search sticks, a thing I didn't even know existed until that moment.

The thing that stuck out to me once that gate was

open was how normal the sump looked. In all those years, with all those stories of drugs and dead bodies, none of us ever bothered to peek over the fence and see that it was mostly just a wet, sunken, disgusting piece of land with overgrown grass and weeds and several large pipes along the outer rim which I suppose were drainage, although they looked big enough to crawl through.

I don't know what I expected it to look like, but it certainly wasn't this. Do you remember the planet Yoda lives on? Dagoba? I was expecting that, fog and mist included, but I have no idea why.

"The way we're going to handle this," the first deputy said, "after we clear the drainage pipes, is we will all walk side by side about six feet apart, up and down the area. To be perfectly clear, despite Sheriff Monroe attempting to put a positive spin on it, we are here to find a body. If you find...her...yell out. Do not touch it. I will take over from there.

"Now, it is really soggy down here, and there are probably bugs. We have a few cans of bug spray for you to shower yourselves in before we take the walk down. Also, please be mindful of your steps. Wet leaves and the like can be very slippery, and it's probably muddy down there. I don't want any rolled ankles. Any questions?"

There were none, just a bunch of nervous glances.

"Alright, go get that bug spray on and head down. My partner and I will walk the perimeter and check those pipes. When we come back up, we will all start. Got it?"

We grabbed two cans of spray off the park bench that was being used as a command center, sprayed ourselves down, then readied ourselves to finally, after all these years, walk down into the sump.

We were all lined up at the far west side, ready to take the plunge. The officer that did all the talking was down on the far end, and the other deputy was standing next to Dave on the opposite end.

"Ready, gang?" The first deputy yelled down the line.

"Ready," several of us yelled back.

"Then let's go! Take it slow and be careful!"

The hill leading down was steeper than it looked, almost like walking down the face of a mountain. I used my walking stick to keep me upright. The last thing I wanted was to fall flat on my big dumb face and roll down into that mess.

When we finally hit level ground again, I was very happy I wasn't wearing my ridiculously expensive Reebok Pump basketball shoes that I just had to have for some unknown reason. I don't even like basketball that much, and when I played, I'd be lucky to make two points. Oh well.

The Converse proved not to be a sagacious decision either because my first step went straight into a mud puddle, soaking my feet. The cheap-ass canvas was no match.

The four of us boys all looked at each other, took deep breaths, then went for it. We took slow, careful steps, using our sticks to feel for any sort of resistance from the ground below.

Mookie's dad must have stepped in something very wet because he sunk about a foot and needed Dave and Dad to lift him out. Leroy laughed and said, "Let's move to Bakersfield, my wife said. Nothing ever happens in Bakersfield, she said." The dads all shared a laugh, and it was nice seeing them all together. I can't count how many times I would come home after school in the years following and see Leroy and Dave plopped down on the sofa, waiting for some sport to start. It was usually baseball, but when that wasn't in season, it was hockey, which was Dave's favorite, of course, being a Canuck. Xavier's dad was never really around, he worked long hours and usually just went home to relax, but every now and then he'd be there, even when Xavier wasn't.

My dad and Leroy died ten days apart, and I don't believe in heaven and hell, but it's nice to think that maybe they're hangin' out somewhere in the great beyond, but who knows.

We continued our trek.

Leroy said, "You know what my wife made us buy?"

"What?"

"A waterbed. Can you imagine? When we left Queens, she didn't want to move our bed and insisted we get a new one. A waterbed. Have you ever heard of such a thing? How the hell you gonna sleep on water?"

"Oh no!" Dad said. "We had one for like five years, and my back has never been the same since."

"Well, shit. How'm I gonna get out of this one?"

"You're not," Dave said, patting him on the back.

Us kids had pulled ahead a little, so I heard only bits and pieces of the conversation between the dads. I distinctly remember the waterbed bit, though. Still kinda makes me laugh because, over the years, I knew just how much Leroy hated that damn thing. One time he asked my dad to break into his house when they were on vacation the following summer and pop it. Dad probably would have done it, but Leroy made the fatal mistake of mentioning this while my mom was in earshot. She put the kibosh on it real fast.

"You think she's out here?" Mookie asked.

"I don't know," I said.

"Only one way to find out," Xavier said, briefly swinging his stick like a lightsaber before returning it to the muck.

We trudged on.

The bugs were really starting to buzz the farther we moved toward the center, making me wish I wore pants, but as Xavier said, "It's hotter than a snake's ass in a wagon's rut."

And it was.

Bakersfield in mid-summer can often border on brutal. That day was no exception. I believe the temp hit 104, and God knows how much hotter it was down in the damp hole.

"Who do you think would win in a fight between Van Damme and Steven Seagal?" I asked.

From far behind us, Dave yelled, "Van Damme!"

We turned and laughed. It was no secret that Dave was a big Van Damme fan, despite his movies being absolute dog shit. Roxy and I were Seagal guys and still are, despite his movies eventually becoming, well, absolute dog shit, too. But, when comparing classics, Seagal gets the win, even in 1990, two years before his true breakout, Under Siege, came out in 92.

When comparing movies that had been out by the time we were down in the sump, Seagal had the massively impressive one, two, three of *Above the Law*, *Hard to Kill*, and *Marked for Death*, followed in 1991 by our personal favorite, *Out for Justice*. It was a tough act to follow.

Van Damme, at that point, had the decent but nothing special *Bloodsport*, *Cyborg*, *Kickboxer*, and the laughably lame *Lionheart*. The following year he would release the somehow even cheesier *Double Impact*, where he played (sigh) twins. *eye roll*

It was a no-brainer, but the question posed was who would win in a fight between the two.

Roxy yelled back at his dad, "Seagal would have both of Van Damme's arms broken in like two seconds!"

"No way! Van Damme would do the splits and dodge Seagal's moves."

"Please! All Van Damme does is wear sweatpants that try to show off his wiener and does terrible dance moves."

That went on for the rest of the way across the sump. In fact, the sheriff next to Dave added that he thought Arnold could wipe the floor with both of them. It was a fair point. My dad then told Leroy about his free steak at Happy Steak. Leroy seemed impressed, which confused me then, but now that I'm older and life has worn me down, that sounds like a pretty amazing story.

When we reached the end of the line, we moved fifty feet down, lined up again, and headed back in the opposite direction.

The conversation had died down by now, and we were focusing on finding poor Bebe. I felt my stick hit something hard, causing me to stop in my tracks. My heart started pounding as I applied a little more pressure to the stick. Whatever was causing the resistance moved slightly, then went back down. I couldn't see anything, but I just knew. I used the tip of my shoe to give it another nudge.

Ugh. It was most definitely something.

"Hey!" I yelled out.

The deputy next to Dave yelled back, "Find something?"

"I...I think so."

My dad told me not to move and not to look. I didn't. Believe me.

"Everybody step back," the first deputy yelled from down the line as he came running towards me the best he could, considering the conditions. When he reached me, he took my stick from my hand and told me to take a step back.

We crowded around. I didn't want to see...but I couldn't not look.

The deputy reached down and pulled back the brush. There was something down there, and it wasn't a clump of leaves.

I could see the yellow hair.

"Oh fuck," the deputy said, my heart sinking into my stomach. He pulled back some more brush revealing a dead golden retriever, half decomposed. The stench was horrible.

I looked down at the poor dead dog, its tongue hanging out of its mouth, its eyes missing.

Dad grabbed me and pulled me back. "Don't look. It's okay. Just a dog."

The deputy repeated my dad, saying, "False alarm, everyone. It's a dog. Shit."

Everyone was staring down at the dead animal. I felt so sorry for it, not only to have died down here and be dinner for who knows what, but for now, being the center of attention for a bunch of gawkers.

"Ortega," the first deputy said, talking to the second deputy, whose name apparently was Ortega, "go call animal control. We've got to get this thing out of here."

"On it," Ortega said, then walked briskly back to the gate and out of our sight.

"Sorry you kids had to see that," the deputy said. "If you want to call it quits, I totally understand."

We all shook our heads no. The truth was, I wanted nothing more than to quit and go home, hide in my room with my friends and play some Nintendo and forget this entire ordeal ever happened. But I couldn't. I thought it was that damn Boy Scout pride again, but actually, I think it was more me wanting to find poor Bebe. I wanted to help her. I was naïve enough to believe that I still could.

"I'm going to stay," I said.

Roxy, Mookie, and Xavier nodded, signaling they were staying, too.

Leroy asked, "You guys sure? Nobody would blame you..."

"We need to find this girl, Dad," Mookie said.

Leroy smiled and nodded.

"Alright then," the deputy said, "let's get back to our posts." To me, he said, "Good job, kid. Way to be alert."

I gave him a half-hearted smile and said, "Boy Scout."

It took at least another hour to finish the search. We came up empty-handed, and I didn't know if that was a good thing or a bad thing. I guess it was simply a thing. Bebe was still out there. Somewhere.

Sweat was pouring down all our faces, our clothes were soaked, and we had bug bites on our legs, but we were out of the sump, and our job successfully completed.

We all went home, proud of a job well done but disappointed that nobody had found poor Bebe yet.

The golden retriever was hauled out and hopefully given a proper burial, but I doubt it.

Dave dropped everyone off at their houses, and I told whoever wanted to come to meet me at my house in an hour after everyone was showered and cleaned up. "We can play video games and... whatever."

"Order pizza," Dad said.

"Yeah," I said, "order pizza."

Xavier and his dad said they were calling it a night. Mookie said he'd be there, but his dad was emotionally drained and was looking forward to getting a good night's sleep on the floor before that "*got*-damned waterbed arrives."

I didn't even need an answer from Roxy. I knew he'd be there. Like always. Especially when free pizza was involved.

The day had been emotionally draining, much more than I ever anticipated, so when Roxy and Mookie showed back up at around 5pm, none of us were particularly in the mood to do much. My dad said he would order pizza at six, so we had an hour and a half to kill before the food arrived.

In the '80s and early '90s, Domino's Pizza had a thirty-minute or less delivery guarantee. If your pizza didn't arrive within thirty minutes, it was free. Here's how boring our town was back then, before Bebe. A little old lady named Esther Brown (don't ask me why I remember that!) ordered a pizza, which took over forty minutes to arrive. Naturally, she got the pizza for free. But you know what else? The local news station showed up at her house to interview her! I swear! Ridiculous! Eventually, drivers all over the country were getting into or causing accidents in order to get those pizzas delivered in a ridiculous time frame. After a few too many accidents, the entire promotion was halted, adopting the current motto of all pizza delivery places; You'll get it when you get it, Fatso!

None of us wanted to be inside (my, how the times have changed), so we took our bikes out front and rode around in circles on my driveway, counting down the seconds until dinner.

The vibe of the neighborhood felt so weird. There were two sheriff cars parked at the end of the street on the opposite side, and we would see more drive by from time to time. Everything seemed a lot quieter, too, like it was the middle of a school day, and no one was home. It was two days until the biggest summer holiday there was, though, and usually, this place is hoppin' with excitement. Every now and then, way off in the distance, you would hear someone yelling, "Beeeee-Beeeeee! Beee-

Beeeee!"

It was heartbreaking, and I didn't like the way everything felt. Have you ever watched a really scary movie, and you know something is going to jump out and scare the audience, but it takes a long time, and the tension just keeps building and building? That's what I felt like.

It was almost time to order the food, and riding around in circles can only hold your attention for so long, so we dumped the bikes and went back to laying on our backs on my lawn.

It was so hot. Like, stupid hot.

When the Guns' n Roses double masterpiece *Use Your Illusion Volumes I and II* were released on September 17th the following year, (causing mall riots at midnight to see who could get the first copy on CD – CDs at the time came in long cardboard boxes, often with unique and amazing art on them.) one song would always stick out to me. It wasn't the best, but it was a solid diddy that really spoke to me. *Right Next Door to Hell* was the opening track on Volume 1, and we made it the unofficial theme song of Bakersfield. To this day, I make a point to listen to it on the first day of the year when the temp reaches above a hundred.

It was almost 6pm by this time, and I would have bet the farm it was at least 102 out still. So laying on the grass to help cool our blazing hot little bodies seemed like the best way to kill the remaining forty minutes until dinner.

"You wanna go play *Yipes*?" I asked as I lazily gazed at the clear blue sky.

"Dude," Roxy said, "you know I wanna play *Yipes*."

Mookie asked, "What's *Yipes*?"

"Oh dude," I said, "it's a Pop-O-Matic game... like *Trouble*, but with monsters. Like, Dracula and Frankenstein and the mummy and stuff."

Roxy said, "It's pretty much the best board game ever. You try to get to the center of the board to turn into the monster, then turn around and try to eat all the other players."

"It's so awesome," I said.

"Let's play it!" Mookie said enthusiastically. Only, none of us moved. We kept lying there, staring into space.

If we had only gone in and been distracted by *Yipes*, or played *Tecmo Bowl*, or watched the network premiere of *The Blob* on USA, anything, maybe we would have missed all the action, and things would have been different for us.

But we didn't.

In the distance and headed straight for the neighborhood, were sirens. The loud blaring kind that moves fast. The kind where you knew something was wrong. We all sat bolt upright when we heard. Down the street, the two sheriff's cars fired up their engines and blared their sirens before taking off in a hurry.

I looked towards Roxy and said, "Oh shit."

"Bebe," he whispered.

Mookie was shaking his head, refusing to believe it. "If they found her, we gotta go."

Roxy and I both nodded, then made our way to our bikes which were just dumped in the driveway next to Neil's stupid Trans Am.

We headed down the street and turned left, the same way the two cruisers went. More and more sirens filled the air.

Something was most definitely wrong, no doubt about it.

We cut across the park to save some time, then made our way to the north exit of the neighborhood, where The Tube was. The sheriff's cars crossed that busy street above and drove straight into the field.

We cut down to The Tube, walked our bikes through, then hopped back on when we reached the other side. The cars, now far ahead of us, were kicking up huge clouds of dirt, leaving a trail.

More cars with sirens blaring blasted past us. We kept peddling. I turned to look back just as an ambulance jumped the curb and headed straight for us. We swerved right to give it a clear path, then continued on.

A hundred yards ahead, at least ten marked cars were parked in a circle, sheriff's deputies and plain-clothed officers stood around, looking at... Something. That *something* had their undivided attention.

We rode up and dropped our bikes. No one noticed. We made our way through the crowd and saw her.

Bebe-Lynn Sanders.

Laying on her back in a mess of mud, leaves, and overgrown weeds, her eyes open but lifeless, staring right at us, her skin an ugly ashen gray.

I was going to be sick.

I would have thrown up right then and there if I hadn't been distracted by a bald man in a pale blue suit yelling at us. I had no idea who he was, and I still don't, even to this day, but he sure was pissed.

"You can't be here!" he yelled, barging towards us. "These goddamn kids can't be here! Get them the fuck outta here!"

I felt hands on my shoulder pulling me back. I looked over and saw Roxy and Mookie being dragged away violently.

We didn't need any more convincing to leave. We got on our bikes and rode home. By now, it seemed that every person in the neighborhood was standing out in the street watching us pedal home, tears staining the side of our sweaty, dirty faces. Once they saw us, they had to have known. I couldn't bear to make eye contact with any of them.

When we got back to my house, my family was out front, my mom yelling at us that we weren't supposed to go anywhere, goddamn it! It was one of the only times I ever heard her use anything, even bordering on foul language.

She was pissed. Dad didn't look much happier, and shockingly, even Neil looked worried.

We dropped our bikes in the driveway, and I'm sure mom was gearing up to read us the Riot Act until she saw our faces. Then she knew and pulled all three of us in for a big hug.

"Why?" she asked. "Why did you go?"

We didn't respond.

We didn't need to.

She knew why.

She was a kid once, too.

Mom ushered us into the house and let us all sit on the sofa and calm down. Within a few minutes, Leroy was knocking on the door. A few minutes after that, Roxy's entire family was there.

Under any other circumstances, this had the makings of a great night. But it wasn't going to happen. Dad still ordered pizza, enough for everyone, but nobody was really that hungry. By the time the rest of Mookie's family arrived (the first time meeting his siblings for me), we all just kinda sat there, not really talking, not really doing anything.

Everyone must have returned home at some point, but I don't remember when. I was lying on my bed, trying so hard to fall asleep, but all I could focus on was Bebe's eyes looking right at me. Even thirty-plus years later, it's still as vivid to me as it was that day, and about once a month, Bebe will show up in my dreams.

I heard the door open, and footsteps approach.

"Hey, little bro."

"Hey, Neil."

"I knocked but you didn't hear me."

It makes me laugh. "Liar."

"Exactly. See how lame that lie is?"

"Yeah yeah…"

Awkward silence. Neil pulls a chair from my desk, drags it across my bedroom floor to the side of my bed, and takes a seat.

"You okay?" he asked.

I nodded silently.

"Hey, dude. I'm sorry. Like, all that stuff I said before… About Bebe… You know, I was just full of shit, you know? I didn't… I was just talkin' trash. I had… I had no idea. Honestly, I figured she found some rich forty-year-old dude, and they ran off to like Mexico or something."

"She was right where you said she would be."

"Come on, man. It's the only logical place in this area to dump a body. The sump is way too obvious, and that field is wide open and has snakes and shit, probably. Nobody is going to walk through it and find her. Not with that new bike trail out there."

"We ride our bikes through it all the time."

Neil sighed. "I'm really sorry. If I had known she was really...you know... I never would have said all that crap. I really figured she was fine. Stuff like that doesn't happen around here, you know. I just..."

Then something happened that I never in my life thought I would scc.

Neil started crying.

Just a few sniffles at first, then eventually actual tears. I was shocked. Since I've known him, this guy has been nothing but a pain in my ass and our parents' ass. Never in my life had I seen him show any emotion like this.

I didn't know what to do. For a ten-year-old boy, emotions are very complicated. Just a few short years prior, I was laughing at jokes made at the expense of a little girl trapped in a well. Now I was unsure if I'd ever be able to close my eyes again.

Reality had hit both of us like a bolt of lightning, and it seemed like Neil didn't know how to handle it either. So, I let him cry. Right there by my bed, I let him cry until the tears dried up.

"I'm... I'm sorry, dude," he said while wiping his nose with his forearm. "I just..."

"It's okay."

"Don't tell anyone or else I'll tell Mom about all those rap tapes you stole from Longs Drugstore and have hidden in your mattress." He smiled.

"How the hell do you know about that?"

He sniffled again. "Big brothers know everything."

"Yeah, I doubt that."

A bigger smile was now on his tear-stained dumb face. "Yeah, well, I know you keep that card Sheriff Monroe gave us in your drawer right there. *Oh, Daphne, I love you, Daphne.*"

"How the hell...."

He put his hand on my head and rustled my shaggy, unkempt hair, still coated in the dirt the cop cars kicked up. "I told you. Big brothers know everything."

He got up, put my chair back, and left the room without saying another word. I rolled to my side and opened the nightstand drawer. The card was still there. I grabbed it, flipped it over a few times, studied it, and looked at the phone number in bold white lettering on a green-colored background.

Of course, I knew the number by heart by now, but that didn't stop me from looking at that damn card about three or four times a week.

Should I call her? Would tonight be the night?

I assumed Sheriff Monroe would be working late, so I had a one in three chance of Daphne answering.

But what would I say?

Tell her how sorry I am about what happened?

She didn't know Bebe any better than I knew her, and as far as I know, she didn't see the body, so maybe she wasn't even that upset. If I called and said sorry and asked if she was okay and she didn't know what I was talking about, I would be humiliated. I'm sure her dad has cases all the time that cause him to work into the night, so maybe this was no different, and she would think I'm some huge wuss-bag.

Yeah, it wasn't the right time. For sure.

Maybe tomorrow.

I put the card back in the drawer, and rolled onto my back. I was tired, so tired, but I was scared to close my eyes.

So I stared up at the ceiling, just hoping I would doze off and not even notice.

No luck.

I rolled over and stared at the carpet.

Nope.

I stared at random objects in my bedroom, like the two-and-a-half-foot long inflatable Ninja Turtles Wacky Attack Blimp displayed by my window or the *Jason Takes Manhattan* poster on my wall that I got for free at Video Network.

Eventually, I got up and turned the TV on in my bedroom. It wasn't cable-ready, so I only got three, maybe four, local channels, and guess what they were all talking about?

It must have been 11pm because Bebe was everywhere on the news. I turned the channel back to 3 and pressed the power button on my Nintendo. Maybe that night would finally be the night I beat *Yo! Noid* once and for all.

It wasn't.

It wasn't until 2003 that I finally beat that game. Seriously. It's the most frustrating game ever made. While it briefly took my mind off Bebe, all it did was replace her with raging anger aimed toward that stupid red Domino's mascot and everyone involved in making that game.

I hit the power button and flipped the TV off, plunging myself back into semi-darkness, the only light coming from the streetlight and moon outside my window and a little slash of yellow under my door.

I crawled back into bed and tried to think of the happiest thoughts I could think of – like Dad pumping quarter after quarter into *Kung Fu Master* and never being able to beat the first stage, despite the Stick Man being impossibly easy to defeat. Or when Roxy and I had an AYSO soccer game one Saturday morning the previous October, and the fog was so thick you couldn't even see your own hands if you put them in front of your face, but still, everyone showed up, and everyone played. Parents on the sidelines cheered, even though I'm convinced they had no idea what was happening on the field. We could have been smoking cigars out there and talking about the stock market for all they knew.

The happy thoughts started working because I felt

my eyelids getting heavier and heavier. I'm unsure if I had just fallen asleep or if it had been hours, but Bebe showed up, as she often did from that day forward.

She stood before me with her gray skin and said nothing. I tried shaking my head to get her to go away, but still, she remained, her eyes looking directly into mine. I was terrified, but I couldn't wake myself up.

Her eyes stayed locked on mine, no matter how badly I thrashed my head around.

I'll never be able to escape those eyes.

The next day I remember not wanting to get out of bed. I tried desperately to fall back asleep, even though I knew what probably awaited me. Didn't matter anyway because my eyes refused to stay shut. Instead, I rolled to my side and stared at my Turtle Blimp again. Eventually, Mom came in to check on me and asked if I wanted to talk. I absolutely did not want to talk, so I told her no thanks and that I was just sleepy and I would be out soon. She acted like she believed me and left, closing the door behind her.

I stayed there for about another hour when my dad came knocking (unlike Neil). I was just going to pretend to be asleep, but it was no use. Dad opened the door and peeked his head in. "Hey, buddy. You awake?"

Zzzzzz.

"Come on, buddy, get up. They caught that son of a bitch... I mean, uh, the potential person of interest."

Forgetting that I was 'asleep,' I rolled over, obviously wide awake, and asked, "Who did it?"

"Come on, they're about to talk about it on the news. They just broke it. Come on, come on."

I rolled out of bed. I didn't know why I was so excited, but I just really wanted whoever did that to Bebe to pay. In the movies, I always root for the bad guys, but in real life, I despised the bad guy and wanted him caught and punished as soon as possible.

When I reached the living room, my parents and brother were looking intently at the TV. Mom and Neil were standing by the table, and my dad was on the sofa leaning forward. I sat beside him, and he put his arm around my shoulders.

On the TV, KGET's primetime heavy hitters Jim Stewart and Robin Mendez were pulling the 11am shift, so you knew something big was breaking.

I was in such a daze I can't remember what they said, which is weird since I remember everything, so I went to the archives and found the report.

Jim Stewart tapped some papers on his desk, looked straight into the camera with a no-nonsense glare, and said, "Breaking news this morning in the Bebe-Lynn Sanders case. We're being told that Trip Windham, the man witnesses say they saw with Bebe-Lynn before she went missing, is now in custody."

Robin Mendez, to Jim's left, took over. "Windham was never formally announced as a suspect in the slaying of the seventeen-year-old Bakersfield High student, but as a 'person of interest,' according to Sheriff Douglas Monroe. We will keep you updated as more facts come in."

Back to Jim. "Bebe-Lynn Sanders was found dead yesterday evening, hidden in the brush and overgrown weeds in a field just north of Truxton Avenue. Initial reports suggest she was beaten and eventually strangled to death. Her body was dumped in a gulch, out of sight from passersby on the newly extended bike trail.

"Bebe-Lynn went missing Friday night after being seen at a popular local hangout...."

Jim goes on to recap everything we already know, hoping to buy time for more breaking news.

I hoped hearing this would make me feel better, but it didn't seem to do anything. Bebe was still dead. Her eyes were still staring at me.

"What a fucking creep," Neil said.

Neil's language caused Mom's jaw to drop.

"Sorry, Mom, but seriously. Fuck that guy."

"Neil!"

"He's got a point," Dad said.

"Gary!"

"What? I hope they fry this son of a bitch."

Mom threw her hands up in disbelief, the language proving too much for her to handle.

Dad looked at me and asked, "You okay, buddy?"

I nodded. "I'm okay."

"You sure?"

"I think so."

"At least they caught the creep. Maybe things can start getting back to normal." He said it with a sympathetic look on his face, and I knew he didn't mean it in a way suggesting we forget about everything and get on with our lives. More like the town can start healing.

I didn't know what to say, so I just returned his same half-hearted smile and mumbled, "that son of a bitch."

Rumor has it my mom is still shaking her head to this day.

Turns out, Trip Windham, person of interest, potential son of a bitch, turned himself in around 10am that morning. I was curious about what happened in that sheriff's department, so just before I started writing this book, I called in a few favors (mooches). I was allowed to dig through all the records of suspect transcripts and recordings until I found Trip's. The recordings had not been digitized, and I couldn't remove the tape (yes, a cassette tape) from the building, so I had to run to a pawn shop nearby and buy a cheap Walkman. For you youngsters, that's like an iPhone but for tapes only.

When I returned, I listened to the entire conversation to get a feel for what actually transpired in there. I ran a few photocopies of the transcript and brought them home to transcribe for you. So here goes.

The sound of a metal chair being pulled out, and the heft of a man sitting is heard. This is, no doubt, Sheriff Monroe. I assume Windham was already seated when Monroe made his grand entrance to intimidate. With Bebe dead now, I'm sure they were no longer interested in their so-called person of interest and were on the hunt.

They're in a small room, probably an interrogation room, based on the slight echo of their words.

Monroe speaks first. He's not subtle.

Monroe: So, Mr. Windham. Care to enlighten us as to why you murdered Bebe-Lynn Sanders?

Windham: I... I didn't kill her.

Monroe: Cut the shit, Windham. If you didn't kill her, who did?

Windham: I... I don't know. But it wasn't me!

Monroe: Oh, of course not. Of course, it was someone else. You're seen with a girl, then the girl goes missing, then you go missing, then she turns up dead, and it wasn't you. So Columbo, who was it then?

Windham: I told you. I don't fucking know!

Unknown: Simmer down! (Unknown's name and words are left off the transcript entirely. I took notes from the tape, but I have no clue who he is. My apologies.)

Monroe: Enlighten us, then, Mr. Windham. We have witnesses that saw you outside of Jimmy's Arcade with Bebe just before she vanished at around 7pm.

Windham: Yeah. Yeah, okay, yeah, I saw her, I don't deny that. I tried... Okay, look, I was in town for a race.

Monroe: What kind of race?

Windham: A race. Cars, you know. At Mesa Marin Raceway.

Monroe: And you drove in from Santa Barbara for a race when, exactly?

Windham: I rode. I rode my bike.

Monroe: Rode *what?*

Windham: My Honda. Motorcycle.

Monroe: When?

Windham: Friday.

Monroe: Who were you with?

Windham: I wasn't with nobody; I was on my bike! I was meeting people there.

Monroe: Do these people have names?

Windham: Yeah, of course they do. Dude, look, listen, I didn't kill that girl.

Monroe: So tell us what happened.

Windham: What the fuck do you think I'm trying to do. I turned myself in for that exact reason!

Unknown: Calm down.

Monroe: Alright. Why don't you tell us exactly what happened, then. We're listening.

Windham: Like I said, I was in town for the races at Mesa Marin. I was meeting a couple of my buddies here from other colleges. We all used to live here a long time ago and go to the races and decided to meet up and hang out for the night.

Monroe: Did your roommate know?

Windham: No. He knew I was leaving, but we're just roommates. We were dorm roommates then we got an apartment together. I'd prefer to live alone, but Santa Barbara isn't cheap, and I dunno. It doesn't matter.

Monroe: Go on.

Windham: So, I get to town and have a couple hours to kill. The race didn't start 'til 8 because it was a night race, and it was hot as fuck, and I left super early because it's the weekend before a holiday, ya know. So I went to where I knew people would be... Mainly, ya know, girls.

Monroe: Okay.

Windham: So, I'm just walking around the movie theater and arcade, killing time, and I see this smoking hot little blonde girl and-

Monroe: (noticeably much more pissed now) Her name was Bebe-Lynn Sanders!

Windham: Right. Sorry. I see her just standing by the side of the building drinking a Coke, so I go and talk to her. I ask her what she's doing, and she says nothing, and I say, a girl that looks like you is rarely doing nothing, and she kinda laughed like high school girls do, so I asked if she wanted to grab a bite to eat with me, even though she was drinking the Coke, but ya know, whatever. She said she wasn't hungry and had something she was going to do, but I didn't want her to go, so I started laying it on real thick. So, like, I tell her what I'm doing in town and ask if she wants to go to the races with me, and she gives me a shitty look like the races are so far beneath her, and I'm just like, okay whatever, princess, then I offer her a ride home. I say it's getting dark, and a pretty girl shouldn't be out alone.

Monroe: Did she tell you she was going home?

Windham: Not then, but eventually, yeah. Like, where she was standing, there was no parking lot, so I assumed she walked there and probably needed a ride. I remember a lot of kids walked there when I lived here. So even if she didn't need to go home, I would have given her a ride anywhere, ya know?

Monroe: Alright, continue.

Windham: So I keep laying it on and finally convince her to let me give her a ride. The arcade was really starting to get busy by this point, but for some reason, she didn't want to stay. Said she had something to do...

Monroe: What did she have to do? Did she say?

Windham: She didn't, but I don't know. I didn't pay much attention to her because I figured at that point she was down to party, you know.

Monroe: Jesus Christ.

Windham: I know. I'm sorry. So we walk back to my-

Monroe: Did anyone see you?

Windham: Apparently, someone saw us because I saw my picture all over the goddamn news.

Monroe: They saw you standing with her. We didn't get any reports of her getting on a motorcycle with you.

Windham: Then I guess no one saw us. What did I care at the time, you know? So, I get her on my bike, and we pull out of the parking lot and park at the warehouses behind Circuit City. She asks me why we're stopped, trying to play all innocent and everything. So I hop off and spin her around on the seat of my bike and start kissing her. She pulls away like she's all offended and shit, so I tell her to knock that hard-to-get shit off.

Monroe: Were you aware of Bebe's supposed reputation?

Windham: Dude, I didn't even know her fucking name. She just looked hot, and I wanted a piece.

Monroe: (his voice is very tightlipped now, angry, like he could snap at any moment and beat the shit out of this arrogant little prick.) So what did you do?

Windham: I made another move. Look, I know this isn't going to make me look good, but... Shit. Okay. I started kissing her again, holding her real close to me... Then... I put my hand between her thighs. She pulled away and spit in my face, so... I punched her. Right in the face, I hit her, and she fell off my bike and landed on the ground.

Monroe: Jesus Christ.

Windham: But, that's it, man. I swear. I swear to God! I was pissed, so I hopped on my bike and took off. She was alive, I swear it. She yelled fuck you at me as I was leaving. I know she was alive.

Unknown: There is evidence she was struck in the face and on the back of the head.

Monroe: I outta beat the ever-lovin' shit out of you, boy, right here and now.

Windham: I know how it looks! But I turned myself in.

Monroe: What took you so long?!

———

Windham: I didn't know! I went to the races that night then... you can verify this. I rode to Las Vegas in the morning. I stayed at the Stardust. I can prove it. When I got back, I saw on the news she was dead and I, apparently, was missing.

Monroe: I don't care where you were. All I care about is what you did to that girl. You wanna know what I think? (Silence) I think you punched her, and when she hit her head, you knew you were finished. Attempted rape and assault. What other choice did you have? You wrapped your hands around her neck and choked the life out of her.

Windham: No...

Monroe: I think yes.

Windham: No, no, listen! If I did it, why would I turn myself in? That doesn't make sense! She was found in a, in a, field or whatever, too. What am I gonna do, sling a corpse over my bike and drive her all the way out there on a busy Friday night?! No, man, no way. If I killed her... why wouldn't I have just left her where she was and gone to the races and acted like everything was totally normal?!

(There is a solid minute of silence.)

Monroe: Maybe you took her out to the field and did it there. Maybe the body wasn't dumped.

Windham: Why the hell would I drive a motorcycle out to a dirt field just to get with a girl? Those warehouses were hidden and dark and the perfect spot. What possible purpose would I have to go out there?!

(More silence, followed by the sound of Monroe pushing his chair back and getting up. Very slight mumbling was heard on the recording, but nothing I

———

could make out and nothing in the transcript, although it's safe to assume he was talking to the unknown person in the room and realizing that Trip Windham was, in all likelihood, innocent of killing Bebe-Lynn Sanders. This did not please Sheriff Monroe in the least. His following words were screamed.)

Monroe: God damn it! Arrest this piece of shit! Sexual assault and battery!

A little later in the afternoon, KGET interrupted the Phil Donahue Show (we were staying close to the TV in case any news broke) and informed us of Trip Windham's innocence in the death of Bebe, though he was currently under arrest.

And that was that. While being a massive piece of shit, a woman beater, and probably a rapist, Windham was innocent of murder. It felt like a kick in the nuts when we all heard the news. If Trip didn't do it, then who? And why?

Jim Stewart and Robin Mendez reported the story of what happened, how Bebe was assaulted, both sexually and physically, and how Trip left her alone and injured in a dark warehouse parking lot. What happened after that was anyone's guess.

My mom, who was working in the kitchen and having just made us lunch, put her hand out on the counter for support and carefully walked herself to the table to sit down. She looked like a ghost.

"That poor girl," she said, looking down at her lap. "I wish I could have done something."

"I'm sure everyone wishes they could have done something," Dad said, standing and walking to my mom. "But there was nothing. Sometimes bad things happen to good people, and there's nothing that can be done."

"If he didn't do it, then who? Is there a murderer just walking among us?"

Dad nodded his head, "Honestly, probably. But we don't have to be worried about anything. Bebe was strangled. Nobody going out murdering will use their bare hands as their weapon of choice. It was probably a crime of passion, just like with Trip Windham."

I knew where dad was going with this, but I had seen plenty of movies where the killer used his bare hands. But again, those are movies, so I kept my mouth shut. Plus, I figured he was saying whatever needed to be said to calm down my noticeably distraught mother.

"Sheriff Monroe and his team are smart," Dad said, "you don't have anything to worry about, I promise. They'll catch him."

"How do you know?" Mom asked, finally looking up.

"Because that's their job, and they're good at it. I bet they want to find this guy more than all of us combined. But ya know what, in the meantime, maybe let's put a pause on showing houses. Or if you absolutely must, I will come with you."

Mom nodded. I sorta figured that she wouldn't be showing anything anytime soon, but I know Dad just had to say it.

"Should I go see her family?" Mom asked. "That poor girl that was over. She must be devastated."

"I'm sure the whole family is devastated, but they need their privacy right now. We're going to get through this."

He looked at me and smiled. "You know what," he said. "There is no reason we can't have a fun holiday tomorrow. Whatta ya say? The usual? Barbequed burgers and fireworks?"

Oh man, with everything that's been going on, we completely forgot to buy fireworks. We rode by the stands fifty times but forgot all about them by the time we got home. Aside from Halloween, the Fourth of July is my favorite holiday. I really didn't want to miss it, even if I knew that year would be a bit different.

"Yeah," I said. "I'd like that."

"Come on. Let's go load up. You wanna call Rox?"

"Yeah!"

"Well, go call him! Xavier and Mookie?"

"I'm on it! Mookie doesn't have a phone yet, so we'll have to cruise by."

"You bet!"

Nobody answered at Xavier's house. I had no idea where they all were, but Roxy picked up on the first ring and yelled out, "Yeah!" as soon as I got out the words, "You wanna." We picked him up right away then my dad went and knocked on Mookie's door, asking if he would like to come out while promising his parents he'd be safe. Mookie came blasting out the door about five seconds later.

For being the day before the Fourth of July, a surprisingly large selection of mini-explosives was available. Apparently, we weren't the only ones whose minds it had slipped.

In a gesture to cheer us all up, my dad told us to get whatever we wanted. This year there would be no limit. It was amazing. Back then, fireworks were much different than what they are today with all these lame safety codes.

If you wanted some shit that spun wildly while shooting fire, get yourself some Ground Bloom Blossoms. Those were banned in the late 90s, but we sure stocked up that day. Who wouldn't want to witness one of those things accidentally shooting off under a car with a small gas leak? It sounded awesome!

Sick of your house and want to try your luck at burning it down and collecting the insurance money? Why not nail some spinning fire to your dry-ass wooden gate. Get yourself a Sparkling Wheel or a Happy Lamp and sit back and enjoy!

Want some ridiculous box that spins out of control and then pops up into a Chinese Friendship Pagoda? Get yourself a few, you guessed it, Friendship Pagodas.

Want to blow up your friend's mailbox? Get a box of Piccolo Petes, split them open with a pocketknife, and dump all the gunpowder into tin foil. Then, fold the foil up nice and tight while leaving a fuse sticking out, and wrap the whole thing in duct tape. Light the fuse and run like hell because something is gonna get destroyed!

Yeah, the 80s and 90s were the heydays for legal fireworks. I can't believe some of these took so long to get banned. It's like nobody gave a shit about all the burned-down houses and scarring.

In fact, several years prior, my grandpa was in charge of the fireworks display on our street, and he kept stressing over and over that adult supervision was required and that kids shouldn't handle these things. Then the first one he lit exploded on him, burned all the hair off both his arms, and singed his eyebrows.

It became a joke after that – Adult Supervision Required!

My dad severely underestimated our ability to spend his money. After about five minutes of all three of us pointing at what we wanted, my dad called it quits. "Okay, that's enough. Fourth of July is only one night, not all summer."

The booth volunteers bagged up all our stuff, and my dad pulled out his wallet and winced at the total.

Our next stop was Albertsons, where we loaded up on burgers and buns and chips and IBC Root Beer, and you name it. (At the tail end of 2003, I would win the IBC Root Beer grand prize for a game they had involving their bottle caps. I won a family vacation to Disney World in Orlando.) My parents were determined to give us the best Fourth of July ever, no matter the cost. Dad paid for the groceries, and we headed back home; Dad now a few hundred dollars lighter. When we pulled up to the house, Mom and Neil were getting into the festivities by decorating our lawn with mini American Flags and red, white, and blue streamers around our mailbox pole. They must have started a trend because several other people on the street were doing the same thing.

Our neighborhood was always so alive on the Fourth, with large family gatherings up and down all the streets, which always provided a lot of fun and very large fireworks shows.

Having just finished lining the sidewalk with flags, Mom looked at us and said, "Whatta ya think?"

"Looks great!" Dad said.

We all agreed. And it did look great. It looked like our typical Bakersfield, Americana Fourth of July celebration, and it couldn't have come at a better time.

"I put the big flag out, too," Neil said, pointing to the full-size American flag hanging from the flagpole holder on the front of our house.

I nodded. "Impressive."

It really wasn't that impressive. A monkey could have done it, but I was happy to see Neil out and actually doing something, so what's the harm in giving him a little pat on the back.

"Yeah!" he said, smiling.

Just a few hundred yards away, unbeknownst to us, while we were unloading and admiring all our purchases, a search of Bebe-Lynn's bedroom was happening. Sheriff Monroe and his team were looking for anything that could explain why Bebe was at Jimmy's Arcade alone that night or who could have murdered her. The department was convinced it was someone she knew, but I'm not exactly sure how they came to that conclusion.

It would be in that bedroom that the case took a bizarre turn. I wouldn't hear about it until later that afternoon. At that moment, we all seemed to have put yesterday behind us, at least temporarily, and could focus on all the fun we would have tomorrow night.

Roxy and Mookie both went home fairly early for dinner, each seeming in much better spirits than the night before. We agreed to meet back at my house at 3 pm tomorrow, leaving plenty of time to hang out and play video games until it was time to move the party outside. Mookie seemed extra excited. The street he used to live on never did anything for the holiday, apparently.

After dinner, my dad turned the news on to get some updates, although I'm sure he'd rather have watched the Dodger game.

This is where we heard about the bizarre turn the case had taken.

In a wastepaper basket in Bebe's bedroom was a note

written from cut-out letters in a magazine... like a ransom note.

Gaylen Young, the newscaster, told us about the strange find, then showed a copy of the note. Sure enough, it looked like a ransom letter from the movies. It also appeared to have been crumpled up and smoothed out. Once I saw it, it was forever burned into my brain.

The note read:

MEET ME AT JIMMY'S ARCADE
7 pm FRIDAY
TELL ME WHAT U KNOW
OR DIE

I heard my mom gasp. "What the hell is going on?"

Dad said, "That's, uh, quite the twist."

"She was being blackmailed?" I asked. I had watched a lot of movies and knew exactly what was going on, even though technically, I wasn't sure if this was a threat, an ultimatum, or blackmail. It didn't matter. My parents certainly didn't know the difference. I phrased my remark like a question because I didn't want my parents to catch on to what a sneaky little shithead I was.

"Looks like it," Dad said, giving me a confused look.

"What in the world do you think she did?" Mom asked.

"Um..." Dad said, thinking. "I... I really don't know."

"Well, I don't care what she did," Mom said, "she certainly didn't deserve the punishment she got. Now I really hope they find the son of a bitch that did it."

Heads turned! All eyes were on mom. It was the first time we had ever heard my mom say son of a bitch.

"What?" Mom said. "I'm allowed to say bad words, too, ya know."

We remained silent for a few moments, mostly just to give my mom a hard time. She rolled her eyes and huffed a bit. Eventually, Neil said, "Nothing worse than a blackmailer."

"A murderer," I said.

"Well, yeah, then nothing worse than a blackmailing murderer!"

I shrugged. Touché

The phone rang, and I knew who it was before Mom answered.

"Hello," Mom said.

Like an icepick straight to my brain, I could hear Ms. Frank's high-pitched squawking through the goddamn receiver.

"Yeah," Mom said, "isn't that strange...(squawk squawk squaaawwwkkkk) I know. I don't know what to think about it. I just really hope they find the guy and throw the book at him. (More squawking from Ms. Franks.) Okay, I will let you know if I hear anything, for sure. Thanks for calling. (Squaaawwwkkkkkkkk!) Okay, yes, I will call you... (Squawk squawk)

Dad said, "You need to tell that old bag to throttle back a bit."

By now, mom was holding the phone so far away from her ear it looked like she was trying to straight-arm it.

Dad yelled, "Ah, my thumb! Honey, help!"

Mom quickly returned the phone to her ear and said, "Oh geez, Gary just hit his thumb with a hammer, gotta go, k bye, thank you!" then hung up fast. To my dad, she said, "I owe ya one."

"Teamwork makes the dream work." Dad switched the TV to the Dodgers.

"We're not going to see what else happened?" Mom said, like continuing to watch the news was the most obvious thing in the world, and my dad was the biggest idiot on the planet.

Dad sighed, "Fine," then switched it back.

Gaylen Young announced that we would be hearing from Sheriff Monroe in a few minutes to discuss the wild twist the story had taken.

"See," Mom said, "aren't you glad you turned it back?"

Dad rolled his eyes and sighed. Over on KTLA that night, Fernando Valenzuela gave up ten hits over seven innings, with Mike Scioscia going oh-for-four at the plate, Eddie Murray going two-for-four, and Kirk Gibson, pulling most of the weight, going three-for-five in a five-to-three loss to the Chicago Cubs. Dad hated missing games, especially when Fernando was on the mound, but judging by the stats, it was as good a game as any to miss.

It took another thirty minutes before we saw Sheriff Monroe on the television. He was out front of the sheriff station, standing at that same podium we'd seen him stand before several times this week. As I did with his previous speeches, I searched the KGET archives and found the footage to correctly relay the transcription to you.

Sheriff Monroe leaned forward into his microphones and spoke.

"While doing a thorough investigation on the murder of Bebe-Lynn Sanders, her family gave us permission to go through her bedroom with a fine-tooth comb, looking for any clue we could find about her final minutes alive.

"One of my deputies, Deputy Tony Bishop, found a crumpled-up note in her wastepaper basket. He immediately handed it over to me. As I'm sure most of you have heard by now, this note, written using letters from a magazine of some sort, threatened Bebe-Lynn. The author of this note demanded Bebe-Lynn meet him or her outside Jimmy's Arcade at 7 the night she went missing.

"We have developed a timeline for that night. We believe Bebe-Lynn left her house on foot and walked to the arcade at around 5:45 pm. While waiting outside for the mystery person, she was approached by one Trip Windham, who talked Bebe into leaving with him, although they did not get far.

"Bebe-Lynn got on the back of Windham's motorcycle and left the parking lot, parking approximately two-hundred yards away in the darkness of a warehouse parking lot located behind the Circuit City.

"Windham tried to seduce Bebe-Lynn, but she wanted no part of it. At around 7:10 pm, Bebe-Lynn, defending herself, spit in Windham's face, causing him to swing at her, knocking her off the bike and to the ground. Windham then got back on his bike and rode off.

"We believe Windham interrupted the intended meeting of Bebe-Lynn and our Mystery Suspect. He did not approach Bebe-Lynn due to Windham being there, instead choosing to follow. But he didn't have to follow very long.

"We believe, after Bebe was knocked down, Mystery Suspect approached in his car. We have no guess what the conversation was about. There is probably only one person in the world who knows that now, and we need to find him.

"Something must have gone terribly wrong because Bebe-Lynn, after being punched in the face and hitting her head on the hard concrete and being left alone, was then strangled to death by the bare hands of a madman.

"We believe this person loaded Bebe-Lynn into his car or truck, drove her out to the first open space he could find, and dumped her body in the brush so it wouldn't be easily found. That brush just happened to be bordering Bebe-Lynn's neighborhood.

"We now know two things for sure. The first is that we know this was a targeted attack. Bebe-Lynn was always the intended victim. She knew or saw something bad enough that the killer decided she must die in order to protect the secret.

"We will continue to search for any clues we can, and we will not stop until this murdering piece of trash is in our custody.

"I am urging any friends or acquaintances of Bebe-Lynns to think, think hard, about anything Bebe said or did that could possibly tip you off to what she knew. Think back to the last days or weeks of Bebe's life – did she ever seem strange or do something out of character? Did she ever mention someone you didn't know or something that she saw? If you can think of anything, please give us a call.

"Now, the only bright spot in this horrible, horrible crime is that we do not believe any other people are in danger. Knowing what we know now, we believe this entire incident was always about Bebe and no one else. So, please, while we are all mourning the death of this innocent girl, let's try to get back to our regular daily routine. This was always about Bebe, so we see no reason not to let your children play at the park, or go to the movies, or the arcade, or waterslides. Tomorrow is the Fourth of July, and I want to see people celebrate. Celebrate Bebe. Do it for her.

"I know it will be hard, and it will take a long, long time to get over this, but we will survive. This town has been through a lot, and I want every single person here to feel safe.

"We will find this scumbag! I promise you that.

"Thank you for coming out and for all your help. We couldn't have gotten this far without all of you. Now, if you'll excuse me, we have work to do.

"Thank you again."

I remember turning to look at my dad. I didn't know what to think. I have seen a million movies like this, where the innocent person witnesses a murder or a mob hit or whatever, then has to go on the run. Only, Bebe didn't seem to be running. Did that mean she didn't even know what she saw?

That would explain her being killed, I suppose. If the killer showed up and demanded to know what Bebe knew, but she insisted she didn't know anything... Well, that definitely could lead to a strangulation.

But the problem with that was, why did she show up in the first place. If she genuinely didn't know anything, why didn't she tell her parents or sister, or call the cops for help?

Something was very screwy about this case, but I didn't know what.

"What do you think?" Dad asked.

"Very bizarre," Mom said. "That poor girl. If I only talked to her on Friday morning."

"We've gone over this a hundred times," Dad said.

"There was literally no reason for you to talk to her. Even if there was, why in the world would she tell you anything, especially if she didn't even bother to tell her folks."

"I just feel awful."

"I know. That girl had a secret, and unfortunately, it got her killed. Believe me, I wish she would have told you or someone, too, but she didn't. The only thing we can do now is hope they catch this guy. I tell ya, I'd like to have a few minutes alone with him myself, not only for killing Bebe but for making Grant see her like that."

"Nobody made me see her. I did it my own stupid self."

"No, if he didn't kill her and dump her there, you wouldn't have seen her. I'd like to punch this piece of shit square in the teeth."

"Okay, okay," Mom said, "that's enough." She laughed a sad little laugh, then said, "I don't know what to do now."

Dad shook his head. "I don't think we do anything now. We move on and let Monroe and his men find him."

Looking directly at me, Mom said, "I still want you guys to stay close for a while. I know what Sheriff Monroe said, but I would feel better if you were here. No bike rides to the arcade or movies or anything, just for a little bit."

I was going to object, but what was the point? Truthfully, I was happy to stay close for a while.

"Neil, the same goes for you. You can stay home."

"What?" Neil said in shock, "I'm an adult."

"Yeah, you're an adult that still lives with mommy and daddy, and as long as you live here and we pay for your car insurance, and your car and gas, for that matter, you can stick around for a while. Tomorrow is a holiday anyway. It would do you good to spend at least one with your family."

"Aw man, that's bunk!"

"Bunk, skunk, or slam dunk," Mom said, "you're staying here."

I have no idea what bunk, skunk, or slam dunk meant, and Mom probably didn't either, but it shut my brother up. I still repeat that line to dumbass Neil whenever he is being a, ya know, dumbass. It usually gets a chuckle.

It was another mostly sleepless night for me.

After I crawled into bed, I pulled Daphne's phone number from the drawer and held it. It would be yet another perfect time to give her a call. I could ask if she was doing okay. Or I could ask if she needed anything, or I could pretend to be nosey about the case.

Any excuse would work.

Tomorrow for sure.

I returned the card to the drawer.

Normally on nights I couldn't sleep, I would put on one of the movies I rented, and by the time it was over, I could barely keep my eyes open. I still had the ones we rented the other day, along with my used copy of *Strange Brew*, but I didn't feel like watching any of those. I guess I didn't feel like watching anything.

Had I known at the time that tomorrow things would get even worse, I doubt I'd ever have fallen asleep, but after an hour or so of staring at that Freddy poster I won and rows of Starting Lineup and M.U.S.C.L.E figures on my windowsill, I finally dozed off.

Bebe had come to see me in my sleep, but I wasn't as scared this time. The entire dream played out with Bebe on the sidelines, always watching with those dead eyes. I tried interacting with her a few times but got no response. She just looked at me, so eventually, I gave up.

When I finally got up, my clock radio said it was almost 1pm. Yikes!

"There he is," Dad said when I shuffled out to the living room. "We were about to give up hope."

I scratched my head and yawned.

"You okay, honey?" Mom asked.

I nodded.

"Pop Tart?"

I nodded again.

Dad said, "You feel okay, pal."

"Yeah, I'm okay. Just couldn't sleep last night."

"Understandable."

I heard mom push the lever on the toaster down. "Happy Fourth of July."

"Oh yeah. Happy Fourth of July."

Dad said, "We figured we'd start barbequing around 5 if that's okay; get a good meal goin' before it gets dark, then do the fireworks. Ya know, the usual."

"Yeah, sounds good."

"*Die Hard 2* starts today."

"Oh, I know," I say, "believe me."

"Tomorrow night at the drive-in?"

"You better believe it!"

It's amazing what I forgot about during the previous five days. I had been so excited about *Die Harder* that I could barely stand it, and then today, I had to be reminded that it was released. I felt some real excitement surge through my body, the first time it had happened since I saw Bebe.

"Are you coming, Mom?"

"Of course. You're not going to the drive-in without me. Just so long as this movie doesn't have naked women in waterbeds."

She was referring to the movie *Nightmare on Elm Street Part 4, The Dream Master*, easily the best of the Freddy movies, as I said earlier. Funny, too, because it was the poster I stared at the night before to help me fall asleep.

Dad had taken me to the matinee of *Dream Master* on opening day, August 19th, 1988. We both loved it so much that we went to the drive-in that night and caught it again, this time with Mom and, surprisingly, Neil.

The moment mom was talking about, a scene that didn't exactly thrill her, especially watching it with a car full of dudes, was when a character falls asleep on his bed, staring at a poster of a sexy girl on his wall. When he begins to dream, Freddy takes over and poses as the girl, now missing from the poster and *in* the guy's bed...

NEKKID!

So awesome. Possibly the greatest scene in any film ever, and that's a hill I will die on. And this was displayed on a massive outdoor screen that was visible to everyone driving down Wible Road, a bustling street through town. I have no idea how there weren't a ton of accidents.

The Crest Drive-In on Wible and Pacheco opened as a single-screen drive-in on May 29th, 1963, with the double feature of *Black Zoo* and *Play it Cool*. In 1977, they added a second screen. On February 15th, 1998, one day after Valentine's Day, they showed their last double feature. *The Wedding Singer* started at 7:05 pm, followed by the Michael Keaton flick *Desperate Measures*. I was there. When the final credits began rolling, the crowd, myself included, started stripping the metal speakers from the poles to keep as a souvenir.

I took three.

Two are hanging in my office as I type this. The other, I gave to my dad. It's still displayed in the garage over at my parents' house, which I guess is just my mom's house these days.

"Alrighty," Dad said, "that's settled. Think your brother will actually go this time?"

"Probably. It's *Die Hard 2*! John McClane is gonna die even harder this time!"

"Kids got a point. I'll ask him tonight. In the meantime, let's try to put the last few days behind us and have a great Fourth. Deal?"

I smiled. "Deal. For Bebe."

Dad smiled. "For Bebe."

The posse showed up at around 3 as planned, and we started the festivities with a *California Games* tournament on Nintendo. When we were all together like this, we usually played a fighting game, *Tecmo Bowl*, *Ice Hockey*, or *T&C Surf and Skate*, but that day we felt like a little *California Games*, which was not only multiplayer but consisted of several different events, such as Hacky Sack, roller-skating, skateboarding, and surfing. At the time, we thought it was the coolest game ever, even though it could sometimes be frustratingly impossible.

Dad had already fired up the grill by the time we were done. We could smell the charcoal burning in the backyard. In the summertime, there's no better smell.

Dad grilled the burgers while Mom got everything ready inside. Pretty soon, all the parents and siblings had arrived, even Mookie's.

Nobody really talked about the latest developments in the case, choosing instead to primarily talk about the Dodgers and the Mets, with good ol' Dave throwing in a few stories about his adventures in amateur hockey with his team, the hilariously named Moose Knuckles.

Once the sun dropped, we ran out front to light some shit on fire. My dad hauled out all the fireworks we bought the day before while my mom filled a bucket with water for discards and readied a fire extinguisher because, deep down, she realized that most men are complete idiots around fire and explosives. (Adult supervision required!)

I had hoped to see a lot of action on the street and wasn't disappointed. The sounds of fountain fireworks screamed from the entire neighborhood while the sparks and smoke seemed to glow in the night sky. I thought briefly of Bebe's family, her sister Skye, and how devastated they must be, but I promised myself I wouldn't linger on it for too long, and I didn't.

I got caught up in the fun and excitement of the night, as I hoped I would. My dad lined up three giant fountains and lit the fuses simultaneously. Down the street, someone was setting off a strobe. I saw Daphne run down her driveway and skitter off away from me. I waved, even though her back was to me.

That's probably why I had the courage to do it.

Dad lit a spinning pagoda, and I watched it spin wildly, sparks shooting in every direction. Xavier grabbed a handful of whirling Ground Blooms and handed them out. This could only mean one thing.

Fire fight!

Now, if you were wondering why these fireworks were

banned permanently, allow me to explain. We, being idiots, would light the fuses on these spinning little maniacs and chuck them at each other. The goal of the thrower was to burn someone. The goal of the dodger was to, well, dodge the fire.

Apparently, this was all perfectly acceptable behavior because our parents just watched in glee as we could have potentially burned down the entire neighborhood.

Xavier lit his first and threw it directly at me. I dodged, and the Ground Bloom hit the street, exploded into a shower of sparks, then spun wildly out of control.

I need some fire and fast.

I ran back up to my driveway and grabbed a punk, which is basically just a stick that stays lit so you can light multiple fuses with it. Kinda looks like a sparkler with no sparkle. My dad lit a match for me and held the flame to my punk.

"Don't throw those in our direction!" Mom yelled.

Mookie's sister Regina got in on the action, and soon, so did Hilary. Everyone was running up and down the street, whizzing lit projectiles at each other while our parents laughed and laughed.

Mookie and Roxy both launched one at me at the same time from opposite directions. I had no other choice but to run up Daphne's driveway. Usually, the sheriff's cruiser would be there for me to hide behind, but Monroe was burning the midnight oil, and I was left high and dry with nowhere to hide.

One of the blooms hit the edge of the driveway and bounced up toward me. I was sure to get hit. In a desperate move to dodge, I dove straight into their trashcan, knocking it over and denting it... badly. My body didn't feel too great either, but the can acted as a shield, the bloom hitting it and skittering off to my right.

I was covered in the Monroe's trash, and my ribs weren't feeling too hot, but I needed to get up fast. If they saw me incapacitated, they were sure to team up on me, and I could potentially kiss my eyebrows goodbye! Above the houses, fireworks from the country club less than a mile away painted the night sky a rainbow of colors.

I got up to a crouching position, stood the dented trashcan back up, and started throwing the refuse back inside... and that's where I saw it. I wasn't sure at first. I thought my mind was playing tricks on me. Another firework exploded above me and shone a divine light upon the most life-changing thing I had ever stumbled upon.

Right there, formerly in the trash, currently on the ground staring up at me, the most beautiful word I had ever seen in my life.

PENTHOUSE.

My eyes went wide, and my breathing got heavy.

Holy shit.

Holy shit shit!

More fireworks from above, casting light on me. If I didn't think of something fast, I would surely be noticed.

I didn't know what to do. I didn't want to throw that glorious treasure back in the trash and come back for it later; that was too risky. But I couldn't be seen carrying it around, obviously.

More fireworks.

I had to act fast.

I grabbed the magazine and tucked it down the front of my shorts. It wouldn't stay for long. It was sure to fall out if I continued dodging Ground Blooms. I needed to get inside and hide it in my room.

Casually, nothing to see here, folks, I was back to my driveway and announced I needed to take a leak. I'd be right back. It was just in the nick of time because turning the corner onto my street was none other than Sheriff Monroe. I hoped, hoped, hoped that he wouldn't notice the trashcan.

"Hurry up," Mom said, "grand finale is coming soon."

I took a deep breath, ran inside, and headed straight to my bedroom. I pulled the magazine from my shorts and just stared at the cover. It was from May of that year, just two months old. I have no idea who the girl was on the cover, but she was wearing a black nightie pulled up over her ass, massive side boob exposed.

I could have died right then and there.

Above the giant black PENTHOUSE lettering, it read: *Exclusive: Eichmann's Secret Confession.*

I have no idea who Eichmann was, but my god, did I want to find out!

I could hear the blasts of the fireworks; my Turtle Blimp was swaying slightly from the vibrations. I paid it no mind. I was transfixed.

The other cover headlines were about boring stuff like peace in the middle east and some bullshit like that. No one in their right mind is picking up a Penthouse to read about the middle east. It was almost laughable.

It took everything in my power to not block my door, sit on my bed, and check it out. But I couldn't. I had made a promise to my friends, so I lifted my mattress and slid the magazine underneath, then returned to the front yard just in time for the finale. The fireworks lit up the sky so bright it almost looked like daylight. I barely glanced up. As excited as I was about the Fourth of July mere minutes ago, I couldn't wait for it to be over. I would make an excuse for the fellas to come to my room with me, and we could sneak a few peeks.

It was our only option. We couldn't leave, and there was no way I could wait. It would have to be done right there in my bedroom, no doubt about it.

After what seemed like hours, when our stash of fireworks was depleted, I let my buddies in on my secret. I thought Roxy would blast off and explode into the night sky like the fireworks we just watched. Xavier yelled, "No way!" and Mookie just stared at me, his mouth hanging open.

We played it cool for about fifteen more minutes while everything got cleaned up, then real smooth-like, made our way to my bedroom. It was the longest fifteen minutes of my life.

I didn't have a lock on my door, so Xavier sat on the floor with his back to it. If anyone opened the door unannounced, it would hit him in the back and buy us a few seconds to hide the mag.

I lifted up my mattress, grabbed the magazine, and presented it to my friends. Roxy covered his mouth and screamed into his hand. Xavier jumped to his feet and then quickly went back down, remembering his job. Mookie's mouth was still dangling. This was no Mom Magazine...this was *the* magazine. The hunt was finally over. It was really going to happen this time, and nothing was going to stop us!

I sat cross-legged on the floor next to them and put the magazine in the middle of us.

This was it.

My heart felt like it was going to burst out of my chest.

I reached for the magazine and flipped it open. My heart sank.

"What the fuck is this?" Roxy said on the verge of tears.

"It's all fucked up!" I said, shocked.

And it was. The magazine was destroyed on the inside. It looked like it had been cut to ribbons. Pages were torn, pictures were ruined.

I was devastated.

We all were.

Until my massive crime and horror movie-filled brain began to process what I was looking at.

I stared at it for what seemed like minutes.

I knew the other guys were talking, probably to me, but I didn't listen.

I heard my brother's stereo playing, so I knew he was back in his room.

"Stay here," I said. "Don't move."

I opened the door and squeezed past Xavier out into the hallway and to my brother's room. I didn't bother to knock – I barged right in.

"What the hell, you dumb fuckin' fartknocker?!" Neil yelled at me over his stupid Unicorn Butthole music. He must have noticed the look on my face and realized this wasn't a typical visit. "What's wrong?"

"Come with me."

He rolled off the bed and followed me. Xavier was still guarding the door, so we had to squeeze behind him sideways.

"Jesus," Neil said, "what did you guys do to that magazine? And where the hell did you get it?"

"I...I found it in Sheriff Monroe's trashcan by accident. But look." I showed him the cut pages, the fonts that matched the so-called blackmail note. It took Neil a few seconds, but eventually, he put it together.

"Holy shit."

My body was trembling. I didn't know what to do. I thought I was going to throw up.

"You've got to tell Mom and Dad."

"I can't tell them. It's a porno mag, Neil!"

"Listen to me, little bro, they are not going to give a flying rat's dick about the porno mag if this is what we all think it is."

I stood silently. The other guys all got to their feet. No one made a sound.

"Come on," Neil said. "Everyone is still outside."

My thumping heartbeat from before was nothing compared to this. I was very concerned I might have a heart attack right then and there. My vision became a little blurry as we made our way to the front yard.

Neil was right. All the parents were still there; Hilary and Regina were sitting in the back of the station wagon with the hatch popped. I was terrified, so I focused all my attention on them. I could hear Hil talking about *Young Guns II*, which would be opening the following month. I'm not sure how much interest she had in the actual movie; her interest lay solely in one of the stars, Balthazar Getty. Regina looked like she had no idea who he was, so Hilary switched topics. "What about *The Golden Girls*?" she asked. Regina practically yelled, "Yeah!"

Neil nudged his elbow into my side. The parents all looked at us, happy as could be. My body felt like ooze, and I was afraid I would collapse in on myself.

"Hey, Dad," Neil said.

"Yeah, buddy?"

214

"Um, we need to talk to you."

My dad's smile disappeared. In fact, everyone's smile disappeared.

"So," Neil said, "Grant found this Penthouse in Sheriff Monroe's trash can on accident tonight."

The smile returned to Dad's face, and he laughed. "Oh geez," he said, glancing at me with a little smirk on his face. Mom's look wasn't so friendly.

"No, Dad," Neil said. "There's more. Look." Neil opened the magazine, revealing the destroyed pages. "All these cuts from these headlines match the...."

He didn't need to finish. My dad got it right away, and that fun, playful little smirk was replaced with deathly seriousness.

"Give me that," Dad said, reaching out his right hand. Neil gave him the magazine. "You guys go inside."

We would have argued, but we knew it was pointless. We also knew we didn't need to actually go inside. We just needed to walk away and give the adults a few minutes alone.

The four of us stood at the top of the driveway between my house and my neighbors. I happened to look down the street and saw Daphne skipping up her driveway and into her house. My heart broke. I wanted to turn back time. I regretted ever wanting to see a stupid porno mag.

"Guys," Dad called up to us. "Hang tight. We need to go have a talk with the sheriff."

So off they went, Dad, Dave, and Leroy, walking down the sidewalk and then up to Sheriff Monroe's house. I wanted to run inside and hide until everything was over, but my legs said otherwise, and they took off down the sidewalk. The guys and I followed. Hilary and Regina could see something was wrong. They hopped out of the station wagon and caught up to us.

"What's wrong?" Hilary asked us, but no one responded. We stood on the Monroe's sidewalk as my dad knocked on the door.

I noticed my dad was holding the magazine behind

his back.

I closed my eyes and silently hoped it would not be Daphne that opened the door, but my hopes were quickly dashed. She stood there in front of our dads, smiling like she didn't have a care in the world. I heard my dad ask to speak to her dad, then she vanished inside.

When Monroe appeared in the doorway, my dad showed him the magazine, and we saw the sheriff's face go slack.

Dad said, "Care to explain what the fuck this is?"

I would love to say that everything was just a giant misunderstanding, but that would be a lie. After our dads confronted him, Monroe stood there, silent and unmoving, for what seemed like ten minutes. Eventually, Dave said, "Judging from your silence, it looks like the jig is up, Sheriff."

And that was that.

Monroe had nowhere to go. He was basically caught red-handed. I didn't know it at the time, but Leroy had already called the sheriff's department and told them we needed a unit out on our street. It didn't take but a few minutes. Once on the scene, they just looked confused. The dads told them the story, explaining how I found the magazine in the Monroes' trashcan. It was weird because the deputies were defending the sheriff, offering possible solutions as to what happened and how it was probably all a mistake.

The sheriff remained completely quiet.

After a few minutes of the deputies trying to think of any alternative solution, Monroe shook his head, waving them off. He walked to the deputy closest to him, held out his arms, and pressed his wrists together.

He was ready to be cuffed.

We just stood there and watched as the deputies led Monroe to their cruiser and opened the backseat door. Daphne, Jeremy, and Mrs. Monroe came running out of the house to see what was happening.

Mrs. Monroe looked into her husband's eyes, her own

filled with tears, and asked what the hell was going on.

Monroe muttered three words and then got into the back of the car.

"I killed her," he said, his voice on the verge of cracking.

Jeremy got defensive, calling the deputies morons and various other, much worse, names. Daphne started sobbing. Before she ran inside, she looked me straight in the face and said, "What did you do?"

I shook my head. I wanted to tell her it wasn't me. I didn't do anything. I just happened to be at the wrong place at the wrong time. But, of course, I said nothing.

With tears in her eyes, she looked directly at me and said, "I hate you," then turned and ran up her lawn and back inside, slamming the door behind her.

It was the last I ever saw of her.

I stood there, frozen, tears rolling down my cheeks. Hilary put her arms around me and gave me a hug as the cruiser took Douglas Monroe away. We watched as they turned the corner and drove out of sight. Hilary's hug turned into a group hug with me in the middle. One last firework erupted in the sky, then everything was over.

The Monroes stayed in the house for a few more months, but I never saw any of them again. Eventually, Mrs. Monroe contacted my mom and asked for the house to be put up for sale.

My mom obliged and sold it in twelve days to a newly retired couple from Arizona that didn't seem to care about the previous owner.

By the next morning, after the fireworks and excitement had died down, Sheriff Monroe had written a complete confession. It outlined exactly what happened. He said he was happy to do it. He didn't know how long he could live with himself, holding on to such a dark secret.

Truth is, Bebe-Lynn wasn't meeting anyone at Jimmy's Arcade. She wasn't even hanging out there. She had decided to walk to Sail-Thru, grab one of their delicious Cokes, and spend Friday night at home watching *Who's Harry Crumb?* on VHS.

What Trip Windham said was true. He did approach Bebe-Lynn outside of Jimmy's Arcade and took her to the warehouse lot, where he ended up sexually assaulting her and punching her in the face.

When he drove off, the injured Bebe-Lynn sat on a curb. Her head hurt, and her black eye was tender to the touch, but what hurt the most was her feeling of shame and humiliation. She didn't know what to do, so she did the only thing that made sense to her. Something that she had been told to do if she was ever in any trouble.

She walked to a payphone and called Sheriff Monroe for help.

She told him what happened.

She told him she was scared.

She trusted him.

Monroe had had a few Friday night drinks by the time the call came in, but he was happy to help. He hopped in his cruiser and met Bebe in the parking lot, where she was attacked.

She got in his car, thanked him, and began to cry. Monroe asked her to detail exactly what happened.

I have no idea what the fuck Monroe was thinking, but sitting alone there in the dark, he leaned over, wiped a tear from Bebe's eye, then kissed her, forcing his tongue into her mouth.

He had heard all the rumors.

He was sure Bebe-Lynn would be happy to oblige him.

But Bebe said something completely unexpected.

Bebe told him she was a virgin.

The tears really began to flow now. For the second time that night, poor, innocent, sweet little Bebe-Lynn, with the cute dimple in her right cheek, had been sexually assaulted. Monroe was panicking. I'm sure he quickly ran through his options, but none of them left him looking innocent. So, perhaps out of disparity, he lunged at Bebe-Lynn again, this time wrapping his hands tightly around her throat.

He squeezed until the light was extinguished in her eyes, then he squeezed a little more.

No turning back now.

When the deed was done, he drove her out to the field, dumped her body, and then started an active investigation to look for her.

His plan was to pin the whole thing on Windham, but when Windham's alibi proved unbreakable, he needed to devise a plan B.

He would write a note.

The note would serve two purposes.

1: It would lead the investigation far, far away from himself. They could chase the lead to the end of the world and never come up with anything. Eventually, Bebe would become just another statistic.

And 2: The note would help ease the worry of the town. By placing blame on the victim, the town could reasonably assume they were safe. Whatever happened to Bebe, perhaps she deserved.

The night after arresting Windham on assault charges, Monroe grabbed a magazine he had hidden from his family, a Penthouse that, according to Jeremy, was locked in a safe, and forged the fake note.

During the search of Bebe's room, Monroe dropped his crumpled note in Bebe's trash and waited for a deputy to find it. It could have worked if he hadn't been so careless with his own trash.

Instead of dumping it in a dumpster, Monroe got stupid and hid it in the bottom of his own trashcan outside.

Under any other circumstances, no one would have found it in a million years. But that night was the Fourth of July, and an innocent kid running from a barrage of spinning sparks crashed into that can and sealed his fate.

So, that's my story.

The press bombarded me with questions in the weeks following, but I didn't know what to say, so I told the truth.

I was no hero. I was just a horny little kid who tripped over some trashcans.

The town felt otherwise.

Time moved on.

The waterslides and miniature golf area closed permanently in 1994 and were replaced with a Walmart that still stands today.

My beloved Jimmy's turned into half arcade, half pool hall in '95, then eventually closed forever in '99. At the time, I had stopped going there. When you're in high school, you always want the next big thing, something better, shinier – you get an inflated ego and think you're too good for such childish things.

I wasn't there when Jimmy's added the pool hall. And I wasn't there the day it closed. I probably didn't even notice. But I would give anything for it to make a comeback – to possibly reopen as a Retro Arcade of some sort. I could make t-shirts and Bob could sell them. Hell, I would work there for free.

When you're young, you think life will always be great. That you'll always be happy and on the hunt for the next big thing. But that's not the way it works. Life beats you down. It beats everyone down. And a new phone or a bigger TV can only provide so much happiness. To find that true happiness, that feeling of drinking Cherry Cokes at the arcade with your buddies, humiliating yourself at the pool, or riding that smelly plastic mat down the waterslide with your old man, to find that happiness, you can do nothing else but think back and reminisce. It's why nostalgia is such a kick in the gut. It's why everything that was old is new again, because people crave it. They want just a tiny slice of their childhood back. They want to go back to the times before adult life kicked in, before your back started hurting, and before you looked at a bill and felt utterly hopeless.

But those times are gone.

All we can do now is remember.

Bebe Forever & Long Live the Arcade!

Above: Dad enjoying at Diet Coke at the beach.
Below: Dad and I work on a birdhouse.

Above: I loved this black and white Vision Streetwear
Beret. Skip McKey said it looked like a bird shit
on my head. Fuck you, Skip.
Below: No idea what is going on.

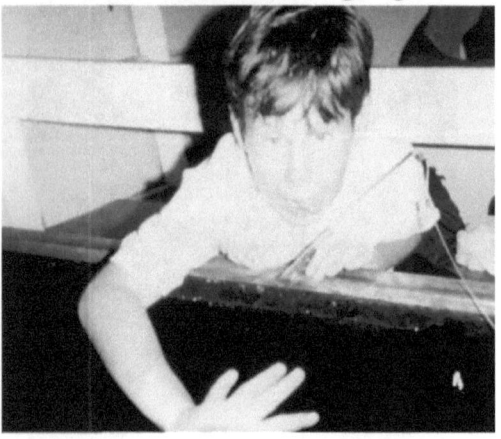

Above: Pinewood Derby
Right: One of the
two speakers
I took from the
Crest Drive-In

Above: The Community Center
Below: The sump looks a lot less scary these days.
It was cleaned and maintained shorty after Bebe.

Thank you for reading!

Oh man, where to begin.

Seriously, thank you all for reading this.
Thanks to Julie and McClane for allowing me to
lock myself in my office and write this thing.
Thanks to Mom & Dad (RIP) for everything,
especially for getting me that Nintendo!
Thanks to Roxy for providing me with a lifetime full of
really juvenile laughs together.
Thanks to everyone in Quailwood! The best
neighborhood ever!
Thanks to Katy O'Rourke for helping me out, and her
brother Trey (RIP) for killing my standup career before it
even began.
Thanks to Chelsey for letting me know what girls really
talked about.
Thanks to Sarah Bender and Bob & Diane Taggart
of Jimmy's Arcade! What a thrill this was!
Thanks to Lindsey Bradley for always helping.
Thanks to Natalie Heyde for the incredible back cover
art.
Thanks to Sarah and Amy Schulz (RIP) for buying me a
Nintendo 64. So amazing.
Thanks to Aryam and Mila Ramos, your laughter outside
my office made being in here so much better.
Thanks to the Bakersfield Reddit Members who helped
me with some details.
Thanks also to everyone who let me use their name,
and to Vanilla Ice, MC Hammer, Jules Bruff, Alethea
Root, Taylor Smith, Ti West, Mia Goth, Greg Kihn, Boy
Scouts of America, Camp Kern, and all my friends over
the years. Without all of you, this story never gets told.

BEBE FOREVER
&
LONG LIVE THE ARCADE!

Follow Grant on Instagram and TikTok
@GrantFieldgrove2.0

And if you'd like some Meet Me at Jimmy's Arcade
goodies, visit his Etsy store at
Etsy.com/shop/GrantFieldgroveArt

If you enjoyed this book, please consider leaving a
review!

Thanks!

#bebeforeverandlonglivethearcade
#meetmeatjimmysarcade

www.ingramcontent.com/pod-product-compliance
Lightning Source LLC
Chambersburg PA
CBHW032115170626
46808CB00006B/1957